Murder on the Bermuda Queen

An Alex Trotter Mystery

by Cheryl Peyton

All rights reserved. No part of this book may be reproduced or transmitted in any form or by any means, electronic or mechanical, including photocopying, recording, or by any information storage and retrieval system, without permission in writing from the Author.

ISBN- 13: 978-1495303746
ISBN -10: 1495 303748

This is a work of fiction. Names, characters, places and incidents either are the product of the author's imagination, or are used fictitiously. Amy resemblance to any actual persons, living or dead, events, or locales is entirely coincidental.

This book was printed in the United States of America.

Other Books by Cheryl Peyton

Six Minutes to Midnight

Walk on Through the Rain: A Polio Survivor's Story

Murder on Bedford Island

Available at www.amazon.com in soft cover and ebooks
In soft cover at www.barnesandnoble.com
Available as signed copies through the author's website at:
www.cheryljpeyton.com
www.authorsguildoftn.org

This book is dedicated to honor the
memory of our college friend

Brenda Miller Mains

She inspired us with her courage,
her character, and her resolute spirit

Murder on the Bermuda Queen

Chapter 1

BRRRNNG!!!

Alex heard the shrill peal of the kitchen phone as she was making her way from the elevator to her apartment. Quickening her pace while digging in her purse for keys she called out, "Keep your shirt on! I'm coming! I'm coming!" Wresting the whole set out of the bristles of a hairbrush, she fumbled through them before pulling out the two that she needed to turn the cranky top and bottom locks.

BRRRNNG!!!

"I said— just a darn minute!" At last, the second tumbler gave way and she flung the door open. Slamming it behind her, she took off running down the long narrow entry hall.

BRRRNNG!!!

"Oww! Crap!" she yelped, banging her hip into a corner of the console, knocking her purse off her shoulder.

Impatiently, she kicked the offending handbag out of her way, sending it skittering into the living room as she limped on ahead.

BRRRNNG!!!

Rounding the corner of the dining area, she lurched into the kitchen and grabbed up the receiver just before the answering machine came on. "Hello?" she gasped into the mouthpiece, panting and holding her side.

"Hi, — uh, Alex? Alex Trotter?" a female voice asked.

"Yes, it's Alex Trotter. Who is this?"

"It's Jasmine Keahi. From art school. Do you remember me?

Alex's mind went back four years to when Jasmine had been in some of her classes at the School of the Art Institute in Chicago. Of course she remembered her. She was unforgettable. The woman was drop-dead gorgeous, for one thing, thanks to her Hawaiian genes that accounted for a creamy mocha complexion, soulful dark eyes, and glossy black hair. Her fashion sense was similarly exotic, even by art school standards where Bohemian, punk, camp, goth, and grunge were all commonplace. Alex conjured up a mental picture of Jasmine coming into the painting studio in a short eyelet skirt paired with high leather boots, and carrying it off.

To Alex, her spectacular looks had made her seem unapproachable, although she had been pleasant enough. As Alex thought about it, she hadn't made much of an effort to get to know her. *So what did Jasmine Keahi want with her after all these years?*

Alex pulled her mind back to the present. "Of course, I remember you, Jasmine. I'm just surprised to hear from you," she added, truthfully. "So, how are you? What have you been up to? Been painting a lot?" She felt like she had started to interview the woman for the alumni magazine.

"Oh, I've worked on a couple of projects, but what I'm calling about is that I'm getting married — to Victor Garza – the art dealer."

Alex's head jerked back at hearing the name of the notorious gallery owner and international dealer. *Victor Garza.* "Of course I know of him." *Who didn't, in the art world? Or, in any world, come to think of it.* "He's a ... a legend and an art authority," Alex offered, avoiding the terms, "con artist" and "art shark," that were normally used to describe the man — but not when one was speaking to his fiancée, she supposed.

"My gosh! You're really going to marry Victor Garza?" Alex's voice had risen several notes. *In addition to being ruthless, the man must be sixty years old!*

"I know what you're thinking, Alex. He has a reputation for being, uh, demanding, and he's much older than me." Alex flushed hearing Jasmine read her mind.

"It's only that he's so discriminating that he's thought to be difficult...even heartless," Jasmine explained. "He's actually a very sensitive and caring man, outside of his professional life. And he's so good to me. I mean, the man puts me on a pedestal."

Alex could imagine Jasmine standing atop a marble base in the art dealer's home, with a plaque underneath that read, 'Idealized Female.'

Pushing that image aside she said, "That sounds great! No doubt the real Victor Garza is much different from his public persona." *He would have to be for anyone to live with him.*

"Well, where are my manners? Congratulations! I'm happy that's you've found true love." She rolled her eyes at her use of such a corny phrase.

"Thanks, Alex. I am very happy. And I'm anxious to have you meet him, which brings me back to the purpose of my call. It wasn't just to tell you about my getting married. I recently ran into Jenna Reynolds — who was in class with us? She told me that you had started a travel business — Globe Trotter Travels, right? And I thought you could help us with reservations for our honeymoon. Or, are you back to painting? I remember you were very talented."

"I was? I mean... I decided to switch careers to make a more regular income. I'm doing pretty well in the travel business. As far as my art is concerned, I sold some pieces out of a small gallery in Lincoln Park, but I never did much beyond that. Nothing on the scale of having my work in the Garza Gallery. I've been there, of course," she added, to sound a little less like a loser.

"If I'm not being too nosy, how did you get together with Mr. Garza, er, Victor?" She pulled out a counter stool to sit down and look out the window at the sliver of the Chicago skyline that was visible. Leaning back, she put up her feet on the other stool to get more comfortable for a prolonged conversation. This was the kind of personal contact with clients that made her love her work.

"Oh, I attended an opening night party at his gallery for that new Spanish painter, Francesca Maria Lazaro Marquez. Do you know of her?"

"Oh, I was talking about her only this morning." *Silence.* "No, I'm kidding. I don't think I could even remember all those names. Besides, I'm not really up on the current art scene, I'm afraid. What does she do?"

"She works in oil, painting swirling designs. Then she sprinkles powdered glass over the wet paint for a dramatic effect. Anyway, she's becoming well-known, thanks to Victor, but she's very temperamental and hard to deal with. She and Victor have had some ferocious quarrels.

"But getting back to how we met, he just walked over and introduced himself at that party. Can you imagine? As if I didn't know who he was! I was dazzled by him, of course, and he asked me out for dinner the next night. That was six months ago, and we got engaged two weeks ago. I'm just so lucky to have met him, and I don't mean just because he's so successful, but he's opened up another world to me: traveling to exotic places, socializing with important people, seeing great works of art. I know that sounds crass, but it's been very enriching and a lot of fun."

"Yes, I'm sure," Alex murmured, feeling incapable of even imagining such a life.

"But, back to you and your travel business," Jasmine continued, making it sound to Alex like it was the other end of the spectrum, "Jenna tells me how clever you are at arranging interesting tours and such, and since we know one another, I'd like you to help us with our wedding and honeymoon plans.

"We plan to be married at sea." She let out a low chuckle. "'Married at sea' – it sounded like I said, 'buried at sea,' didn't it? Anyway, as part of the celebration, we'd like to have guests join us on a cruise to Bermuda on the *Bermuda Queen*. I've looked into it and that ship is one of the few that offers a complete wedding package after leaving port, including the captain officiating. Most ships don't allow ceremonies once they leave port, as I'm sure you know.

"Anyway, we'd like to hire you to do all the bookings and to plan excursions for the two days that the ship will be docked in Bermuda. Would you be interested?"

"Sure. No problem. I'll be happy to reserve the staterooms and help your guests with their travel documents. I've been to Bermuda, so I know all the main attractions that most people are interested in. How many guests are we talking about and what sailing date are you looking at?"

"We'd like to be on the August 4th cruise leaving out of New York. After that I know we get into hurricane season. As far as the reservations are concerned, we should have about thirty people, including Victor and me. Since we need to know the number earlier than for a wedding at home, I sent out those 'Save the Date' cards right away. In the two weeks since then, I haven't gotten any regrets. I don't know if that's good or bad. Is that number doable for you?"

"Sure. That's a manageable number."

"Good. Unfortunately, I'm worried that many of the guests are quite *unmanageable*. My two maiden aunts can be a handful, but most of the guests are Victor's business contacts with whom he's had a rocky relationship from time to time. The wealthy collectors are probably quite finicky; the artists are temperamental to varying degrees; Walter Sneed, the art critic, has offended nearly all them at some point, and Victor's ex-partner hasn't really spoken to him since losing his lawsuit after their break-up.

"Besides those in the art world, there are a few relatives that have multiple problems. I'll make notes for you about those who shouldn't have staterooms across from one another. And a couple of them who should stay on a different deck than ours.

"I guess the one I'm most worried about is Victor's daughter, Sonia.

"'Sunny,' as she's called, is anything *but*. She's the most caustic person I've ever met. She's made no secret of her disapproval of my marrying her father. I think she suspects me of having ulterior motives because of Victor's wealth and the difference in our ages.

"Plus, she's afraid she might stop getting her allowance, or lose out on some inheritance. Her husband, the 'count,' is always getting into financial trouble, so she comes to Victor for money and he can't say 'no' to her. Anyway, now that I'm in the picture, she does her best to try to get under my skin, like calling me 'Mother,' although we're the same age, and reminding me that she's in her father's will and I'm not — yet. It's laughable how she tries to worm out of me what's in our pre-nup."

"Oh, geez!" Alex exclaimed. "Sounds like the Anna Nicole Smith saga, except that she married a ninety-year old."

"Yeah, and he *died*," Jasmine added. "A little different.

"But Sunny's brother Tony and I are great friends. Lucky for me, Sunny hasn't been able to poison his mind against me. Unfortunately, Victor is always upset with *him*. Tony's very likable, but he's a bit of a dreamer. He can't seem to settle on doing any one thing. He's very charming, though, but that's worn a bit thin for Victor, I'm afraid.

"Anyway, I need to send out invitations and you need information to be able to reserve the staterooms as soon as possible. We'd like all of our guests to have balconies, if possible, and we'll need suites for a few of them, but we'll go over all that later. As I said earlier, I'd like you to meet Victor so you can get a sense of him and what he has in mind for our trip. You and I can get together and work out the details after that."

Alex broke in. "Don't worry about the guests not getting along. There are always personality clashes among strangers on tours. I'm used to dealing with that. Anyway, it's a big ship, and there are plenty of excursions in Bermuda if we need to keep people separated."

"I've heard about the pink sand beaches and the beautiful old towns and British atmosphere. I'm dying to see the place! And then, to be getting married, as well!"

"How about your plans for the wedding, itself? Did you need me to help you work with the ship's social department?"

"No. I've already arranged with the wedding consultant to have the captain officiate, and I've reserved the chapel and one of the private party rooms. I don't want you to worry about the wedding and reception. In fact, I want you to be one of the guests in every sense of the word. Are you seeing someone you'd like to invite to go along?"

"Oh, well, maybe. On my last trip I kinda hit it off with the detective who was investigating the murder of one of my tour members."

"Murder?! Of someone in your group?"

"Well, yes, but that was my first one. My first murder, I mean. Well, my only murder— after many tours." Alex cringed at the reference as it wasn't a subject that would exactly inspire confidence in a client. "Arlie Tate is a very decent sort. And a good detective. Anyway, we've stayed in touch and I know that he wants to join me on one of my trips, so . . ."

"By all means, invite him. Come to think of it, his presence could be useful. Might help to keep everyone in line. I hope he doesn't mind not having any official business, though. I know

Sunny would like to get rid of me, but I doubt that she'd actually push me overboard."

"Don't kid about people going overboard! It happens once in a while. My reason for having Arlie along is for him to experience my usual kind of tour, where everyone has a great time and nothing goes wrong. The *Bermuda Queen* is a luxury vessel that's practically new, and the island is safe with many first-class amenities. Quite a change from my last destination, I might add."

"Well, that's good. So, I hope to get going on this as soon as possible. Victor and I would like you to come over to his home for dinner. We were thinking about this Friday evening, if you're available."

"Sure. That'd be great." Alex winced, wishing that Jasmine had suggested a brief business meeting at the gallery instead of a long social evening. She was hardly looking forward to spending any time with the notoriously rude and demanding gallery owner.

"Okay. Let's say seven o'clock. I'll let the cook know to expect you. Victor's place is at 1232 Astor. Do you have a car?"

"Of course. And he's only a couple miles from my apartment building."

"Good. There's an extra parking space behind the house so you don't have to look for street parking.

"I'm really looking forward to seeing you again, Alex, and for you to meet Victor."

"Yeah. Me, too. Bye."

As Alex replaced the receiver she sank down in her seat. "I'll let the cook know to expect you," she said aloud in a mocking voice. *I suppose if I had said I didn't have a car, she'd have the chauffeur pick me up. What have I gotten myself into? I have to spend an evening trying to impress Victor Garza? He's the most successful dealer in the art world, and he didn't make his fortune or his reputation by being nice to people.*

On the other hand, Jasmine has invited me, and he really likes her, apparently. Maybe the man will go easy on me for her sake. Well, I have only a couple of days to find out.

Chapter 2

FRIDAY EVENING, after Alex had finished dressing for her dinner meeting with Victor Garza and Jasmine Keahi, she was pacing around the apartment trying to calm her nerves before it was time to leave.

As she passed by the entryway mirror, she paused to pat down her cloud of reddish-brown hair that tended towards frizzy unruliness with the slightest up-tick in humidity. Leaning over, she inspected her gray blue eyes, noting that they were slightly bloodshot, probably from an uneasy night's sleep. At least the color hadn't risen in her cheeks. That would come later, she thought, after a glass of wine or when Victor Garza started picking apart her plans for their cruise.

Giving her image a passing grade, she turned and shuffled back into the living room, mumbling to herself what she planned to say to her clients. Circling the room and going over her lines, she fingered the pearls on her necklace like a supplicant rubbing rosary beads.

Concentrating on her presentation, she didn't hear her roommate Beth enter the apartment or notice her standing in the hallway watching her.

"Where did you say you're going, again?" Beth asked.

Alex jerked. "Wha?! Oh, Beth! Don't scare me like that! I'm a nervous wreck as it is!"

"I thought you were meeting a client for a business dinner," Beth responded, calmly. "Isn't that your best dress you wear to weddings?"

"Yes, I am and it is," Alex answered, a little piqued at the interruption and the characterization of her outfit. "And it's not just *any* client. I told you that I'm having dinner with Victor Garza and his fiancée, Jasmine Keahi from the Art Institute.

"Maybe I should have bought something new," Alex fretted, looking down and tugging at the skirt of the turquoise-blue dress. "This isn't hanging right, is it? Is this necklace too much? Maybe I should just change. Do you think I should?"

"Calm down. The skirt's fine. The necklace is fine. It all works. In fact, you look like a million bucks. I shouldn't have implied that you look like you're not properly dressed for the occasion. I was just teasing. Geez. Relax. What's the big deal? Who's this Victor Garza, again?"

"Victor Garza of Garza Galleries," Alex intoned slowly and distinctly as though she were speaking to someone slow-witted. "He's only the Titan of the art world. Not only does he own the gallery on the Gold Coast, but he has one in London and another in Hong Kong, I think —and maybe more. I mean, the man knows kings — and I have to do business with him!"

"Relax, Alex. You've been invited by *them*. They want *your* services for planning their wedding cruise, right? You know that you're capable of taking care of that, so go as the professional that you are, and not as a blubbering sycophant."

"'Blubbering sycophant'! Hah! Thanks for that disturbing image. I know I'm just making myself crazy about how I'll come across to the guy. But, you're right— they're not auditioning me for their social circle, or for their billionaire clientele. I'm just a hired hand to make their travel arrangements. Jasmine has already told me that their guests will be difficult, so that's a concern. But, I can only put people in nice staterooms and offer them the best excursions. They'll have to work out their own relationships."

She drew in a deep breath and slowly let it out. Nodding, she smiled feebly at Beth. "Okay, I'm ready. Let's get this over with. I'll see you later. Hopefully, not too much later. I don't want to prolong the evening by getting into some esoteric discussion with Victor Garza on the philosophy of art, after a couple glasses of wine. Not that I could. I don't know what I'm talking about *before* I start drinking."

Chapter 3

AT SIX-FORTY Alex was driving her red Fiat south on historical Astor Street. En route, she slowed down to take a gander at the Cardinal's palatial mansion and gardens that took up an entire city block. Passing that, she couldn't help but gawk at all the other impressive brownstone and limestone mansions; many formerly owned by wealthy founding families of Chicago. She thought about how the street had been named to honor John Jacob Astor's financial success, although she knew that he had never lived there.

It was interesting to see how all the small yards were privatized and protected with perimeter wrought iron fences that featured spear-pointed pickets and locked gates. Some of the residences were almost completely hidden by their inner courtyards, while others were just well set back and concealed by lush landscaping.

When she got to the 1200 block, she turned right and then left into the back alleyway, as Jasmine had instructed, and started looking for number 1234. Easily spotting the numerals on one of the back fences, she pulled onto the adjacent concrete pad and turned off the motor.

Okay. This is it. A couple of hours and I'll be back home, having been well fed and looking forward to a nice commission coming my way.

Getting out of the car, she cautiously approached the locked gate where a neat sign requested that one push the bell for admittance. When she did, a refined male voice came over the intercom and asked, "Yes? Who is it?"

Identifying herself by stating her name along with that of her business, she breathed a sigh of relief when the gate slowly swung inwards allowing her to step into the backyard. *At least they still want me to come in.*

Following the brick path around the side of the mansion, she passed by the stone-pillared porte cochere, a nineteenth century forerunner of the carport. Looking up at the original exterior, it wasn't hard to imagine carriages pulling up under its roof to discharge ladies in bustled dresses who would step onto the high stone step in their buttoned shoes. Bringing her mind back to the present, she noticed the silver Mercedes coupe parked in the spot where real horsepower had stood a hundred years earlier. The vanity license plate read, "JAZZY 1."

Coming around to the front of the home, she was startled at the sheer scale of the structure. Peering up at the facade, she had to crane her neck to see all the architectural elements of the Gothic Revival style above her: the deep porch, the massive quarried stones that went up to the roofline, and the turret with its curved glass windows. *How could the laborers even pick up those granite blocks, much less set them in place two stories up? It must have been like building the pyramids.*

She mounted the broad steps and tentatively approached the heavily framed, recessed double doors where there was another discreet sign that requested that one ring the buzzer.

This time, pushing on the button didn't elicit a disembodied man's voice asking for identification. She realized that she must have been in view of mounted video cameras from the time that she came onto the property. She only hoped that her gawking hadn't made her look like she was casing the place.

After a few moments, one of the paneled doors opened to reveal a sturdy redheaded man with a bushy mustache, standing at attention. His ample girth was corseted by a plaid vest stretched across him under his dark suit.

Is that a weskit he's wearing? she wondered, amazed that she even knew the proper name of that style of vest.

Why do I feel like I've just stepped onto a "Masterpiece Theatre" set, being met by a "gentleman's gentleman?" She suddenly had a mental picture of the man holding open a dinner jacket for his "lordship" to slip into for the evening meal.

"Miss Trotter, is it?" the man asked.

"Uh, yes, it is. That is, I'm Alex Trotter. Jasmine Keahi and Victor Garza are expecting me," Alex managed, trying to get her brain and her mouth coordinated.

"Quite right. Mr. Garza and Miss Keahi will receive you in the drawing room. Follow me, please."

Oh, of course — the 'drawing room.' Alex was feeling giddy at being surrounded by such opulence in a private home.

Following behind the butler, she gasped at the museum-quality artwork they were walking by. *Was that a Giacometti nude standing there in the wide central hall? Of course, it was!* she chastened herself. She was in Victor Garza's home where all of the art was original and nearly priceless. She'd better sharpen up in a hurry before she said something stupid to Mr. Garza, whom she was sure didn't suffer fools gladly.

"Excuse me, Miss," her guide gently intruded on her thoughts as she was ogling a Monet painting of the artist's gardens at Argenteuil. Mesmerized by such a treasure, she didn't immediately respond. *One could actually buy one of these masterpieces for their house? Hardly anyone would ever see it here! And how much would you have to pay for it? — like fifty million?*

"Uh, Miss, I'm sorry to disturb you, but Mr. Garza is waiting for you."

"Oh, quite right," Alex responded, feeling ridiculous for parroting the man's English expression. Turning her attention to the closed door where they were standing, she put back her shoulders, brought up her chin and gave her hair one last pat-down.

"Yes, I'm ready," she said, resolutely. Stepping forward, she felt more like she was being sent to the principal's office, rather than meeting her host for dinner.

Entering the richly appointed room, she first noticed the rounded outer wall and realized that she was in the turret. She recognized the elegant Victor Garza striding toward her across the sapphire-blue Chinese rug. He was taller than he had appeared in photos, but more striking with his dark hair, silver at the temples, and his neatly-trimmed mustache.

"There you are, Miss Trotter! We've been waiting for you. Come in and sit next to Jaz. She's anxious to talk to you. Thank you, Simmons. We'll eat at seven thirty." Alex took note of how easily her host exerted his command; welcoming her but intimating that she was late, and directing what everyone in the room should be doing and when.

Clasping Alex's hand with his soft manicured fingers, he squeezed it firmly for several seconds, causing Alex to stiffen uncomfortably as she felt the man's electricity. Looking at his face, she noted how his hooded dark eyes bore right through her, while giving nothing away.

Jasmine Keahi was standing by the sofa, as Victor Garza led Alex over to her.

"It's so good to see you again, Alex," she enthused, hugging her briefly. "You look marvelous. I love your dress. And you have so much hair!"

Alex instinctively pulled at her wild curls while enviously eyeing the other woman's sleek, sweptback hairdo. Taking in the expensive perfume, haute couture clothes, and expertly applied make-up, Alex thought that Jasmine Keahi was more stunning than ever, and had become much more sophisticated; which should have been expected.

"Jazzy and I are so pleased that you'll be putting together this little wedding cruise for us and our guests," Victor Garza purred, unctuously. "I understand that you're also an artist. I'm sorry, but I'm not familiar with your work. What is it that you do?"

"What is it that I do?" Alex repeated, dumbly. "Oh, mostly representational art — landscapes and street scenes. In oils," she replied, with a slight shrug. "I'm at the Lorenzo Gallery."

"Lorenzo Gallery...?"

"In Lincoln Park."

"Oh, of course. I'm sure it's a nice little gallery.

"Well, let's get down to the matter at hand, shall we? Jaz and I have finalized our guest list, which I'll get to in a moment. We're prepared to advise you of the broad concepts of how we would like the week to play out, and you can inform us on how it can all be accomplished.

"But first, let me get you a drink."

"I'll have a glass of chardonnay, thanks," Alex said, guardedly, wondering what the man expected her to be able to do. Most clients were happy to choose from the offerings that were readily available. Of course, this man was used to getting everything customized

"So." Victor Garza audibly exhaled and leaned back in his leather club chair, once they were settled with their drinks. "We have twenty-eight on the list. An even thirty with Jaz and me. I expect very few, if any, regrets."

Who would dare turn you down? Alex thought, but said, "I've checked with the cruise line about space for that sailing, and there are still sufficient choices in all categories."

"Good. Glad to hear you're on the ball. Do you know the *Bermuda Queen*?"

Alex had to repress the urge to say, *'Hum a few bars and I'll try to join in.'* Instead, she responded, "No, but I'm familiar with the Olympus line and I've cruised on a couple of their other ships that are very similar. I got a schematic of the *Bermuda Queen* for locating facilities and desirable staterooms."

Victor Garza waved her off. "Jaz will get together with you another time to make selections for accommodations for everyone. For now, you can just tell us about the ship. I mean, what's special about it— if anything."

"Well," Alex began, noting the skepticism, and trying to recall her rehearsed lines, "the cruise line is known for having a more relaxed, spontaneous atmosphere than many others. For instance, there are no set times for dining, and you don't have to eat in the main dining rooms. There are several specialty restaurants where you can eat whenever and with whomever you please — without table assignments."

Victor Garza nodded curtly, so she went on. "There's an emphasis on high-energy activities like modern exercise facilities, Vegas-style acts, and live bands that play every night for dancing. Of course, there's a fully-equipped casino and several bars, including one with karaoke.

"I think the ship and the destination will be perfect for a honeymoon." No reaction from the black eyes looking through her. She thought maybe she should start doing a 'soft-shoe number' to put on a better show.

Plowing ahead, she said, "Your guests will be enjoying the perfect vacation to celebrate the occasion with you."

She sat back, deciding to quit while she was possibly ahead, thinking that she had gotten through her practiced lines reasonably well, and hoping that she had made the cruise sound enticing.

She saw that her host was staring at his drink, scowling. "I'm not really a party guy."

"Oh, Victor!" Jasmine chided. "You have a wonderful sense of humor when you allow yourself to relax! Remember, you're not making any deals or talking business on our honeymoon. I don't think we should even attend the onboard art auctions. This is *one week* that's just for pleasure and I want you to enjoy it with me."

"You see why I'm marrying this woman? It's not just that she's beautiful, but she actually *likes me* and wants to spend time with me. Frankly, I feel that I'm at the age where if I'm ever going to get a softer edge and stop to take a breath, it's now."

He suddenly patted his breast pocket, pulled out a cell phone and squinted at the screen. "Oh, sorry. I have to take this. Excuse me, ladies, while I step out in the hall for a couple of minutes." With that, he sprang up out of his chair and was gone.

Jasmine leaned in towards Alex and patted her knee. "Victor is very impressed with you, Alex! Believe me, he doesn't usually compliment people. . . unless they're buying something very expensive. I think everything is going to work —" Jasmine's voice cut out as they heard Victor Garza shouting from right outside the door.

"Listen, you chiseler! We agreed on the price of that piece before you started it! I told you, I've got someone for a mil and not a penny more! Don't finish the damn thing if you think you're putting in too much time — they won't know the difference! I've sold them on *you*, not that slab of stone. Retitle it 'Unformed Creation' — I don't give a fuck! But I'm sure as hell not taking less for my commission! I'm the one who made you into a collectable sculptor who gets the big money, so what I say goes. Are we clear, now?!"

A moment later the door reopened and a smiling Victor Garza strode back in. "Sorry, ladies. Just had to do a little business with Bruno Rasconi, the sculptor. Wonderful talent. Oh, and he's one of our wedding guests! I'm sure he's looking forward to it.

"Why don't we go in to dinner, now? I believe we're having some nice Dover sole. We can talk about your plans for us in Bermuda while we eat. The ship sounds fine, Alex. A lot of live music and showy entertainment is good, although I wish there were some big names. Well, we might have to live with some limitations — but, getting married again at my age, I want to make sure that this is the best wedding and cruise ever, if it's the last thing I do."

Chapter 4

"OH, THANK GOD, I'M HOME!" Alex declared later that night when she flopped onto the living room sofa. "I'm telling you, Beth, that man sucks all the oxygen out of the room! Everyone serves at his pleasure at all times. It's exhausting!

"First, he doubted that the ship would offer anything worth his time and money, even though it's luxurious throughout and has top-notch entertainment. But there aren't any 'big names.'" She made air quotes. "I was afraid he was going to demand that the cruise line bring in Michael Buble to sing for them every night — and him only because Michael Jackson is dead."

Beth shook her head and smiled, sympathetically, her pony tail waving back and forth. "He was really that bad? How was he with what's-her-name — Gardenia? Or doesn't it matter, since she's only marrying him for his money?"

"*Jasmine*. And she appears to genuinely like the guy. And he seems to be devoted to her in his own chauvinistic way. I mean, he's very attentive to her and all that, but he also tells her what to do — in a passive-aggressive way. It's obvious that he pays for her clothes, her jewelry, her Mercedes; so that all figures into her opinion of him, I'm sure.

"But I'll give him this, he's charming enough when everything is going his way, but I saw what he's like when someone displeases him. He took a couple of phone calls out in the hallway. He was loud enough that we could hear what he said, and believe me, I wouldn't have wanted to be on the other end of the conversations.

"One was a sculptor whom he accused of 'chiseling,' which I thought was pretty funny. 'Sculptor...chiseling' —get it?" Beth smiled crookedly and rolled her eyes.

"Anyway, I think the second call was from his son — at least I hope he doesn't get that personal outside the family. Apparently, Tony Garza was asking his father for a loan, or to invest in some business enterprise of his. Victor told him that he'd have to wait until he was dead before he got anything. Then he said that he'd never amount to anything, and had done nothing but mess-up everything he'd ever tried' — except that he said it in stronger language.

"After that, the man came waltzing back into the dining room, all smiles, and made a toast to his 'two lovely dinner companions.'"

"See -- I told you you looked good!"

"Yeah, well that compliment comes at a price. I don't know what he expects from Jasmine, but he expects *me* to make sure the sun shines everyday and that the ocean's calm. In Bermuda, I'm supposed to come up with excursions that are exciting, but not tiring; interesting, but not too cerebral; exotic, without being too foreign.

"Anyway, I rattled off as many trips as I could think of and he objected to something about all of them, like: the evening glass-bottom boat cruise, where you see fantastic marine life illuminated through the darkness under the boat. He thought his guests might have 'had enough' of boats. I mean, it's only an hour and a half cruise. It's an island, for Pete's sake. A lot of excursions are by boat.

"Of course, he wasn't that impressed with the land trips either. I mean, *everyone* visits the beaches! I don't know where else the sand is pink and you can watch pods of dolphins jumping through waves from your lounge chair."

"I could tolerate that," Beth deadpanned. "Can you swing an invitation for me?"

Alex made a face. "That's very kind of you... but no. Anyway, then there's a bus tour that visits all the favorite tourist stops like Somerset Village and the botanical gardens, but he couldn't imagine riding on a bus for several hours. Frankly, I couldn't imagine him sitting on a bus for most of a day, either."

"The man can't always expect to be chauffeured around like he's some kind of dignitary," Beth protested.

"*You* tell him that," Alex retorted, "but I plan to have him chauffeured around. There are horse-drawn carriages and private taxis in Bermuda. For a price, you can arrange for either of them to take you most anywhere on the twenty-square miles of land. And that's how Lord and Lady Garza are going to tour the island. Their guests can take buses and scooters, or walk, for all he cares.

"For instance, I suggested the Verdmont House museum in old St. George. It dates back to 1710. It has beautiful Georgian architecture and is full of the original family's English and Chinese porcelain collection.

"After the house tour, they could walk around the gardens before they have lunch at the Specialty House just across the street. The afternoon could be spent visiting the local perfumery and then shopping in town for cashmere sweaters, tweed jackets and Wedgwood — you know, the British imports that are all over the place. He didn't seem that impressed."

"Maybe they need a chance to catch their breaths. I'm exhausted just hearing about it."

"Well, I have to be ready with options in case they feel like being on the go. But, you're right, I didn't tell them about everything. Like — the next day, they could be escorted around Hamilton by carriage. There's even better shopping there at designer houses right along Front Street, and tons of first-rate outdoor restaurants.

"Maybe, for exercise, they'd like to visit the Gibb's Lighthouse where they can climb to the top to see the whole island; although it's quite an exertion.

"Really, just walking around and soaking up the atmosphere in Hamilton is the best way to experience commercial Bermuda.

"And then I could arrange for a little party on the beach for everyone on our second night there. What do you think?"

"I think it's too bad that I'm not going. I'm sure you'll pull it all together and it'll come off without a hitch. Not like your last island adventure, we hope," Beth mugged.

"Oh, thanks for bringing up the murder on Bedford Island. That reminds me — I need to call Arlie Tate and ask him to be my date for the week. I told him my next trip would be smooth sailing, so a week's cruise to Bermuda on a luxury liner is perfect. He'd have to be impressed with my handling of this, not that he'd admit it, of course.

"I'll call him tomorrow after I know where we'll be staying. I'm meeting Jaz at the house to decide on staterooms for the guests."

"Oh, so now it's *'Jaz'* and *'the house'*?" Beth flipped her pony tail up with her hand.

Alex batted her eyes. "Oh, sure — we're BFFs, The truth is, Victor won't be at *'the house'* tomorrow, so I'm taking advantage of working alone with Jasmine who appears to still be a normal person.

"Geez, after tonight, I know what it was like to audition in front of David Merrick for the lead in *Promises, Promises.* Tomorrow, at least, I'll be out of the spotlight."

Chapter 5

THE NEXT MORNING Alex retraced her route back to the Garza home. The front door was answered again by Simmons who was wearing another plaid vest. This time, he greeted her by name before leading her down a hallway. Showing her into a light-filled room he identified it as the "morning room," and assured her that Miss Keahi would be with her shortly.

Left alone, Alex looked around appreciatively at the sunny yellow and white decor that was set off with pots of ferns and palms. *How many rooms do you have to have in a house before you started naming them for times of the day? Does this become off-limits in the afternoon?*

Alex had just walked across the sea grass rug to inspect a small still life when Jasmine called out a greeting from the doorway.

Turning, Alex was surprised at how Jasmine's appearance had changed from the night before. Today, her dark hair was worn down, with soft curls skimming her shoulders. She was dressed much more casually in a crisp white short-sleeved blouse and slim grey slacks — the kind of designer clothes that are very expensive but appear understated.

"Thank you for coming back again so soon, Alex," Jasmine gave Alex a quick hug. "I'm really glad you're here to take care of this chore. There are *so* many details when you have your wedding guests stay for a week! Anyway, let me get us coffee and some rolls to munch on while we work on this." She pushed a button on the wall, before inviting Alex to sit in one of a pair of striped lounge chairs.

After they were seated, Jasmine handed Alex two sheets of printed copy paper. "These are all our guests. I've put a star by the ones we need to reserve suites for. I know I told you the other day that we have to separate people who don't get along, but I've decided we won't worry about that. They're all guests on the same wedding cruise, and they'll just have to make the best of it. But some of them are quite particular about their accommodations and Victor is willing to cater to them."

Alex glanced at the two typed pages, trying not to react to how many asterisks there were. "Okay, I can work with this. You know, people have different ideas of what's desirable on a ship. Like, some think that there's a "better side" of a ship but, in crossing the Atlantic to Bermuda, there's no difference. It's not like cruises that travel alongside land. "You may have heard that the word 'posh' was originally an acronym that stood for 'Port Out, Starboard Back,' referring to roundtrip sailings from Southampton to India in colonization days." Jasmine shook her head.

"Oh, well the story goes that *POSH* was stamped on certain first-class tickets for the passengers to have shade each way, but that may just be a legend."

"Very interesting. What are the *undesirable places* to stay on a ship? I've heard that some people don't like cabins located in the aft part of the ship, but I don't know why."

"Well, if you're on a lower deck in the back, there can be a lot of noise from the engine; just as when you're on a lower deck at the fore you may not be able to get to sleep with the sound of the waves hitting the bow. But the aft cabins higher up have balconies that are larger than on the ship's sides, and are very much in demand. Sitting outside at the back of the ship, you have a 180-degree view of nothing but water, which becomes a restful, private world of your own."

"Ooh, that sounds wonderful! I would love a suite in the aft. Maybe some others would, too. I'll check the list."

"There are a few things you'll want to consider first," Alex cautioned, "like, the fact that the aft decks are 'stepped out,' meaning that the balconies below are overlooked by the balconies above, so that even a public deck, like the Sun deck, can look over your balcony."

"Oh." She pause, thinking. "But I still like the idea of a large balcony perched over the sea, all to itself. Tell me about a couple other nice locations, and I'll go down the list and write in some assignments"

"Sure," Alex agreed, digging in her purse for the schematic of the ship. I've high-lighted all the cabins that were available when I called this morning. We'll avoid anything directly over the lounge and casino, or staterooms near the white areas on the plan that indicate housekeeping areas, laundries, or crew-only elevators." She held the ship's plan for Jasmine to see.

There was a soft knock at the door, causing both women to look up. "Come in, please," Jasmine said, as a plump, rosy-faced young woman entered carrying a large silver tray.

"Oh, fine, Annie. I'll pull up the leaf on the table over there so you can put it down." Jasmine lifted up the spring-loaded side of a pine table. "We'll help ourselves. Thank you, Annie."

After the maid had left and closed the door behind her, Jasmine poured two cups of coffee. "Here, Alex, put in what you'd like and take a couple of pastries." She pointed to a napkin-lined basket. "The cherry rolls and the kringle are made by our Danish cook. You can't go wrong with either kind."

"I don't need any encouragement," Alex said, piling several pastries onto her plate. "I don't get home baked goods very often. Thanks."

"Anyway, where were we?" Jasmine asked as she sat down and looked at her copy of the list. "I'm going to mark a few names for suites near ours, if possible. There's Edmund and Juliana Devers. They're major collectors who live in New York and London. Then, there's Dame Edith Herrington. She's English and travels with her assistant, Eloise Brown. Uh, here's Rudolph Perino and his partner, Damien Loren —theatre people. Very nice, but quite dramatic, of course. Let's see— my cousin Cindy Carmody, who's my matron of honor, and her husband Michael should have a suite. She's been a big help to me. She's insisting on doing all my flowers, for instance, and she's very creative. Let's see — how about Victor's attorney and his wife — Morrie and Shirley Feldman? Yes — I think those are all of the A-listers." She flipped the page and looked at the second sheet.

Putting her finger on the page, she looked up. "Oh, and now we come to the guests from hell. Here's one of my favorites — Roman Gregg, my husband's former business partner. He and Victor have barely patched things up since their court case, but I hope to avoid him as much as possible. Roman sued Victor first and then Victor counter-sued, and it got really ugly and expensive for both of them.

"I hate to say it, but I think Victor is only inviting Roman and his wife Monica so that he can gloat about how happy he is, and that he's moved on with his life. Probably, that's why they're being given a suite, too."

As Jasmine looked down again, Alex scurried over to the table and grabbed a couple more wedges of kringle. Back in her chair, she demurely crossed her legs at the ankles before biting off a hunk. "Maybe we'll put the Greggs in a forward suite, farthest away from you —and using a different elevator," she advised, between chews. "Any other guests who might want to throw something at you besides rice?"

"Ha! Yes, as a matter of fact, there are. I've already told you about Victor's daughter, Sunny. Then there's her gambling, former playboy husband, *Count* Carlo Giovanni, who I hope will be spending all his time in the casino. Victor can't abide the man. Of course, Victor has little patience for anyone with a weak character and no self-discipline. And Carlo is the poster boy for vices and over-indulgence. Sunny seems to find it exciting to be married to a Count, even if it means that they're in debt most of the time. Like it's a big deal that he's a Count — in Italy. Do you know how many counts there are in Italy?"

"I think they're countless," Alex responded.

Jasmine broke out in peals of laughter. "You're so funny, Alex. 'Countless!' I love it! And this one shouldn't be 'counted!'" she squealed. "I'm sorry. Now I'm getting silly. But this guy has never worked an honest day in his life, that I know of. He inherited some money, along with his title — but he's lost more than he's won.

Jasmine continued. "So Sunny will show up and sweet talk Victor into giving her 'advances' on her allowance. Carlo wouldn't dare ask himself since Victor would probably kill him."

Alex started to squirm. "I don't think Carlo will be either winning or losing big on this trip, Jaz. In fact, he'll most likely be very disappointed in the gambling, period. There's a casino on the ship, but they don't offer "high-roller" stakes. Once we're docked, the casino will be closed, and there's no gambling on the island."

"Do they have nightclubs in Bermuda where they serve alcohol?" Jasmine asked, dryly.

"I think you could scare up a little rum in a lounge or two," Alex replied, in kind.

"Well, then, Count Giovanni will be fine. Let's move on.

"Since we've taken care of the Count and 'Countess,' as Sunny likes to call herself, we should find something nice for her brother. Tony will be coming by himself, but I'd like him to have a suite. He's the sweetest guy in the world, and I feel bad that his father is so hard on him all the time. Besides being so nice, he's also very handsome. Wait till you meet him— you'll fall in love with him. Oh, wait a minute —you're bringing a date — a detective, as I recall."

"Yeah. Arlie Tate. I've caused enough grief already, so I think flirting with some other guy in front of him is out of the question. He's good looking, too, in his way, but I wouldn't call him sweet — more like acidic—or even rancid, but I like him. Anyway, who else do we need a suite for? Certainly not Arlie and me. We'll be happy with standard staterooms."

"Well, the next group is the artists who have exclusives with Victor who I'd like to have nice rooms with balconies. They're people who get astronomical prices for their work, so they're used to having the best of everything. Let's see — there's Bruno Rasconi, the sculptor; and painters, Lydia Corbin, Marcel Longine, Jonathan Welles and Francesca Maria Lazaro Marquez. Lydia and Jonathan are married — to other people, I mean. These people are all high-strung and difficult, but I'm hoping they'll be able to relax and be nice for a few days while they're on the cruise. They constantly put a strain on Victor. They think their talent entitles them to make their own rules regardless of contractual obligations to him or his clients.

"Anyway, I think that's it with the artists. Who else? Oh, that's right. The only art critic in the world who proves that the pen can be deadlier than the sword —Walter Sneed. I'm always afraid I'll call him Walter 'Snide' to his face."

"Hah! That's a good one! You know, you're a lot sassier than I realized when we were at the Art Institute. I'm sorry I didn't know you better when we were there — I think we could have been good friends."

"I think so, too. And call me Jaz. Jasmine sounds too exotic in Chicago, don't you think? It fit me better on Oahu. It's like a Hawaiian shirt — the tourists all buy them on the island to wear to a luau on the beach, and then they go home and never wear them again because men don't wear bright floral prints in Cleveland or wherever. You should tell your clients that they should buy Hawaiian shirts at Goodwill — they're like new."

"That's a great tip, Jaz. Everyone should try to save twenty bucks on a $10,000 vacation."

Jasmine made a face. "Oh, all right, it's not much. Anyway, back to the business at hand. Talking about Hawaii brings me to my two aunts who live here — but they're from there. You know what I mean. I lived with my Aunt Lola when I first moved to Chicago ten years ago. She and her sister, Aunt Alaana, are the ones who are very close, although they occasionally get into silly, but heated, arguments. They're on good terms now so they can share a balconied stateroom.

"I think that's everybody at this point. Let me take another look to see if someone else should also have a suite...no, not them...no..."

There was another knock on the door.

"Anna?" Jasmine inquired, looking towards the sound. No response. She turned to Alex and shrugged. "Anna must be here for the coffee service. Have you had enough kringle?" Alex stuck out her tongue at the jibe, but brushed her shirt to remove any tell-tale crumbs.

Jasmine turned back to the door. "Come in, Anna! It's fine."

But, as the door swung open, it wasn't Anna standing there. The woman who came charging into the room was about as different from the modest serving girl as it was possible to imagine. About ten years older, she had close-cropped impossibly red hair, heavily fringed dark eyes, and a lean, hard body that was outlined in a stretchy black top and long slim skirt, giving her the appearance of a jungle cat. Frozen in front of Jasmine, she looked ready to pounce.

"Well, look who's here —it's Mother!" her husky voice growled in mock surprise.

"Sunny," Jasmine responded, flatly. "What are you doing here? I'm in the middle of a business meeting regarding the wedding."

"I'm here because it's my father's house. And how many hours a day do you spend working on that ceremony of entrapment, anyway?"

"Sunny, please. I'm just trying to make your father happy and take care of our guests. Don't you have a nail-sharpening appointment or something to go to?"

"Uh, excuse me, but I really should get going," Alex broke in, wondering if she had somehow become invisible.

"Oh, don't leave on my account," Sunny purred. "Who are you, anyway? You're not a friend of Mother's, are you?"

"This is Alex Trotter, our travel consultant," Jasmine said, walking over to stand next to her. "She's taking care of our reservations on the ship and arranging for land tours," she continued, squeezing Alex's arm in a 'you-can't-leave-me-now' grip. "Alex, this is Victor's daughter, Sunny."

Alex leveled her gaze at the rude woman. "Is that spelled with a 'u' or an 'o'?" Jasmine covered her smile with her hand.

"*Countess* is spelled with both," Sunny answered, coolly. "So, where did Mother put Carlo and me? Do they still have steerage?" She glanced at the lists in Alex's hand.

"We've assigned everyone where we thought they'd be most comfortable," Alex answered, picking up the papers. "Let me see— I believe that you're not on the same level as Jasmine. That's right — you're beneath her and your father, and on the opposite side," she finished, curling up her lips in a wicked smile.

Sunny screwed up her face while considering the remarks before she opened her mouth to speak. "I assume that means that we're on a more *stable* level."

"You could say that," Alex replied. "At least, from my point of view, and in the interests of other guests, there better *not* be any 'rocking the boat' down there."

"*Okay!*" Jasmine broke in. "As pleasant as this is, you'll have to excuse us, Sunny, so we can finish up. Alex, would you please come with me to the office? I'd like to show you the invitations." She pulled Alex towards the door as Sunny glared after them, her eyes becoming two slits.

Only when they were out in the hallway, did Jasmine let go of Alex's arm. "Whew! I just had to get out of there!"

Alex looked at her watch. "Yeah, well it was time to move on to a different room, anyway.

"What?"

"Nothing. Just something silly. Do you really want to show me the invitations, or were you just getting me out of the boxing ring before I put that woman on the ropes?"

"I know how you feel. Actually, I was loving that you were getting the best of her. I usually think of a comeback about an hour after she insults me, but you didn't miss a beat! I just figured, since we had gotten through the list, you'd rather get on your way than stay and do battle with Sunny."

"Yeah, it's just as well," Alex mused. "I must admit I was enjoying myself, even though I wasn't being very professional; but *you're* my client, really — not her, right?

"Anyway, I'll go home and start making reservations for the cabins we've picked. Hopefully they're all still available. I got the credit account numbers from Mr. Garza last night so I'm all set. I'll be back in touch, soon."

Driving home, Alex mentally reviewed the last couple of hours. How was Jasmine going to survive that bunch? Alex had met only two of the family members so far, and both of them spelled trouble for her: Victor was totally controlling and Sunny wanted her out of the way to get the man's money. And now, the blood-sucking Count had to be added to the mix. Alex decided that she'd better keep a close eye on *all* of the Garza family members on the cruise. And maybe on some of the guests.

Chapter 6

"HEY, ARLIE. It's me. Alex."

"Are you in trouble?" Arlie Tate asked in his soft southern drawl.

"No, of course not. Just the opposite, in fact. I have good news! An acquaintance of mine from art school is hiring me to make the travel arrangements for her wedding guests on a cruise to Bermuda, and wants me to bring a guest. So, how does that sound?"

"That depends— am I the guest?"

"Of course you're the guest! Do you think I'd call you to tell you I'm taking someone else on a cruise to Bermuda?"

"I never know with you, but, yes, Bermuda sounds really good. When?"

"Leaving out of New York on August 4; returning August 10."

"Bermuda's just a short flight for me outta Jacksonville. I could meet you there."

"It's a *cruise*, Arlie. The purpose of a cruise isn't just to transport people —a *cruise* is an entire vacation! You get fine dining and quality entertainment all in one place that's convenient and luxurious; and made affordable due to the high-volume. A *plane* is solely for transportation. Do you see the difference? Besides, we're only two days in Bermuda. Even the wedding is on the ship." She heard a low chuckle on the other end of the line.

"I can really get you going, can't I? But thanks for the spiel on the advantages of cruising. You should be a travel agent. Okay, seriously — I'd really like to join you on *the ship*, of course, and that week shouldn't be a problem to take off. I guess I'll need to bring a tux, then, right?"

"You have a tuxedo?!" Alex thought back to when she first met the detective and compared him to the scruffy TV character, Lieutenant Columbo.

"Yeah, I do. Just because I like to be comfortable most of the time, doesn't mean that I don't own any decent clothes and know when I need to wear them. I bought a tux after I was in a friend's wedding a few years back, and I wore it to some affairs when I lived in Atlanta. Now, I'm not saying it doesn't need some serious going-over, but it might pass. I'll see. What's the ship's dress code? Any formal nights, or just the wedding?"

"Arlie Tate— you keep surprising me. It's Freestyle cruising, so it's more casual. I'll give you all the particulars later. I just wanted to let you know as soon as possible so you could put it on your calendar, and I could reserve our staterooms."

"Was that 'staterooms'— plural, or is this a bad connection?"

"*Adjoining* staterooms, Arlie. I'm working on this trip, so I need to be discreet. Don't worry — we'll be able to visit back and forth."

"You bet your sweet a— we will. I mean — that's fine. We'll work it out. Should be a great time, you know — for you and me."

"I think so, too. Even the bride is glad you're coming. Most of the wedding guests are warring with one another, so Jasmine hopes your presence will encourage good behavior. I've met a couple of the family members who are dangerous sorts, and I haven't even *laid eyes on* the people that Jasmine's talking about. I'll need to closely observe what these people are up to, I can tell you that."

"Alex— don't go getting any foolish ideas about playing peacemaker or social director. You know how you are —you always want to get into everybody's business. These people are all adults who have managed their lives before you arrived on the scene, and can take care of themselves now. You hear me? We've talked about this before. Let's just have a good time enjoying a wedding and a vacation together. No meddling!"

"You're not going to say, 'You beat everything, did you know that?'" Alex asked, reminded of a line from the old Andy Griffith television show. "Yes, I hear you. I'm just saying that it turns out that Jasmine is a really nice person who is marrying into a treacherous family, by all accounts, and I'm just going to be on guard so that no one starts any trouble."

"*You* just stay out of trouble, okay? I've gotta go, now, babe, but we'll talk later. Oh, and by the way, Sheriff Andy said that to Barney when the guy had done something really foolish, so it's more appropriate than you think. How's this impression— 'You beat everything, did you know that?'"

Arlie's uncanny imitation of the Andy Taylor character gave Alex a good laugh as they hung up.

Chapter 7

ONE WEEK LATER Alex found herself back at the Garza mansion for another meeting with Jasmine. Since it was a warm afternoon, Jasmine had suggested that they sit outside on the flag-stoned patio.

Once there, Alex took a seat at one end of a sofa while Jasmine sat in a lounge chair across from her.

"I've reserved all the staterooms," Alex said after some small talk. "Here's a copy of the names and room numbers. Also, I've brought some documents you can review later, but some require Mr. Garza's signature, where I've put an 'X' on the contracts, agreements, waivers, and application for travel insurance and cancellation insurance, those last are optional, but recommended.

"Then there are some statements of legal protections you can review. I've also sent this packet to all your guests. Pretty boring stuff. Basically, they say that cruise ships have 'strict liability' coverage, meaning that they have to take special care to keep passengers safe on board between ports. Of course, having protection and collecting are two different things, but people have won suits when they've been raped or robbed by crew members — that kind of thing."

"Good grief! I hope that doesn't happen very often!"

"No, but with an average of 2,500 passengers and 800 crew members, there's potential for trouble just by the numbers. Add to that, excessive drinking during late hours, the relaxation of normal rules of behavior — and, well, every night can be like the office Christmas party.

"As for security measures, all the cruise lines run criminal background checks on every crew member and passenger, but that doesn't mean that people don't lie on job applications, or that all troublemakers and deviants have arrest records. There are other safety precautions taken, too, like ID cards issued for getting on and off the ship, security personnel on board and mounted cameras."

"That's true for any hotel, isn't it?" Jasmine asked. "I wouldn't think that being on a ship poses any special threats — or does it?"

"Well, you would certainly think so if you read their disclaimers," Alex replied. "Since ships go all over the world, they can encounter especially dangerous situations at foreign ports and they take *no responsibility* for them. Things like: 'perils of the sea,' 'piracy,' 'acts of war,' 'terrorism,' 'political coups,' and 'revolutions.'"

"Oh, I see. I guess you don't worry about any of those things at the Hilton," Jasmine said.

"Well, maybe at the *Cairo* Hilton," Alex deadpanned.

"But, even if you're on board and become the victim of a crime or injury due to negligence, there's a problem suing because of the uncertainty of jurisdiction. In international waters, you have to sue in the country of registry, and American citizens have to report serious crimes to the FBI, but authorities don't usually comes on board during the cruise.

"Anyway, we're getting a little carried away here, considering that we're going to peaceful Bermuda that hasn't been involved in a conflict since our Revolutionary War when they offered George Washington salt for protection from his forces that could attack, because they didn't even have gunpowder to fight back.

"But back to the present— along with the contract, I've sent everyone a statement for them to sign stating that they're physically able to travel. I mean, you don't have to be able to do a back flip on deck — just a front aerial with the splits." She paused. "Kidding. Just wanted to see if you had fallen asleep."

"No, I'm paying close attention,. I was just thinking of my Aunt Lola who sometimes uses a cane when her arthritis flares up. I know she's never been on a cruise before. You think she'll have a problem?"

"No, she just needs to tell the cruise line that she uses an appliance for walking. It's a low bar for 'fitness for travel,' believe me. I've been on a couple longer, more expensive, cruises where the only people who could walk were the private-duty nurses. On one Mediterranean cruise, there was an elderly man at my dining table who was so hard of hearing we had to have a microphone on the table. When you picked it up, you felt like you either had to sing or tell a joke."

"Ha! So, I gather, a handicap is not a problem."

"No. A passenger just needs some means of mobility — and must be able to feed himself, or have someone there to assist him. There's one physician, and at least two nurses, on every voyage, although the ship isn't liable for their malpractice, if it exists. And I hate to mention it, but all cruise ships have morgues below. People don't realize how many times passengers die on board. As I said, on longer cruises there are more elderly people, and they can die from natural causes like heart attacks or strokes.

"Again, I don't think you have to worry about too many people dropping over dead on a one-week cruise to Bermuda —

unless you count the people who go back for thirds at the midnight chocolate buffet."

"Sounds like a harrowing trip!" a male voice interjected. Jasmine and Alex turned to look at the speaker — a handsome dark-haired man walking towards them from the back of the house.

"Tony!" Jasmine called out, springing up from her seat with open arms. Alex also stood, facing the visitor.

"Jazzy!" the man responded as he approached and embraced her. "What a nice surprise."

Turning towards Alex, he nodded and smiled. "Sorry if I'm interrupting. I didn't realize Jasmine had company until I came outside."

"Tony, this is my friend, and our travel consultant, Alex Trotter of Globe-Trotter Travels. She's taking care of all the reservations for the wedding cruise."

He reached out and to shake Alex's hand but held it while he studied her. "Pleasure meeting you. I like your business name, by the way. Clever." Alex felt uncomfortable under his scrutiny, being reminded of the probing, deep-set dark eyes of his father. But, unlike Victor Garza, Tony seemed more accepting and cheerful.

"Hi," Alex replied, standing a little taller and patting down her hair. "Nice to meet you, too, and thanks for the compliment...about my business. The name was kind of a natural."

"Yeah, but it's perfect," Tony said, indicating the sofa. "Sit. Please." Alex did so and Tony dropped down next to her. "I know you must be really good at what you do because you're working for my dad. I'd like to talk to you sometime about how you got started. I know it's tough — I've tried a few ventures myself but, so far, nothing's really taken off."

"I hope that you don't get discouraged and give up," Alex said, suddenly feeling sympathetic with this appealing stranger. "Maybe my best advice would be to have some kind of job so that you have income while you're starting up your business —

something to fall back on. Like, I had a couple part-time jobs and sold a few paintings in between taking people on trips —you know, just enough to pay the bills." *I'm telling the son of a multi-millionaire that he should wait tables to make ends meet?*

"That makes sense," Tony said, thoughtfully, "but for what I want to do, I need a lot of venture capital for equipment, commercial space, employees' salaries, products — the list goes on. Right now I'm trying to get a loan or line up some investors. I thought I could convince my dad, but..."

Alex recalled Victor Garza's harsh insults that she had overheard in his phone call. "Would you mind telling me your idea? I'm interested."

"Yeah, I'd like to hear, too," Jasmine added. "Your dad never told me, and I thought I'd rather hear about it from you, anyway."

"Oh, that's okay. I don't want to take a lot of time away from your visit."

"Don't worry about it, Tony. Alex was just giving me some legal documents to read over later. Frankly, I think we'd both rather hear about your business plan at this point."

"Well, all right, if you're sure. I just hope you think it's worth your time after I explain it. It's not like a break-through invention; just a concept, really. But I haven't seen the model that I have in mind anywhere."

"Okay." He leaned forward with his hands clasped on his knees. "We're all familiar with how successful Starbucks is, right? In fact, every day, two more Starbucks stores are opened somewhere in the world. And that's in a world where the favorite drink is *tea,* not coffee. Think about this: the overwhelming number of people in Asia, the Middle East, Australia, Africa, all of the United Kingdom, and much of Europe, are tea drinkers. Of the more than seven billion people in the world, two and a half billion live in China and India, alone, and their populations are *all* tea drinkers."

"If it weren't for the outrage about the tea tax," Alex inserted, "*Americans* might still be tea-drinkers."

"Maybe. It would help if there were teahouses here, too — or anywhere — that are comparable to Starbucks for coffee. By that I mean warm, cozy, meeting places with a strong branding that offer consistent quality and variety of their product. I'd like to include uncommon teas like East Frisian, Honey Bush from South Africa, with the more familiar White, Green, Yellow, Oolong, Black, and even post-fermented tea known as Pu-erh, that's a staple in China."

"Wow, you know a lot about teas — or tea," Alex put in. "Would you be processing it like Starbucks roasts their coffee?"

"Eventually. But, for now, I've researched where the best leaves are grown and the best methods for wilting the leaves to remove water, the best machines to macerate them, how and when to oxidize for the best aroma and flavor, and on through the rolling and drying. My plan would be to buy select leaves that I'd ship to certain facilities that are currently in operation."

"I think you have a very interesting idea, Tony!" Jasmine enthused. "How do you see the places looking? You know, colors and — well, what would they be called?"

"I've given that a lot of thought, too. That's why I commented on how good your business name is, Alex. As you know, we all react to names, either positively or negatively. So, figuring out a name that will attract people is very important. One reason the founder of Starbucks picked that name is that he thought an 's t' sound was strong.

"I've mulled over different ways to go, but I keep coming back to naming the tea shops simply, 'Tea Leaves.' That's the focus — quality tea leaves. Plus, it's a soft sound and it's associated with telling one's fortune. At least, I hope they foretell mine."

"I like it!" Alex broke in. "Just say it out loud, *Tea Leaves, Tea Leaves*. Why does that remind me of laughing? Oh, yeah — 'Tee Hees,' like in a comic book. Well, never mind me. It's a good name, anyway." She felt her face redden at her theatrics.

"No, that's not a bad association, Alex!" Tony responded, giving her a little pat on the arm. "And as for colors, I was thinking of pale greens and tans, grounded by plum — you know, the colors of tea. Then, of course, I'd have warm lighting, natural materials like wood for tables and chairs, and bamboo for the floors. For guests I'd have free Wi-Fi, newspapers, and great ethnic and regional sweets like kugelhopf, knafeh, jalebi, tea cakes, biscotti, and kringle."

"Ah, *now* you're speaking Alex's language," Jasmine chimed in, cheerfully. "I like it all, Tony, and I'm impressed with the amount of research you must have done. Did you get a chance to explain any of the details of your plan to your father?"

Before he could answer, they all turned at the sound of the back door slamming.

"Victor!" Jasmine called out. "I didn't expect you now."

"Apparently not. What's going on here?"

"What do you mean?" Jasmine queried, frowning. "Alex brought over documents for the wedding cruise, and then Tony stopped by. He was just telling us about his idea for a chain of teahouses. Alex and I both like the concept. Just now, I was asking him if he had had a chance to go into the particulars with you."

"I heard enough," Victor groused, cutting her off. "Nothing different from his usual pipe dreams. Personally, I've never been in need of a cup of tea that wasn't readily available. *Starbucks sells teas*, you know. They bought a goddamn tea company, in fact. And I don't want any more of my money going over to China. We send enough there as it is."

Alex cleared her throat to remind them that she was there. No one seemed to take any notice. *Doesn't anyone in this family bother keeping their arguments private?*

"Dad," we don't need to discuss this here," Tony urged. "Alex was just giving me some suggestions for starting up a business, and asked me about my ideas for a new venture. I told her a little about my plan. That's all."

In the tense silence that followed, Victor Garza turned and stared balefully at Alex. *Oh, Great!* Alex thought. *Now they notice me. If that man looked at me with any more fury, I'd catch on fire.*

"Victor," Jasmine broke in, "I was interested, too, and I think Tony's ideas have merit. He just needs a start; maybe one shop here or in London. I think it would be worthwhile to see how that kind of a business would be received, don't you? Couldn't you consider loaning him enough for start-up expenses for one 'Tea Leaves' shop? See how it goes? You help out Sunny when she asks for money."

"Leave Sunny out of this! She has her own cross to bear. You're getting all emotional about this, Jaz — and it's something you know nothing about. It's between me and Tony. I told him that if he wants to fritter away my hard-earned money, he'll have to wait until after I'm dead and he inherits enough to do what he wants. But I can see that he's gotten you on his side, as usual."

"Wait a minute, Dad. I wasn't going behind your back to *influence* Jasmine, if that's what you're insinuating."

"Mr. Garza, it was just as Tony says," Alex added. "He asked me about how I started my travel business, and I asked him about his idea. I just want to set the record straight on this."

Victor's gaze hadn't left Jasmine. "Let me just say this, Jaz. After we're married, I don't want you giving Tony any of your allowance. That money is to be spent on you, and I can see now that I'll have to ask for an accounting."

"Victor!" Jasmine gasped. "Please! Let's not discuss these personal matters here. We're making Tony and our guest very uncomfortable. You must have had a tortuous day that you're in such a foul mood. I know you'll regret your remarks later."

"Tony, I'm sorry about all this," Jasmine said, moving over to him and putting a hand on his arm. "Thank you for describing your plan to us." In a barely-audible voice, she added, "Apparently, I shouldn't have taken it upon myself to let your father know. I hope you get the opportunity soon to make it a reality."

"Thanks, Jazzy. You're the best," Tony murmured, covering her hand with his.

"Well, I need to get going," Alex said, jumping up. "It was nice meeting you, Tony. And nice seeing you again, Mr. Garza. Call me with any questions you have, Jasmine. No, please, stay where you are. I'll just let myself in the back door and Simmons can show me out."

A minute later Alex was out in front of the mansion taking deep breaths as she walked to her car. *That man is a selfish, controlling tyrant! He doesn't deserve a son as decent and nice as Tony. And he certainly doesn't deserve to marry someone as sweet and loving as Jasmine. I would suggest he buy cancellation insurance, because I think Jasmine is getting a good look at what she's marrying into.*

Chapter 8

August 4— three months later.

SITTING IN THE NOISY, congested Manhattan Cruise Terminal, Alex tried to find a comfortable position on one of the bolted-down molded plastic chairs, but found it impossible. She had just gotten there from the airport on the cruise line transport bus and, as she was earlier than expected, had decided not to go directly to the ship. It was only a little before noon and she knew from experience that the staterooms weren't usually clean and ready before twelve-thirty, at the earliest.

Being that it was a Sunday the early-morning plane from Chicago to JFK hadn't been full, and she hadn't had to wait long for her suitcase to appear on the carousel. A porter had taken it out to the bus for her. After the bus was loaded, it took off for New York City. With little traffic, the ride had taken just thirty-five minutes to arrive at the passenger terminal on 12th Avenue.

Now, seated inside, she dutifully took the "Globe-Trotter Travels" sign out of her carry-on and held it in front of her. It was unlikely that any of the wedding guests would need assistance from her at that point, but she felt obligated to identify herself, just in case. Mainly, she just wanted to sit quietly for a few minutes and collect her thoughts.

The *Bermuda Queen* would be sailing at four o'clock and the wedding was scheduled for six-thirty. Alex still couldn't believe that the ceremony would actually take place, but now that it was less than seven hours away, it had to be a near-certainty. Thinking back over the past three months of going over the plans with Jasmine, Alex had to admit that she always seemed happy about the upcoming nuptials. Maybe Victor had mellowed like he had said he was going to do. Or maybe Jasmine felt that the 'good outweighed the bad.' Or maybe she was being temporarily distracted by the fun of planning the event and the cruise.

That certainly was how Alex was feeling. Whatever misgivings she had about the marriage, she was certainly looking forward to the party tonight and the week's cruise, especially since she'd be with Arlie. Thinking back to his visit with her in Chicago over the Fourth of July, she had to shake her head in wonderment.

The first thing Arlie had wanted to do was to visit the Field Museum to see 'Sue,' the largest intact dinosaur skeleton in the world, and then to stop by the fossil prep room and the DNA center, where scientists performed the extraction of genetic material from bones. That was his idea of a romantic weekend, apparently.

Alex had never seen his eyes light up as they did when he viewed the seventy-five-million-year-old remains of some herbivore that lived on a pre-historic swampy continent. *Who could compete with that?*

Before the weekend was over, there were a few fireworks besides the ones that exploded over the lakefront, but Alex had seen that Arlie Tate was still a little bashful with her. Besides being highly intelligent, and insightful, she was discovering how guarded he was. She wondered, now, what it would be like spending an entire week with the man.

Thinking about her reunion with Arlie today, she did a quick assessment of the condition of her white slacks and blue knit top, then pulled out a small mirror, scrunched her hair and patted her moist face with a tissue. *Good enough, hopefully.*

From where Alex was sitting, she could see the waves of arriving passengers coming into the terminal as they either took seats to wait, or swept through to their next destination. Arlie might show up any minute now, but she should be more concerned with the members of her group who might be around and needing help to find their way to the ship that was docked at Pier #37.

Just then a couple, lugging suitcases and leading a young boy, started down her row of chairs to get to vacant seats. Alex turned sideways to make a little more room for them to get by. After the threesome passed, she held up her sign again.

"I can read that," a small voice said.

"Huh?" Alex brought down her sign to look into a pair of bright blue eyes set in a cherubic round face that was four feet off the ground.

"I can read your sign," the young boy repeated. "I'm seven years old and I can read. It says "Globe-Trot-ter-Tra-vels." He pointed a stubby finger at each syllable. "Are you a basketball player? You don't look like one."

"What? A basketball player? Oh...no, you're thinking of the *Harlem* Globetrotters. You're right, though — they're a basketball team, but I'm someone who helps people who are on vacation. Are you on vacation with your parents?"

"Yeah. We're going to the Bermuda Island for my mom and dad's anniversary. I was goin' to stay with my gramma but she couldn't take care of me on account of her having surgery. But she's okay, really."

"Oh, I see. Well, you'll have a lot of fun on the ship. I'm going to Bermuda, too, on the same ship you're going on; *The Bermuda Queen*. I'm Alex Trotter. What's your name?"

"Toby. Toby Wilson."

"Toby!" his mother called out. "Come back here, honey," she motioned to him. "Sorry about that," she said to Alex.

"Not a problem. I'm enjoying talking to him."

"Well, I better go now," Toby said. "It was nice to meet you. If I need help on my vacation, I'll let you know."

"Okay, I hope you do," Alex said.

Toby looked up then, causing Alex to start to turn to see who was coming, when she felt hands placed firmly on her shoulders.

A deep Southern voice drawled, "I leave you to your own devices and you pick up another guy."

"Arlie!" Alex exclaimed, grinning up at him. "Hi! Uh, this is Toby Wilson. He read my sign and wanted to know if I was a Harlem Globetrotter. Anyway — Toby, this is Mr. Tate who's going on the boat, too. Maybe we'll see you later on board, okay?"

"Cute kid," Arlie remarked after Toby had gone back to his seat. "Is he your only customer so far, 'Meadowlark'? Maybe you should stand near the door where people could see you."

"Thanks for the suggestion, but I don't really want to be seen. I'm not even expected to be here— I was just making a half-hearted effort in case anyone needed directions. I'm only sitting here because I was early, for one thing, and looking for you, for another. You look good, by the way." She took a moment to admire how his sandy hair and deep-set blue eyes were set off by the navy blazer.

"Thanks," Arlie mumbled. "I guess you got through to me that some of my clothes went beyond 'casual.' Maybe more like 'homeless.'"

He sat down next to her. "So, the wedding's still on, I assume. You thought your friend would back out, right? From what you've told me, we should have quite a lively evening if the guests are as bad as Jasmine says they are."

"Alex!" a man's voice called out, causing both of them to look up. "So good to see you! What a day, huh? Have you seen my dad and Jasmine, yet? Oh, I'm sorry — I'm Tony Garza," he said, addressing Arlie who had stood. "Are you with our group?" He extended his hand.

"Arlie Tate. I'm with Alex," Arlie said, nodding towards her as he firmly shook hands with the newcomer.

"Oh. Alex hadn't told me that she had invited someone."

Alex jumped up. "Well, we weren't talking about the wedding when I saw you *months ago*, Tony. But, to answer your question, I haven't seen your father or Jasmine— or anyone else I know. You all didn't travel together? What about Sunny and the Count?"

"No, they're coming on their own. I know Jaz and Dad flew in yesterday. They were planning to be boarding early to meet with her matron of honor, the wedding consultant, and the captain. I haven't texted or called them today as I figured they'd be too busy or couldn't get reception on the ship. Sunny and Carlo were coming in from the Cape today. I'm sure they have a driver to take them directly to the ship, so you won't see them here."

Arlie was looking at Tony with interest, moving his gaze from the smooth tanned face, to the cream linen suit, the open-collared pink shirt, and down to the soft leather deck shoes worn without socks. "Sounds like your family is pretty self-reliant, Tony. Alex should be able to get on board, then, don't you think?" he asked, slipping an arm around her. "Oh, sure. Uh, I'll just see you later then, Alex, okay? At the wedding? And you, too— I'm sorry, was that Artie or Arlie?"

"Arlie. Arlie Tate."

"Arlie — got it. It's not a common name. Well, glad you could join us."

"Thanks. Should be a great time."

"Arlie," Alex said, "I think you're right that it's time to get on the ship. All the staterooms should be ready by now, anyway. We'll see you at the wedding, Tony. I'm looking forward to meeting all the guests and seeing your family again. Should be a quite a night."

Chapter 9

"YOU NEVER MENTIONED Tony to me," Arlie whispered in Alex's ear they moved through the crowd, heading for the exit of the terminal.

"Didn't I? Well, I guess I didn't because there wasn't any reason to. I only told you about the family members I thought might cause trouble. You'd really like Tony, if you got to know him. Not that I know him well — I hardly know him at all, in fact. I'm mostly going by what Jasmine has said about him. She thinks he's wonderful."

"Well, he's good looking and well dressed, I'll say that. He seemed to think a lot of you, too."

Alex peered into the deep blue eyes under the heavy brows. "You sound jealous, Arlie. Can I tell you that you have nothing to worry about. If I were interested in Tony, believe me, you would never have heard about this trip. Besides, I compared you favorably to Tony when Jasmine was bragging about what a handsome, charming guy he was."

"You said I was charming and handsome?"

Alex chewed her bottom lip for a moment. "Well, not exactly, but I said that I liked you the way you are. Almost the same thing. Here we are at check-in, ready to go through the scanners and board the ship. This is great, isn't it? I can't wait to get underway!"

* * *

A HALF HOUR later Arlie and Alex were entering their connecting cabins on Deck Thirteen. The two staterooms were identical, each comprised of a king-sized bed with a white eiderdown cover, a white laminate-topped dark wood dresser with a mirror above, a pale blue tweed armless sleeper sofa with storage space underneath, and a flat screen TV mounted in one corner.

Each bathroom was equipped with a clothes rod on one side across from a dark wood vanity with two porcelain sinks. Through an adjacent doorway were a shower and commode.

The blue-carpeted balconies were each furnished with a round table, two cushioned chairs and two chaise lounges.

Alex looked around appreciatively. "I love the décor, don't you, Arlie? The white walls and blue draperies look clean and modern. And the abstract artwork is quite nice. It' looks bigger than only 185 square feet, doesn't it?"

Arlie nodded. "Let me put it this way— I think it's big enough for both of us. You did notice that everything in the place is doubled— the sinks, the dresser, the bed. There are even two chairs on the balcony. Seems a shame not to use it the way it was designed."

"Arlie. We' might as well spread out a little. Believe me, we'll be seeing *plenty* of each other. Anyway, let's plan what we're going to do. If you don't mind, I'd like to tour the ship right away to see how to get to all the public spaces —the the main dining room, the art gallery, the theatre, casino —all those things."

"You wanna go on your own?"

"No, of course not! I mean, *we'll* tour the ship together, if that's okay with you. We can grab something to eat, too, since dinner won't be until at least eight o'clock. I'd also like to just check on Jasmine and see if everything's going as planned."

"You mean, you want to find out if she's backed out yet because you think she should. Alex, she's marrying a very wealthy, powerful man. Without even meeting her, I can tell you she'll go through with it."

"You're so crass, Arlie Tate. Anyway, she and Victor are one deck up, near us, but all the way aft. I'd like to see their unit. It's the largest deluxe suite and all the way around the back of the ship, so all they see is water. Can you imagine?"

"If you go out far enough onto our balconies, all you can see is water," Arlie said, peering out the sliding glass door. "Just don't lose your balance."

"The railings are about a foot higher than the ones on land," Alex said. "Which is much better. Did you ever notice that railings on people's decks are always right at eye level? But I digress. What was I saying? Oh, yeah, I want to check in on Jasmine. We might run into some other guests, but I don't know most of them. The rest are on our deck — some very important artists and collectors, but further aft. Sunny and the Count are on our deck, too, but —"

"I know, 'further aft.'" Arlie finished. "We should get going, but you probably want to take a few minutes to put your things away. Then we can go wherever you want."

"See how nice you are?" She gave Arlie a kiss on the cheek. He put an arm around her neck and kissed her on the mouth.

"Well, that's better," Alex breathed.

"It's the only way I know to get you to stop talking for a minute."

"Oh. Well, let's get unpacked, like you said. It's only a little after two so, if we leave in, say, fifteen minutes, we can get something to eat, tour the ship and still have plenty of time to relax and take our time getting ready for the wedding.

"Oh, and I need to locate the chapel! I understand it's very small — seats only thirty people, if that. Good thing that Jasmine and Victor will be standing. Also, we should be on one of the upper decks at four o'clock to wave at everyone on the dock as we pull away from New York City."

Arlie looked at the ceiling, shaking his head. "We don't know anyone on the dock. Just promise me that we can get a drink up there and I'll wave like the Queen of England. Right now I'll leave you to organize yourself and I'll see you in a few minutes." He gave her a pat on the behind, turned and walked away.

After Arlie had left, Alex opened her suitcase and took out the tissue paper-covered dress that was on top. Taking it our of its cocoon, she couldn't help but stroke the smooth copper satin and run her fingers over the intricate iridescent beading on the bodice. It was the most beautiful dress that she had ever owned, she thought. Of course, it probably wouldn't measure up to the couture designs on most of the other guests, but she was confident that she could hold her own in it.

* * *

OUT IN THE HALLWAY a few minutes later, Alex and Arlie had to walk only a short distance down the carpeted hallway to get to the stairwell. Climbing up one flight they reached the landing, and opened the fire door. Alex motioned for them to go to the right. Going along the quiet corridor, she had to peer at each room number they passed to make them out in the soft lighting. "14872 — this is it."

She knocked twice. No response. She knocked three times more and called out Jasmine's name. No response. She turned and looked at Arlie, quizzically.

"Knock once more," he advised. "She might not hear you in such a big apartment."

Alex gave a little shrug and knocked again. This time the door was cracked open. Jasmine took a step out. "Alex!"

"Hey, Jasmine! Thought I'd see how you're doing. Are you all right? You look a little pale."

"Oh, I'm fine." Jasmine opened the door further to reveal herself standing barefoot in a white terry robe, her dark hair falling in ringlets over her shoulders. "Oh, hi. You must be Arnie."

Alex spoke up. "Artie. I mean, *Arlie,*" she corrected herself with a shake of the head. "I'm a little flustered right now. I feel like we've disturbed you. Did we wake you?"

"Oh, no, I wasn't sleeping. I probably didn't hear you when you first knocked. The bedroom is over on the other side of the suite. It's a pretty big place." Alex felt a pinch on the back of her arm.

"I was just resting until the hairdresser and beautician came to do my hair and put my face on. That's all. But, I'm fine, really. Isn't it amazing that we women can look sick when we don't have any makeup on?"

"Yeah, well that's true with me," Alex agreed. "Is there any errand you need me to run? Anything you need from the pharmacy? Victor's not here, I assume."

"No, he wanted to look around the ship and to give me some privacy. But, as to your offer, thanks, but I have everything I need. I'll tell you what, though, I do have a favor to ask of you. At the cocktails reception, before dinner, I wonder if I could ask you, as I've asked Cindy, to circulate among the guests, introduce yourself and make some conversation. I just don't know how well these people are going to mix, and I'd feel more comfortable with you and Cindy sort of hostessing. Of course,

Victor and I will be walking around talking to everyone, but the more of us covering the guests, the better."

"Sure, I don't mind. I need to meet everyone to do my job, anyway. If that's all right with you, Arlie," Alex added, a little late.

"Oh, right," Jasmine joined in "I should have asked if you minded, Arlie."

"No problem, but Alex doesn't need my permission. I'll go around with her, if that's all right. She's very social. I'm sure she'll do a good job talking to everyone."

"Yes, well, I guess we'd better be running along," Alex broke in before he said anything embarrassing. "I can't wait to see you in your dress, Jaz. Oh, where is the chapel again, by the way? I want to find it before the wedding."

"It's on Deck Seven, right near the casino, which is interesting, isn't it? Wait till you see it — Cindy has decorated it beautifully. So, I'll see you later, then. Thank you both for stopping by."

Chapter 10

"LET'S GO UP AND EAT FIRST," Alex suggested when they got to the elevator. "I thought it would be nice to get something in the Garden Cafe on the Sun Deck. Okay?"

"Fine, if you're sure we can't find a tofu stand somewhere."

"What? Oh. Funny. I assume you mean that you don't want a salad. Let's just check it out," she said as they stepped into the empty elevator and she pressed the 'up' button. "If they don't have sandwiches, we won't stay. I just thought it'd be nice to sit outside on the top deck and look over the city and harbor while we have the chance.

"So, what did you think of Jasmine? Isn't she beautiful?"

"You're just as pretty."

"Oh, I am not at all!" She paused. "Wait a minute — I'm arguing against self-interest. I think I'll let you say what you want. Jasmine didn't look her best just now, that's for sure. You'll see how gorgeous she is at the wedding."

"I didn't buy her story of why she looked so pale," Arlie commented, standing back to let Alex off the stopped elevator. "Shall we take that table?" he asked, pointing at a round table under a yellow umbrella on the other side of the pool. "Looks like you'll have your view from there."

"Sure, that's fine. But, what do you mean you 'didn't buy her story'? You didn't think it was because she wasn't wearing makeup? You've never even *seen* her before to know how she should look. Some people are very fair, you know. So, what did you think was wrong with her?"

"I'm not a doctor — I'm a detective, so I can't give you a diagnosis. But I know that she was unsteady on her feet, maybe dizzy."

"How could you know that?" Alex challenged. "It didn't look to me like she was losing her balance."

"She wasn't, because she was holding onto the door the whole time we were talking to her. Didn't you notice that she never let go of the handle and was bearing down on it? You could tell that she was pitching forward a little onto the balls of her feet since she wasn't wearing shoes."

"Wow. That's pretty good, Arlie. I didn't notice any of that. But why wouldn't she just tell us that she felt lightheaded or whatever? What's the big deal?"

"That's what makes it suspicious. Another thing, didn't you think it was strange that she didn't offer to let us even step inside so she could show off her fancy suite? She must have noticed how you were trying to look past her to see into the room. I'm not saying she has a fatal illness. I'm just saying that she wasn't feeling well and didn't admit it."

"Yeah, maybe so, but there are many innocent explanations for that. She might not have wanted me to pry, or to pester her to see the medic, or whatever, considering that she just wanted to relax to prepare for the ceremony and the long evening ahead. She could be a little unsteady due to nerves, or be exhausted from working on the wedding, or shaky from not having eaten enough today — lots of reasons she wouldn't necessarily share with me."

"That's true," Arlie conceded. "Could be something very trivial. I'm just saying that she wasn't suffering from lack of lipstick. Let's eat. I'm going to have a Reuben. What would you like?"

* * *

FORTY-FIVE MINUTES LATER, Alex and Arlie were easing their way through a crowd of people in the Atrium on Deck Six. Everyone seemed to be coming towards them. Glass-walled novelty shops and boutiques that bordered the open space were doing a brisk business as tourists stocked up on items they had forgotten or wanted as souvenirs. The light pouring in from the glass ceiling brightened the whole space.

"Seems like everyone got the same idea at the same time," Alex remarked, pulling Arlie over to a protected spot under the suspended circular staircase. "Of course, this is always the busiest place. There's the Internet cafe over there. Back that direction I know there are several smaller restaurants, like a steak house, and an Italian cafe. Across from us is, as you see, the customer service desk and the bank. Those people are lined up to exchange dollars for pounds, while the other long line over there is for people asking questions, like, 'What time does dinner start?' 'When does the Casino open?' 'Where can I smoke on the ship?'"

"So, only fat wheezing gamblers have questions?" Arlie asked, drolly.

"Those are just some examples," Alex sniffed. "I'm sure *someone* wants to know where the fitness center is — it's up on the Sun Deck, where we were, by the way.

"I think the theatre is all the way aft, past the restaurants," she continued. "We don't need to see that right now. We should go up to Deck 7 so we don't run out of time to check out the chapel, the casino and the art gallery before we go back up to the Sun Deck for departure."

"Let's just go up the stairway," Arlie suggested. "I'm starting to get a crick in my neck under here, anyway."

* * *

"WELL, HERE'S THE CASINO," Alex said as they approached a wide opening off the dark blue carpeted hallway. "Some of the lights are already on so we can see in. Pretty alluring, isn't it? That purple cast on everything makes people feel like they're in a fantasy land. That's the idea. Nothing is too real — like how much you're betting with plastic, on plastic chips and plastic playing cards."

"It's a cool-looking room, though," Arlie said, impressed. "They've nickel slots, anyway. Can't get into too much trouble with those. I'm sure we'll come down and try our luck a few times."

"Look at all the places where you can set your drink by the slots and tables," Alex remarked. "These cruise operators know what they're doing. But it's a fun place to be as long as you set a limit on how much you're willing to lose — and win, and walk away. That's the trick — leaving with winnings. Anyway, let's go find the chapel. Jasmine said it's close by."

Back out in the hallway, they found a small brass sign reading 'Chapel' with an arrow. Coming to the dark wood paneled doors, Arlie opened the right one and they both stepped inside the cool, fragrant room.

"Ooh! Look at this place!" Alex gasped, grabbing hold of Arlie's coat sleeve.

The high-ceilinged room was bathed in tones of amber, ruby, and emerald that emanated from back-lit stained glass windows of abstract design. Three were set opposite one another in each side wall. At the front of the chapel was a spotlighted mural of a sunset on the ocean reflecting its rosy sky and its gold and silver waves.

For seating, there were half a dozen dark wood pews fitted out with tufted burgundy velvet cushions. On each of the pew ends at the aisle was a bouquet of flowers, including stalks of Bird of Paradise, purple and white orchids, and ferns, tied together with wide lavender ribbon that fell halfway to the floor. On the altar was a huge bouquet of pink phalaenopsis orchids, red calla lilies, orange proteas, hot pink ginger, Birds of Paradise and ferns.

"It looks like these flowers are native to Hawaii," Alex gasped, in wonderment. "I can see why Jasmine was so pleased with the chapel and Cindy's decorations. They're exquisite. And the chapel is so ethereal. I can't imagine anything happening here that isn't sacred."

"Well, I wouldn't go that far," Arlie said. "It is beautiful, though."

"It is." Alex took a last look around. "Well, let's just look in at the Art gallery and then we'll head up to the Sun Deck, okay?"

* * *

FIVE MINUTES LATER, they were walking through the gallery space, gazing at dozens of lighted works of art on the white walls.

"I'm surprised to see Dalis and Picassos — they're prints, right?" Arlie whispered.

"They're *limited* prints and lithographs, probably with original signatures," Alex explained. "That makes them quite valuable. There's some question as to *how* valuable they are. They go for thousands of dollars at auctions on ships. I mean, like twenty five thousand, thirty thousand, or more."

"People will pay that kind of money for artwork on a cruise?" Arlie asked. "How do they know they're authentic and that they're worth so much?"

"Well, they don't, really. The free wine and champagne they serve at the auctions goes a long way, from my experience. The auctioneer always says that everything's at least 20% less than on the open market, but, I've heard that people have found those claims to be untrue after they get home. Just the opposite, in fact."

"Seems like a scam, no?" Arlie asked, quietly, looking closely at one of the Dalis.

"Well," Alex started, "Maybe evaluating art is like anything else — it's worth what someone is willing and able to pay for it. Of course, that isn't what our host Victor Garza would say. He'd probably tell you *exactly* what you should pay for any of these. I wouldn't venture to say, myself."

"Excuse me. Could I offer some assistance?"

Alex and Arlie spun around to face the speaker: a thin, bronze-faced man with a blond pompadour. He was carefully dressed in a navy pinstripe suit and white silk shirt. A lavender handkerchief was artfully arranged in his breast pocket. Standing there, the man suddenly pulled back his lips to display a mouthful of large teeth that were chemically whitened well beyond nature's capability.

"I'm Horatio Krumm, art dealer and auctioneer," he announced through his blinding dental work, as he proffered a brown manicured hand to each of them. "I noticed that the gentleman was interested in one of our fine Dalis. There's an auction scheduled for tomorrow night and that presents an opportunity for you to posses a piece of museum-quality art at a bargain price." He beamed at Arlie who couldn't help but wince a little in response.

"Well, I don't —" Arlie started.

"No, no. I must caution you not to feel that you don't know enough about art. I'm sure you know what you like and, fortunately, I can advise you as to quality and rarity, which are the elements of value in all things — am I right?" He revealed his glittering teeth again. "Depending on the bidding, you could be doing much better than you'd ever do at the casino across the way. Not that I discourage anyone from wagering in our well-run gaming room. It's just a comparison.

"So, tell me, is this the Dali that has won your heart?" Horatio Krumm gestured to the framed print that Arlie had briefly looked at. "Brilliant choice, if I may say. It's one of our *Divine Comedy* Dalis. Salvador created one hundred illustrations for the Dante classic between 1951 and 1960 for an Italian limited-edition reprinting. Since then, they have become his most famous and most sought-after series. Thirty-five hundred woodcuts were made to make reproductions; that many as they degrade over time and use. But we are privileged to be able to offer many of them to the cruising public — all signed by the artist.

"And you, sir, have shown discriminating taste in selecting one of the best, and one of my favorites. It's titled *Original Perfection,* which is exactly what it is."

"Well," Arlie jumped in, "my girlfriend, here, is quite a good artist in her own right. I think I'll talk this over with her. However, we need to be going now. Thank you for the information. Maybe we'll see you later." With that, he took hold of Alex's elbow and started steering her out of the exhibit.

Once outside, they started walking briskly in the direction of a bank of elevators. Arlie looked back over his shoulder once before confiding to Alex, "Could you believe that guy? Talk about a used-car salesman!"

"Did you mean what you said to him?" Alex asked.

"What did I say? I barely got a word in."

"That I'm your girlfriend and you think I'm a good artist."

"Of course. You know I like your paintings." He paused, looking at her without expression. Then, tapping her nose, he allowed his lips to curl up slightly. "But the only discussion we're going to have about buying a print is that we're not going to buy one, right?"

"Certainly not a signed Salvador Dali. At least I'm not." Alex answered. "But I think we should go to the auction tomorrow night and see what goes on. Maybe not take our credit cards. I know how champagne affects me."

"Okay with me, but I just thought of something, Alex. The auction is *tomorrow* night when we'll be in international waters. There are no consumer protection laws there, you know. I don't think that's an accident, do you?"

"No, it's not. Good call. The auctioneers on ships aren't regulated by any U.S. jurisdiction. But Mr. 'What's his name'? Horatio? has to give a buyer some kind of Certificate of Authenticity describing the piece.

"I remember a discussion back in art school about the Dali Divine Comedy' engravings; something about authenticating them. I don't remember now, but those looked real to me.

"Speaking of real, do you think that's his real name — Horatio Krumm?" Alex queried.

Arlie gave her a little smirk. "Never mind his name. You don't think those are his real teeth, do you? I'm not sure I can trust anyone who has teeth whiter than his shirt.

Here's an elevator that goes to the top. Let's go get a drink and wave to all the people in the harbor who are so happy to see us off on our cruise to Bermuda."

Chapter 11

BY SIX O'CLOCK THAT EVENING Alex had finished with her hair and makeup and had stepping into her copper-colored satin dress. After pulling up the short zipper in back, she slipped on her sandaled heels and walked out to appraise herself in the dresser mirror. *Not bad,* she thought. *Not bad at all.*

Gazing at her reflection, she had to credit her curling iron with a great victory over her frizz-prone hair, even with bringing out more red highlights and giving it some shine. But it was the dress that was really beautiful. If she wasn't getting carried away, she thought she might even be considered a little sexy, what with the form-fitted beaded top and plunging neckline. And the skirt followed her curves to just past her hips where it flared out to the floor. After a few turns, she stopped to inspect how the low-cut back looked in the mirror, and thought, *pretty daring for me.*

While admiring her dress, she was startled by a tap on the connecting door. "Alex? Are you there? Could you help me with my studs when you're ready? The damn things are giving me fits. I keep dropping them on the floor and I can barely bend over in this get-up."

"Sure. I'm finished. C'mon in." She turned and struck a pose that she hoped was vampish — one shoulder and hip forward. She licked her lips and smiled.

After a moment the handle turned as Arlie continued his tirade. "I mean, I'm stiff as a board in this shirt and then these ... Alex! My God!"

"What?!"

"You're beautiful! You look fantastic!"

"Geez ——the way you yelled I thought my hair was on fire! And look at *you,* anyway — you look like ..."

"Like a maitre d'," he finished as she searched for a metaphor. "That brown dress is great on you. I mean ..." He slowly moved his gaze down her body and back up to her face.

"It's *copper*," Alex corrected him, "but thanks. You're looking at me like you looked at the bones of that prehistoric swamp creature. I'm very flattered."

"Trust me, I'm not thinking about a 'prehistoric swamp creature'? You beat everything, did you know that?"

Alex chuckled at their private joke. "Well, hook me up in back, will you? And then I'll snap on your studs. We've gotta get going pretty soon. She turned around for him to connect the tiny fastener. "Be sure you get it to grab onto something. That's all that's keeping me from indecent exposure."

"Not in my book, but I've got it."

* * *

TEN MINUTES LATER they were downstairs standing with a small group of people outside the closed doors of the chapel. Every couple of minutes one door would be opened by an usher to allow another couple inside. The strains of Bach's Jesu, Joy of Man's Desiring could be heard being played in organ tones on a keyboard.

"Don't forget — we're 'friends of the bride,' Alex whispered to Arlie as they moved up to be next in line. "We want the usher to seat us on Jasmine's side."

"Shouldn't we tell him that you *really dislike* the groom?" Arlie whispered back. Alex elbowed him lightly in the ribs.

When the door opened, a short balding man in a tuxedo came towards them, holding a program. Alex stopped him and announced, "We're friends of the bride," and reached for his order of service.

The man pulled it back from her grasp and sneered, "Good for you. I'm a friend of the groom. I'm his attorney."

The usher came up behind him and quickly handed Alex her own program. "Ma'am, there is no 'bride's side.' As you see, there are three pews on each side. Everyone has to sit together. This way, please." He proceeded to show them to a space at the end of the last row on what would have been the 'groom's side,' as the keyboard player got to the end of the cantata.

After a few moments, the musician launched into the Canon and Gigue for Three Violins and Basso Continuo, commonly known as Pachelbel's Canon. "That's the music for the bridal party," Alex whispered, excitedly, pulling a camera out of her purse. "And there's Victor Garza coming out of a door in front with the Captain and Tony."

Arlie patted her knee and whispered, "Okay— take it easy, now."

In response to the musical cue, the wedding guests turned around to see Cindy Carmody enter. She was moving very slowly to extend her walk down the abbreviated aisle giving everyone time to admire the striking color combination of her coral dress, blond hair, and bouquet of purple orchids and pink phalaenopses.

As Cindy got to the front, the captain smiled and nodded at her as she gracefully turned to face the wedding guests.

Moments later, the keyboard player added another string instrument's low tone as the music swelled into a great crescendo. In eager anticipation, the guests again swiveled in their places and stared at the back of the chapel. As the seconds ticked by, several women started shifting in their seats — straining to see something, or to get a better sightline of the door.

Alex held up her camera and focused on the doorway, repeatedly checking the image in her screen. Not satisfied with what she saw, she felt around for the zoom button, but hit the flash, instead. The resulting click and blinding white light seemed like an explosion going off in the hushed, darkened church. Two women across the aisle wearing similar floral dresses turned to stare, openmouthed.

Finally, both doors were thrown open and Jasmine Keahi made her grand entrance. Dressed in a strapless mermaid-style gown in pure white organza, the bride seemed to float like the mythical sea creature that had inspired the design. The slim dress was elegantly tailored down to the knees where it burst out into ruffled layers like a can-can dancer's crinolines. The frills were longer in back to trail behind her like a frothy wake. Completing the outfit was a fingertip-length tulle veil attached to a pearl headpiece that crowned her upswept hairdo. Her bouquet of lavender, white orchids and baby's breath added exotic color and fragrance.

Other cameras were now flashing, accompanied by several 'oohs' and 'ahs' from the crowd. In response, Jasmine glanced around as she walked, her dark eyes glistening, and the color rising in her cheeks.

Alex elbowed Arlie, looking pointedly at him for confirmation of Jasmine's glowing beauty. "See what I mean?" she asked, gloating.

Leaning in close, Arlie said out of the side of his mouth. "Okay, you win. She doesn't look that sick right now." Alex exhaled in exasperation, shaking her head.

As Jasmine arrived at the front, Victor Garza stepped towards her and offered his arm. They both approached the altar.

Captain Thomas commanded attention as he looked over the assembled guests and cleared his throat to begin the liturgy of the wedding ceremony. Alex noted that the floral-dress women were dabbing their eyes with a tissue. She wondered what Sunny was doing then, if she was even there.

Sunny came to her mind again when the Captain gave the traditional charge, "If any of you has reasons why these two should not be wed, speak now or forever hold your peace." Someone coughed causing everyone to look around, suspiciously. Alex gripped the pew for the five long tense seconds until the Captain resumed speaking. It was only after the couple spoke their memorized vows and were pronounced "man and wife," that Alex felt she could breath normally, again.

Following the kiss, and the introduction of "Mr. and Mrs. Victor Garza," Captain Thomas announced that all of the guests were invited to make their way up to the VIP room on the Sun Deck. The bridal party would be delayed a little with the photographer, but would soon join everyone upstairs as the celebration continued with cocktails, followed by a sit-down dinner, and would conclude with dancing under the stars to the music of "The Four-Sea Sons."

Alex nudged Arlie. "C'mon, let's get up there before the others. I need to get my head together before I'm ready to take on this group. Just follow my lead. It could get pretty snarky up there."

Chapter 12

ALEX AND ARLIE were the first ones to arrive at the outdoor area of the Sun Deck that had been partitioned off for the party. The space had literally been lit up like a Christmas tree with strings of clear lights suspended overhead. In the center of the space was a large tiered fountain lit by lavender-colored floods. Adding to the garden atmosphere were bistro tables and chairs set off with up-lit potted palms and other tropical greens. Piped-in orchestral music played in the background as waiters and bartenders stood by the Tiki bar waiting for the guests and the bridal party to arrive.

"I see some of the wedding guests getting off the elevators already, Arlie. There are those two little ladies in the flowered dresses we sat near in the chapel coming out — I bet they're Jasmine's aunts."

"They look a little confused."

"Yeah. I'll go introduce myself and see if I can be of some help. Would you mind getting me a glass of chardonnay?"

"No problem. I'll get myself something, too. Be right back."

As Arlie walked off, Alex waved at the two women who each held up a hand and tentatively wiggled a couple of fingers. As the women approached, the one in the pink floral two-piece dress asked, "Do we know you, dear? You look familiar."

The lady in glasses, in the lavender floral outfit chimed in. "Yes, yes you do. I was asking Lola who you were in church when you took a flash picture before Jasmine came in."

"Yes, well, I'm sorry about that," Alex said. "But you probably saw a picture of me on some of the paperwork I sent you about the cruise. I'm Alex Trotter of Globe-Trotter Travels. I'm helping Jasmine with the arrangements for the cruise and setting up excursions when we get to Bermuda. So, are you her aunts?"

"Yes. I'm Lola, and this is my sister, Alaana. We know you from your picture, of course! You look so different tonight, though."

"Oh, yes, I recognize you now," agreed Alaana. "And Jasmine told us that you had become friends. It's so nice to meet you. Didn't our darling girl make a beautiful bride? We're very happy for her."

"And worried, too, of course," Lola inserted, lowering her voice. "It has all happened so fast, and Victor is *so much older*, don't you think? I think he's older than *we* are. And he can be so brusque. We don't understand these people from the *art world*, anyway. They're all very *different*, aren't they, dear?"

"Well, actually, I'm also an artist — like Jasmine. Artists can be like anyone else," Alex explained, as two men in tight black pants walked by; one with spiked frosted hair wearing a cape, and the other with a pink streak in his crew cut, wearing a long black scarf. "I mean, Victor is more of a *business man* than an artist. And a very successful one at that. From what

I've seen, he appears to love Jasmine, and she seems to love him."

Just then Arlie walked up with two glasses of wine and handed one to Alex.

"Thank you. Ladies, this is my guest, Arlie Tate. And this is Aunt Lola and Aunt Alaana. Can we call you that?"

"Sure, of course. Makes us feel like family," Lola said, looking between them. "You two make such an attractive couple. And close in age, too."

"Okay, Lola," Alaana, cut in. "We should let them move on and meet other people, now. Go ahead and look around, sister. I'll be right with you. I just want to tell Miss Trotter something."

Pulling at Alex's elbow, Alaana stretched out her neck to whisper. "Don't tell Jasmine that we think that Victor is too old and unpleasant. Lola shouldn't always say everything that pops into her head. I always have to smooth things over."

"No problem," Alex whispered back, and then said aloud, "Uh, why don't you ladies get a drink, or iced tea, if you prefer. Just tell one of the waiters what you'd like. We'll see you a little later."

"Characters, huh?" Arlie said under his breath after they'd gone off.

"They're cute, but I can see how they get into arguments and have misunderstandings. They're so much alike. I've already forgotten who's who. One of them says, 'of course' a lot. Of course, I don't know which one." she added, rolling her eyes.

"Oh no! Here comes Sunny. Don't go anywhere, Arlie. And I mean even if you have to go to the john."

Arlie turned to look at a woman with flaming red hair in a long skinny black dress bearing down on them like a charging bull.

"Well— if it isn't Alex Trotter," the deep voice said in greeting, without acknowledging Arlie. "Aren't we all dressed up tonight? In that dress you look like pure money — pennies, but that's money, isn't it?"

"Nice to see you, too, Sunny. And I was just thinking that black is really your color. It suits you. But, enough about us. Didn't Jasmine look beautiful? I thought she looked like a movie star on the red carpet in that dress."

"A movie star? Maybe like a dark-haired Daryl Hannah in *Splash*. That mermaid thing can only go so far, can't it?"

"It's a big look right now, and a clever choice for a shipboard wedding, I thought," Alex countered.

"I'm sorry — we haven't been introduced," Arlie put in, raising his hands like a referee. "Arlie Tate. And you must be Sunny Giovanni. You'll have to excuse us, but Alex needs to get around to meet everyone, so we'll have to continue this later. Maybe meet your husband, too, if he shows up."

"The Count will soon be here," they heard Sunny say as Arlie was steering Alex away at breakneck speed.

"That woman is downright nasty," Arlie said.

"Don't say that I didn't warn you. Here comes a waiter. Why don't we grab a couple of hors d'oeuvres and sit down for a minute. I'm starving. And, by the way, I could have taken care of myself with Sunny; but thanks, anyway."

Having selected a few rolled canapés, they sat down next to a table occupied by a middle-aged couple they hadn't met. The man was paunchy and nearly bald, but sported a trim grey mustache and goatee. The woman had stiff blond hair and was wearing a multi-colored sequined jacket. They hadn't seemed to notice Alex and Arlie as they continued their conversation without looking up.

"I mean, can you believe this?!" the man was saying. "How does he have the balls to even invite us on this fucking cruise? It's costing a fortune and he's rubbing my nose in it, the son-of-a-bitch!"

"Shhh! Roman! And watch your language! We didn't have to come, you know. I would have been content if we had never laid eyes on the man, again. Besides, why are you getting so upset *now*? The case is settled. You're not getting another dime from him, so forget it. I thought we came to take advantage of a free cruise to Bermuda."

"Listen, Monica, don't kid yourself — this is *no free cruise*! Victor is using *our money* to pay for this, so I hope you're enjoying the hell out of it. And the case may be settled, but it's not over with for me. He cheated me after we broke up the business and he took the best artists with him, and had them sign exclusives. Then he took the clients who were buying their work!"

"I never understood how he got by with that!" his wife hissed. "But you went to court and settled. Why did you settle?"

The man took a bite of a stuffed mushroom and chewed on it, looking out on the crowd. "You could say he just had the better lawyer. And I didn't settle as much as I gave up when I ran out of money. Feldman convinced the judge that Victor's associations pre-dated mine, and that Victor had done more business with them, and some other bullshit. A lot of it came down to his word against mine."

His wife sat still, pursing her lips. "You know— some of those artists are here, Roman. What would it hurt to go and talk to them? You know better than anyone what a bastard Victor is to work with. You can bet your sweet ass that his artists all feel that way. We already know he has a feud going with that sculptor, Bruno Macaroni, or whatever. And someone said that Francesca 'whats-her-name' threw a fit about her exhibit at Garza's."

"Yeah, I hear ya. Why shouldn't *I* try to steal them back? We still wouldn't be even, but it'd help." The man looked pleased with himself. "Hell, I should talk to the collectors, too. Why the fuck not? Victor invited me as a guest — I'm *expected* to talk to the other guests." He put his hand over his wife's. "Monica, I swear to God, if I get a couple of deals going, I'm going to buy you some diamond jewelry in Bermuda. Right now I need another drink. Want anything else, babe? Might as well indulge ourselves. Like I said, I already paid for this."

Arlie looked over at Alex. "Should we move along?" he asked in a low voice. "I'm not sure you can make this couple feel any more welcome here than they already feel."

"Let's go talk to the guy in the cape and his friend," Alex suggested. "They look more approachable."

Moments later Alex had introduced herself and Arlie to the two men: Rudolph Perino and Damien Loren, who were set designers from New York City.

"Wasn't the chapel divine?" Rudolph asked, after the introductions. "Whoever did the flowers had a good eye. Loved the touch of Hawaii, too. Of course, baby's breath is only native to Europe, Asia and North Africa — but we shouldn't quibble. "Oh, waiter!" He turned quickly, causing his cape to swing out. "I'm finished with this plate. Thank you. Love the red cummerbund! Not everything is black and white, right?" He flashed the waiter a coy smile.

"So, you're taking care of the land excursions," Rudolph said to Alex. "Damien and I simply adore Bermuda, don't we, Dame?"

"Oh my God, yes! The shopping is fab! Stores are open till midnight in Hamilton. And Marks and Sparks has the best inventory of British menswear you'll find anywhere. More conservative than our usual fare, of course. *You* might do very well there," he added, giving Arlie the once over.

"Thanks for the advice," Arlie said. "Maybe I'll get some Bermuda shorts.

"Alex? I guess we better move on if we want to get around the room before dinner."

"Okay. Well, it was really nice meeting you both. Let me know if I can arrange any special sightseeing for you in Bermuda, since you already know the island pretty well. I'll be sending around a listing of what I've planned so far."

"Interesting guys," Arlie said in her ear as they walked away. "I wondered about the inclusion of baby's breath with native Hawaiian flowers in the bouquet."

"Very funny, Arlie. C'mon, let's go talk to that group of people over there."

Chapter 13

"WE'RE VICTOR GARZA'S STABLE of artists — not that we're 'stable,'" cracked a man with a ponytail and square glasses, in response to Arlie's introductions. "I'm Bruno Rasconi." He turned to look at the others. "Why don't the rest of you give your names, so I don't embarrass myself." He indicated several people with his outstretched hand.

A small woman with flyaway long dark hair wearing a white cotton shift and turquoise jewelry said, "Okay, I'll start. I'm Lydia Corbin, and this is my husband, Craig." While she looked very much the artist, Tom looked like an accountant in a three-piece suit and round tortoise-shell glasses.

"I'm Jonathan Welles and this is Christine." Jonathan had a pleasant, open face with slicked-back dark hair. Christine was petite and pretty with small even features set off with china blue eyes.

"I'm Marcel Longine. Enchante." He took Alex's hand. "I live in France but, as I visit New York often, I was able to accept Mr. Garza's invitation." He was of slight build with dark good looks and an easy smile.

"And I am Francesca Maria Lazaro Marquez. I guess I am the last horse in the barn, or, how you say, 'stable.'" Francesca had a mane of wild, dark curly hair that surrounded an animated face with strong Castilian features. She wore a long, tiered dress of fine cream-colored lace that was accessorized with multiple strands of pearls of various lengths, a heavy gold chain-linked bracelet, and jeweled rings on several fingers.

"We were just, uh, comparing notes," Bruno Rasconi said, looking around the group with a wry smile. "Seems that we've found common enemies as we've all been ripped off by Victor Garza and insulted by Walter Sneed, the art critic. We were shocked to see Sneed here, considering how he's treated all of us."

"I know he's no favorite of Jasmine's," Alex responded. "She calls him Walter 'Snide.' Anyway, your best critics are your buyers, right? You just need to please them, and you have."

"Even so, I don't like to be referred to as 'a gauche painter in gouache,' Lydia said. "That's just word play and not honest criticism."

"True," agreed Bruno. "And I don't like to be described as 'chipping away at marble that looked better when it was on the side of a cliff. That prick is willing to destroy careers just so he can sound clever."

"Oh my God, you're so right!" Francesca exclaimed, her dark eyes flashing. "He doesn't care what he says or how he finds things out. I know he sneaks around bribing poorly-paid gallery workers to give him some gossip. Just because I, how you say, 'make a scene' when Victor Garza cheats me out of my earnings to take more for himself, I shouldn't be the one criticized as 'hot-tempered and cold-blooded.' Meester Sneed no esta un amigo de artistas."

"As you can see, we're not shy about expressing ourselves," Bruno cut in. "When you both came along, we were just talking about having a nice little chat with Sneed. Except it wouldn't be nice. Garza, too. He's our host, but he owes us a lot more than a cruise to Bermuda.

"Anyway, we should be thanking you for taking care of all of our bookings and the land excursions. You've done a good job. Everything's gone very smoothly so far. The rooms are great. Jasmine tells us that you're an artist as well as a good tour operator."

"Yes, but I'm not in your league. I'd feel complimented if Walter Sneed bothered to insult my art, and Victor Garza never even *heard* of the gallery that sells my work. But I know that both of them are very difficult to deal with.

"For the record," Arlie put in. "Alex is being modest about her work. Walter Sneed should criticize her, too." Alex gave him a bemused look.

She turned to the others. "Maybe you all can work through some of your issues with them on the cruise. I mean, they're on vacation. They could be in the mood to be more reasonable."

The conversation was interrupted with shouts and clapping behind them. Everyone looked in the direction of the commotion to see a man in a ship's staff uniform in the center of the area introducing Cindy, Tony, and the bridal couple to those who were gathered around. The applause was sustained as people started moving forward to congratulate the bride and groom.

Alex and Arlie started drifting towards the scene as well. Alex leaned in to say, "After we're through the receiving line, we should be going in for dinner. Wonder who we'll be sitting with."

Arlie smirked, "Odds are it'll be someone who's pissed off at the groom. I can see why the guy brought his lawyer with him. Maybe he should have brought a body guard, too."

Chapter 14

THE DINING ROOM glistened with glass and silver that reflected the glow of dozens of candles. Five tables set for six were covered in snowy white linen cloths on which stood tall crystal vases containing stalks of rouge-colored hibiscus and purple lilies with all the blooms above eye-level. Submerged in the water with the stems were bunches of purple and red grapes.

White bone china with gold edges was surrounded by crystal stemware and repousse silver. The impression of the table settings was one of luxury and discriminating taste.

Arlie and Alex were the first to arrive at their table, awaiting the arrival of Dame Edith Herrington, her assistant, and Edmund and Juliana Devers. "The Devers are big-time art collectors who live in London most of the time, but have a townhouse in New York," Alex was saying. "And Dame Edith is a benefactress of the arts on both sides of the pond," she added, just as a sturdy-looking middle-aged woman in a navy blue ensemble approached.

Thrusting out her hand, the newcomer smiled broadly at them, showing crooked teeth. "Hello, there. I'm Eloise Brown. Dame Edith's assistant. I see your name cards — Alex Trotter and Arlie Tate," she read upside down, cocking her head. "Yes, nice to meet you. It's really quite lovely, isn't it?" She scanned the room, appreciatively, before returning her attention to them.

"Yes, it certainly is," Alex inserted quickly, having an opening.

"Yes, quite. Well, I'll pop off now. Just wanted to see where we would be sitting so I didn't have to drag Dame Edith all around Robin Hood's barn to find our seats. I'll go get Milady and we'll be back straightaway and join you."

After she walked away, Arlie commented, "Well, she's certainly friendly. We don't have to try to make her feel welcomed."

"Right. I can see where she'd make a great assistant — a real take-charge, competent type. And how about her language — so veddy British, huh? Looks like we'll be the only Yanks at the table. You better hold onto your bowler, old bean. I think we're in for the full monty."

"I hope that doesn't mean what I think it does."

A minute later, true to her word, Eloise returned, guiding an elegant lavender-haired octogenarian who wore a black jeweled over a dark dress. A stately middle-aged couple walked on her other side.

After introductions had been made, and enough effusive observations had been made about how charming the setting was, what a beautiful bride Jasmine was, and how generous the groom was to treat everyone to this cruise, Alex opened up a new subject.

"So, are any of you attending the art auction tomorrow night? I'm aware of the reputation of inflated prices at ship auctions, but Arlie and I thought we'd go and see what sells for how much. There are some nice Dali lithos from the Divine

Comedy. The dealer claims they're from the original wood cuts. And they're signed, of course. You all would know their value better than I."

Edmund Devers put down his glass. "Oh, my word! We haven't been to one of those in donkey years, have we Juliana? Like to stay away from those kinds of things when we're on holiday, you know. Last time we went to one, I thought the dealer was all mouth and no trousers. Know what I mean?"

"That he didn't know what he was talking about?" Alex guessed.

"Yes, yes. Talked a good game, but it all seemed a bit dodgy to me. I'm not an expert, though. Rely on old chaps like Victor, there, to make sure I don't splash out and end up with the dog's dinner, besides."

"Something that's not of good quality for a lot of money," Alex translated, hesitantly.

Devers nodded. "Pretty sure the last piece I bought from him was quite overpriced, though; but yes, usually he's on the square. But art's a very personal thing, isn't it? Buy what you like, but don't be a chancer. It's 'horses for courses,' I always say. I'd be gobsmacked if you found a real buy at the auction. Oh, I, say! Look who's here!"

Everyone at the table turned to stare at a rumpled young man standing unsteadily in the opening to the dining room. Squinting out at the space, he appeared to be looking for something recognizable to determine whether or not he should come in.

"I say, Carlo!" Edmund Devers called out. "You're in the right place, old chap! Glad you could make it."

As the newcomer pitched forward a little, he grabbed onto the door frame and stepped forward to steady himself. After testing his balance, he started over to Arlie and Alex's table, taking small uncertain steps.

When he got there, Edmund Devers made the introductions. "Juliana, Dame Edith, Eloise— you remember Victor's son-in-law, don't you? Carlo, this is Alex Trotter, our tour agent, and

Arlie Tate. This is Count Carlo Giovanni." Everyone murmured greetings, as Carlo looked slowly from one to another, blinking dull dark eyes to focus on each face.

"Pleazure," he intoned, still blinking. Putting a hand on the table, he leaned down close to Edmund Devers. "Have you seen Sunny? My wife? She's going to be pissed that I'm a little late. I got into a poker game in the casino. Man, I had full boats for two hours! I could tell the dealer was bleeding. You know you can't walk away from that."

"She's right over there with Tony," Edmund Devers replied, pointing across the room. "But, in my country, you're the one who's 'pissed,' and she's the one who's 'cheesed off.' I think we all 'get the picture,' as you say, here.

"I suppose the old man is 'cheesed off' too," Carlo continued. "But I don't think I should have to answer to him. Well, here goes. I better make nice to Sunny first and then congratulate Victor for getting such a hot piece. See you later."

"He's always been a good lad," Dame Edith commented after Carlo departed, "but he'd better practice some temperance more often and become a little more responsible. Time to grow up and get a job. Is he still up the spout, Edmund?"

"I suppose so. At least I never heard that he was gainfully employed. Pleasant chap, though, as long as he's not *my* son-in-law."

Alex and Arlie watched as Carlo weaved his way over to Sunny's table, flopped over her back and attempted to kiss her on the neck. Wriggling out of his grasp, Sunny stood up and gave him a murderous look as she got into his face. Shaking her finger at him, she said something before she started pulling him over to the bridal table.

Jasmine just nodded at Carlo when they got to the bridal table, and resumed her conversation with Cindy Carmody.

As Sunny dragged her husband over to her father, Victor threw down his napkin, jumped out of his chair, and grabbed the man by his loosened tie. Carlo flailed his arms, his face reddening as he made choking sounds.

"Dad! Don't hurt him!" Sunny shrieked.

"Victor!" Jasmine called out. "That's not going to help anything!"

Conversation in the room had ceased as everyone sat staring at the scene, openmouthed.

"This is my wedding, goddammit!" Victor screamed, giving Carlo one more good shake before releasing him. "If you don't have respect for me, you should have respect for your wife. And if you don't have respect for either of us, you should at least have respect for yourself! Look at you! You're drunk as a skunk and probably lost big again. Well, don't come to me to bail you out, and don't send your wife. I'm through with you both! In case you haven't noticed, I have my own wife to take care of now."

An ashen-faced Sunny slumped against the table with her head down. After a few moments she straightened, squared her shoulders, and started back to her seat, looking grim-faced. Carlo followed behind, looking miserable.

Everyone turned back to their own tables and started conversing again, with animation.

Eloise Brown smoothed her navy jacket and cleared her throat. "Well, Miss Trotter, I'm sure that we'd all love to hear about the Bermuda excursions you have in mind for us. Will they all be by coach? I know it's not possible for many, but I wouldn't mind riding shank's pony for touring the towns."

"What a frightfully good idea to hear about visiting the island!" enthused Dame Edith. "Leave it to Eloise to come up with such a practical suggestion at just the right time."

Chapter 15

FOLLOWING DINNER, after the guests had moved outside again, the Four-Sea Sons band played, "I've Had the Time of My Life," for the bride and groom's dance, with the lead singer crooning the lyrics.

Remarkably, the wedding dinner had proceeded without another incident after the angry confrontation between Victor Garza and his son-in-law; although the tension had remained palpable, causing people to converse non-stop, with forced cheerfulness, throughout the meal. It had reminded Alex of luncheons that followed funerals, where people were just happy to still be alive and were easily amused by any casual comment or uninspired observation.

When Tony Garza had stood and asked for attention to propose a toast to the "happy couple," everyone held their collective breath. After he had finished, they still weren't sure they should exhale, considering the emphasis the young man had placed on how beautiful, intelligent, and talented Jasmine was, while his father was characterized only as being *lucky* that she had married him; as though the man had done nothing to be deserving of her.

The groom's attorney, Morrie Feldman, had immediately followed with remarks that reflected a more balanced appraisal of the union and lavished accolades to both the bride and groom. However, his statement that *he*, Morrie, was lucky to have Victor Garza for a client due to all the suits that the art dealer had brought his way could best be seen as being a left-handed compliment. When he was finished, everyone had heartily applauded, most likely out of relief to get past the awkwardness, and with the hope that they were marking the end of the toasts.

* * *

"THANK GOD FOR DANCING at weddings," Alex remarked to Arlie as they watched the bride and groom moving gracefully around the floor. "Wears off the effects of alcohol and puts everyone in a better mood."

"Yeah, as long as they don't play, "We Are Family," and remind everyone of the feuding Garzas," Arlie cracked. "Of course, Victor doesn't seem to be on much better terms with these so-called friends of his. Hard to imagine who didn't make the cut for the cruise."

* * *

ALEX AND ARLIE HAD DANCED several numbers when they decided to take a break to catch their breaths and sip their drinks. As they sat at their table, the band wrapped up "Can You Feel the Love Tonight?" so it was expected that the next number would be another up-tempo one which was another reason for a rest.

The keyboard player and drummer started playing a familiar series of three notes that went up in pitch and volume, into a crescendo.

"C'mon, let's dance, Arlie!" Alex said to the collapsed man. "Those are the first bars of 'Sweet Caroline' —the greatest wedding dance song, ever! Look, Aunt Lola and Aunt Alaana are already out there."

"Dame Edith is allowed to sit and watch," Arlie countered, slowly getting to his feet but not moving from his chair. "Besides, you'll say the same thing about 'The YMCA' and 'Proud Mary,' and every other loud, jumping song."

"Dame Edith is at least eighty-five and you're thirty-five. And this is my favorite!" She grabbed his hand and pulled him out onto the dance floor, even while she started moving to the music and singing along with many others.

"Where it began, I can't begin to knowin',
but then I know it's growin' strong..."

* * *

AN HOUR LATER they sat having another drink while the band was taking a break. Arlie had leaned back in his chair with his legs stretched out. They had danced every number both fast and slow in the last set.

"Oh, Oh," Alex said, nodding towards the other side of the dance area. "There's Victor and his former partner, Roman, going at it. Let's go over and eavesdrop. Looks like they're talking loudly enough to hear them if we get anywhere close. They're in each other faces. You see that? C'mon, let's go!"

"Let's not, Alex. It's not our business. Besides, if you want to eavesdrop on someone, why don't you go over and see what Morrie Feldman is talking to Count Carlo and Sunny about? Whatever it is, the Giovannis don't look too happy. After hearing Victor's tirade, it could be about a change in the will or, at least a loss in Sunny's allowance."

"Oh, good call — that's even better. Sunny looks like she's ready to spit nails. I'll just wander over—"

Arlie put a hand on her arm. "Alex, I was kidding. If you want to walk around, let's go over and talk to Jasmine who's sitting there by herself. You haven't talked to her since the reception line."

As they made their way over, they found the bride staring off into space, unaware that she had company.

"Jasmine, hi!" Alex said, cheerfully, to get her attention. "You okay? You look a little out of it."

"Huh? Oh, Alex, Arlie— hi. No, I'm fine. Just taking a breather. You know — all the excitement. You keep asking me how I am, Alex. Maybe I need to get out in the sun more."

"No, you look great — gorgeous, in fact. I only meant that you looked a little distracted."

"Can I get you something to drink, Jasmine?" Arlie asked. "Maybe a little brandy for a nightcap?"

"Oh, thanks, but I'm not drinking. I've got water here, so I'm fine. I probably shouldn't say this, but I'm looking forward to tomorrow when I can just sit out on our balcony. There's been a lot of tension here tonight, starting off with that scene when Carlo came in late and drunk. Was everyone talking about that? It was so embarrassing!"

"Oh, don't worry about it," Alex said, with a wave of her hand. "No one took much notice. People were more interested in the decorations and the food and everything to pay much attention. Besides, there's always a scene at a wedding. I think people just felt relieved to get it over with."

Jasmine chuckled. "You always know the right thing to say, Alex. I only hope you're right."

"Alex is good with words, isn't she? — and she has so many of them," Arlie teased. "Seriously, you and Victor have done a great job with the wedding and that didn't spoil it. The Count should be the one who's upset since Victor has apparently reached a breaking point with him."

"I really don't know what Victor has decided," Jasmine said, "but I know that we're meeting with Morrie Feldman tomorrow afternoon, so that should tell you something."

* * *

"WELL, COULD I?" a man's voice whispered in Alex's ear from behind her.

"What?" Alex turned to see Tony Garza.

"I'm asking you to dance, and was trying to be clever by using the lyrics of the song, 'Could I have this Dance?' Wasn't it a big hit for Anne Murray years back?"

"Oh, Tony! Sorry — I was daydreaming. I hadn't even registered what the band was playing. Of course, I'll dance with you. I'm guessing you know how to waltz, so I'll just follow. I've been wanting to talk to you, anyway. We really haven't had a chance to talk since that day on the back patio." She took his hand and they started twirling to the three-step dance.

"I know, and I regret that, Alex. I haven't wanted to interfere tonight with you and your date, but I saw you were alone just now."

"Oh, don't worry about Arlie. We're not joined at the hip. I see he's over talking to the bartender right now. I'm just sorry *you're* not with someone. I know from experience that it's not much fun to be alone at a wedding."

"Oh, well, I had some duties to perform to keep me occupied. Besides, I'm not seeing anyone, and you can't invite a casual date to a wedding that goes on for a week."

"How are your business plans coming along? Has your father reconsidered making you a loan, or investing?"

"No, in fact, Dad is making it almost impossible for me to find other investors. He's advised all his friends and contacts, who are basically the only wealthy people I know, that they shouldn't risk their money with me."

"That's hardly fair! If he doesn't like your business idea, that's one thing, but why close off your other opportunities?"

"I hope that's a rhetorical question. You saw how he was with Carlo tonight. Not that I blame him, but once he decides that you're off his list, that's it. There's no going back."

"But now that Jasmine's his wife, couldn't she exert some influence over him? She believes in you and your ideas."

"I know that Jasmine would do anything for me, but I can't believe that Dad will show her any more respect now than he did during their engagement." Alex looked up at Tony and saw that his expression had hardened.

"Well, the song is over, Alex. Thanks for the dance. I see that Arlie is back, but we'll talk later, okay? I promise I won't be such a downer."

"Of course, Tony. I wish I could offer you some real help, but maybe we can just have a drink together sometime this week. I'd like that."

* * *

THE BAND QUIT PLAYING at about eleven-thirty, sending everyone home with the last dance, which was their version of Jennifer Lopez's, *Waiting for Tonight.* Jasmine gave her bouquet to her aunts, Lola and Alaana, and departed with Victor to the applause of the remaining guests. Alex noted that Carlo and Sunny were no longer around.

Several of the artists were still there by the fountain conversing with the art critic Walter Sneed. Bruno Rasconi seemed to be button-holing the writer, his voice rising in anger.

"The least you can do is stick to criticizing the artwork!" Alex heard him say, but couldn't hear Walter Sneed's response. Then more from Bruno. "You're not supposed to be some kind of 'shock columnist' to build your readership. These are our livelihoods you're using to play games with!"

Several others surrounded Sneed, who started waving his arms in an effort to hold off the group that was crowding him.

At that point, Francesca Maria Lazaro Marquez, who had been at the bar, became aware of the commotion and hurried over to join in, and tripped inside the circle with her drink held aloft.

What happened next was unclear, but just as Francesca disappeared into the group, there was what appeared to be a domino-collapse of people, with bodies falling forward from the back to the front, as voices cried out. "Oh, no!" "Stop pushing!" "Ow!"

Alex and Arlie raced over to the pile and started helping them up, one by one. As they worked their way though the group, they became aware of someone frantically splashing in the pool.

"You people are crazy!" Walter Sneed screamed as he lay helplessly in the water, kicking his feet in the air while concrete nymphs squirted water onto his head. "I won't forget this!" He sputtered, spitting out mouthfuls.

"I'm a police officer," Arlie advised the crowd. "Please step back so I can get in and help this man." As people slowly backed away, Arlie bent over the fountain and reached out to the nearly-hysterical man.

"You're the police? Oh, thank God!" Sneed cried out. "Thank you! Thank you! I hope you're here to arrest these imbeciles. You can see that they tried to kill me!"

"Look, I'm a guest here, but from what I saw, it looked like it was an accident. Let's just get you out of the fountain, okay?

"Alex, would you go get a couple of towels by the bar or the pool?" She nodded and took off in the direction of the bar.

"All right, Sneed. Grab hold of my hands. And on the count of three you're going to rock forward. Got it? Okay, here we go — one, two, three!"

Fortunately, Arlie was able to assist the heavy man up to a sitting position on the first try. Then, grabbing him under the arms, Arlie clean-jerked him to his feet.

Alex came back with a pile of terry towels and handed one to the soaked man who started patting his head and chest with it. He was still standing in water up to his knees.

After the man had gotten his bearings, both Arlie and Alex took hold of an arm and assisted him to step out of the fountain. Back on the floor, Alex gave him another towel, which he grabbed in disgust.

"Okay, now?" Arlie asked the obviously still distraught man. Walter Sneed nodded, curtly, his lips tightened into a thin straight line.

"I think you just need to go back to your stateroom," Arlie advised, "and take a hot shower and get a good night's rest. Looks like your tux is a goner, though," he added, lifting up the hem of the dripping jacket.

"All right, folks!" Arlie said, turning toward the onlookers who still hadn't dispersed. "The party's over. We'll just consider this an accident, but be more careful in the future. Mr. Sneed could have been badly injured. I think it's time to leave the area, so I'll wish you a good night."

After escorting Walter Sneed to one elevator, Arlie and Alex got on another, still shaking their heads. "I guess Jasmine was right," Alex said, once they were inside. "She thought you would be useful in keeping order."

"I don't think there was any order, but at least no one was badly injured," Arlie said. "Look, I get why those people would like to do some damage to that sniveling creampuff, but I hope they keep their cool for the rest of the cruise. I really don't want to play cop this week."

"Like you said," Alex put in, "it didn't seem like they intentionally pushed him into the fountain. It looked to me like that Francesca woman lost her balance and she plowed into the group, and some people fell into Sneed. At least after tonight the artists will be able to avoid him. We'll see how it goes. Oh, here's our floor."

Walking down the hallway, Alex tugged at Arlie's coat and whispered close to his ear, "I don't know about some of the other guests, but *I* had fun tonight. Thanks for all the dances. You're pretty smooth, Mr. Tate. You'll have to tell me sometime how you got so much practice."

Arlie looked at her with a sly smile.

"Oh, here we are at our rooms, Arlie, so... uh, I'm sorry, but I'm going to need your help in undoing the back of this dress, if you don't mind."

"Mind? I've been planning on it."

Chapter 16

"ISN'T THIS THE LIFE, ARLIE?" Alex stretched on the chaise lounge and took a deep breath of sea air. "Here we are having breakfast on our balcony overlooking the Atlantic Ocean bound for Bermuda, without a care in the world."

"I'm glad you're so relaxed." Arlie patting her knee. "Of course *I* was the one who got up early and went down seven decks to fight a mob scene at the buffet table to bring back our food. And then, I wasn't even sure what you'd like."

Alex lazily waved her hand and leaned back in her chair. "Oh, we can take turns. And you made all the right choices — everything that could hold up in transit— fruit, breads, and coffee. Love all these miniature sweet rolls. Thanks again."

"No problem. The coffee is right down the hall, anyway. So, what's on your agenda for today?"

"Well, I haven't made any plans for the group. I would imagine most everybody slept in, like I did, and they'll want to leisurely explore the ship on their own. We should do that, too. We didn't see everything. Maybe later we can go up on the Sun Deck and relax by the pool. It's warm and sunny, but not hot. Perfect for sitting out. Tonight, after dinner, we're going to the art auction, right?"

"Yeah, I'd still like to, even after Edmund Devers said that he'd be 'gobsmacked' if there'd be a good deal. I'd like to get up to the gym at some point today, too. Wouldn't you?"

Alex paused a moment, considering. "I was kinda hoping to get enough exercise walking in and out of gift shops, but your way is probably more effective. Here, you take this blueberry muffin. You've earned it and I don't need it.

"But what I'd really like to do right now, Arlie, is to learn a little more about *you*. I've told you all about my past, dull as it is. Like, how is it you're still single, or were you married before? You must have done your share of dating as I could see you've spent a lot of time on a dance floor."

"Well, last night I certainly did." He took a sip of hot coffee. "My left leg has been cramping up ever since."

"Seriously." Alex took off her sunglasses to look him in the eye. "You lived in Atlanta a long time, right?"

"I was born and raised in Atlanta. My folks are still there. My dad, Emery, is a lawyer, and my mom, Abby, is a psychologist. It was expected that I would go to law school after college and join my father's firm."

"But you didn't. What happened?"

"Well, after I got my undergraduate degree in Criminal Justice at George Mason, I realized that I was more interested in studying criminal behavior and evaluating evidence than in prosecuting or defending an offender. I figured that if I did *my* job well, I could do more for the cause of justice. So, after graduation, I went on to grad school to study criminology. With my master's degree, I got a job with the department in Atlanta. Eventually, I took the job in Camden County, Georgia, where I met you.

"Wow, that's impressive, Arlie. You gave up a lot of money for your principles. You didn't do a stint in the Peace Corps, too, did you?"

"No. And I'm not that noble. Just did what I was interested in. But I think you want to hear about my social life. Can I heat your coffee?" he asked, raising the pot to add to his own cup.

"No, thanks. But yes, I'd like to hear about your social life. I mean, not the particulars. Whatever you feel like telling me would be fine. You know, like if you've had any special girlfriends — or wives. "

"No wives. Actually, I was engaged for one summer after college. She was very pretty. A society deb. Her parents were country club friends of my parents. Anyway, when I told Alicia — my fiancée — that I wouldn't be going to law school because I wanted to be a policeman, she broke off our engagement. Not immediately, but that was the reason. I guess she was marrying a lifestyle rather than me."

"Oh, Arlie, that's very sad!"

"Yeah, well, it was years ago, and, honestly, if Alicia was superficial about what she wanted in a husband, I wasn't any better. I got together with her because she was very attractive and was in my family's social circle. Not exactly a love connection for me, either.

But, the whole business soured me on relationships for quite a while. I got into my studies and my work and I was satisfied. I've dated some since then, of course, but I've never been serious with anyone else. And now— there's you."

"Oh, you don't have to say anything about me," Alex said, fidgeting with her shirt, equally torn between wanting to hear what he would tell her and dreading it.

"I should," Arlie said, putting down his cup. "But you're the one with the words. You know I really like you, and we get along great now, don't we? I know it was a little rocky when we first met..."

"A little *rocky*? You considered me a murder suspect!"

"Well, that's true. But after I got to know you better, I hoped that you weren't guilty."

"Oh, that's so sweet," she mocked. "Listen, before you get any more complimentary, why don't we finish up here, and go down to Deck Six and check out the stores— just to get it over with," she finished, noticing Arlie's sardonic grin.

"Okay, but we don't have to rush," he said, putting his head back and closing his eyes.

A moment later a high-pitched scream from somewhere above them shattered the calm. "What the hell?" Arlie got to his feet. "That came from up there, didn't it Alex?"

"Yeah, from a balcony over that way." She stood and pointed toward the back of the ship. "Oh my God, Arlie! You don't think someone went overboard, do you?!"

"I doubt it. You were just looking in that direction, weren't you? But *something* happened. I hear voices. We'd better go up and check it out."

Once they were out in the hallway, they headed for the stairwell and took the steps two at a time up to the next floor. Starting down the hallway they saw a small crowd of people talking together in the hallway.

"This is the way to Jasmine's and Victor's suite," Alex said, breathily, trotting along to keep up with Arlie's longer strides.

The door to 14872 was standing open when they got there, making Alex gasp. "Oh, no! Something's happened to Jasmine!"

They pushed their way into the suite. "I'm a police officer," Arlie said to several people standing around. "What's the problem here?"

"Oh, Detective Tate, Miss Trotter!" It was Eloise Brown. "Dame Edith and I were just sitting out having a cuppa, when we heard a crash, and then screams, and then all bloody hell broke loose! I came out in the hallway just now as Victor Garza dashed past, leaving the door open. A couple of people already went out onto the balcony. How did you two get here?" Arlie took off, leaving Alex to explain.

"We heard a woman's scream from our balcony. too. We're one deck below. Excuse me, Eloise, but I'd like to go out there and make sure Jasmine's okay."

Alex hurried across the sumptuous sitting room and exited at the sliding glass doors. Catching a glimpse of her friend standing at the other end of the balcony talking to Arlie and her two aunts, she paused a moment and took a deep breath.

"Alex!" Arlie called out and started towards her.

"What happened here, Arlie? I see Jasmine's okay and—wait, what's all that? A plant was knocked over?'

"That potted palm came over the railing from the deck above— the Sun Deck. Right about where we were last night. "Listen, I need you to do me a favor. Victor's gone to check the area above us, but I'd like you to go up, too. See if anyone's around that you know. I need to stay at the scene and wait for security. If you don't see any of the wedding guests, ask whoever's there if they saw anything suspicious. Find out whatever you can. I'll see you later. Oh, security's here now. Good."

Two uniformed men stood in the doorway to the balcony as Alex eased past them. The older one, whose nametag read, 'Leonard Marks,' said, "We got a call that something fell off a railing?"

Arlie nodded and indicated they should go inside to talk. Turning towards Jasmine he called out, "I'll be inside for a few minutes with security. Just stay where you are. Be sure none of you disturbs anything."

Once inside, Arlie addressed the officers. "I'm a detective with the Camden County, Georgia, Sheriff's Office. I'm here as a guest of Mr. and Mrs. Garza who were married on board last night. According to Mrs. Garza, that heavy potted palm tree you can see out there, crashed onto their balcony from the Sun Deck, while they were sitting out there. It missed them by inches. Hard to believe it could be an accident, but I haven't been up there to look for any other explanations. I can tell you that several people at the wedding hold grudges against Mr. Garza, which could point to a motive."

"Yeah, well that may be," Officer Marks said, "but we aren't authorized to get too involved in this. If the Garzas are U.S. citizens, they can report this to the FBI after they get back to their home port. You're welcome to look into it if you want to, of course."

"Do you guys have any fingerprint kits so I can dust for some latents?"

"Nope. Sorry."

"Well, for now, I'll just bag the pieces of pottery and wait till we get to Bermuda. Can you put up some tape while I process the scene — and if you'd get housekeeping to bring a few paper bags and clean this up after I'm done."

"Sure. We can stand outside till you're done, too."

"Okay, fine. I need to go back out and meet with Mrs. Garza now. Thanks."

Once outside, he crossed over to the three women. "Ladies, I'd like to speak to Mrs. Garza alone, now."

"Oh, of course, Detective," Aunt Lola said. "We're just glad we could see that Jasmine's all right, aren't we, Alanna?"

"Yes. We're just down the hall and heard the commotion. Well, bye dear. You're in good hands now. But we'll be around if you need us."

When they were gone, Arlie said, "I know you'd like to go back in, Jasmine, and you can in a minute, but first, just show me exactly where you were and where Victor was right before the pot landed."

"Well, I was lying in this chaise lounge, here, and Victor was in this one. Although, I think that he had just stood up. He said that he was going in for another cup of coffee and asked me if I wanted one. I started to tell him that I needed a fresh cup, and he turned back to have me repeat what I said, and that was when it crashed right between us. I know I screamed and ran over to the railing. It was so unbelievable that an object would fall like that, barely missing us."

"What did Victor do then?"

"He came over to check on me. I guess I was crying. In fact, he thought at first that I'd been hurt. When I said I was okay, he left to go upstairs to see if he could find out who had dropped it. Whoever it was must have meant to *kill him.* But why? I mean, my God!"

"I don't know, Jasmine, and there may not be much to go on. The matron's here now and Victor should be along soon. Why don't you go in and I'll get this cleaned up, and we'll talk again later."

* * *

AFTER ARLIE HAD COLLECTED the shards of the ceramic pot in several paper bags, he went back inside the Garza's stateroom to meet with Victor and Alex who had both returned from the Sun Deck.

"That bastard Rasconi did it!" Victor brayed, waving off Jasmine who was making protesting noises. "I know it! Probably did it with Roman Gregg. They were up there together. Sitting there having breakfast by the pool, acting like nothing happened, until I walked up. You should have seen the shocked looks on their faces. Of course, they figured I was dead."

"Maybe they had hoped to keep their meeting a secret from you," Arlie suggested. "You have an exclusive with Rasconi, don't you? Did either of you see any other wedding guests?"

"Yeah, I did," Alex answered, "Those two guys from the theatre were there, and Jasmine's matron of honor, Cindy, and her husband. Oh, and the Devers, who we sat with at the reception. No one claimed to have seen anything suspicious; like someone running away from that area where we were last night.

"Victor, I know you got up there a couple minutes before I did, but I think we'd have to rely on someone who was there at the time the pot was pushed over. One could probably get away from the railing and hide behind something in seconds."

"I'm telling you it was Rasconi! Why don't you just go and grill him, Detective! I bet he sings like a canary."

"I think you've read too many Dashiell Hammett novels, Victor. That's not how it works, usually. Anyway, we're at a dead end here. I'm going to talk to your neighbors, Dame Edith and Eloise. See if they saw or heard anything helpful. Then I'll take a look at the mounted cameras on that deck. We may get lucky that one's in the right position."

Jasmine's face lit up. "Oh, wouldn't that be something? Although, it'll be awful, too," she added, shaking her head. "I remember when Alex warned me that the balconies at the end of the boat were stepped out so that the next deck up can see them, but I never thought…I guess I can't believe someone would actually want to kill Victor."

"Have you thought that it might be *you* that they wanted to kill?" Arlie asked.

* * *

"OKAY, ELOISE. Take your time and tell me *exactly* what you remember," Arlie said, as he and Alex sat in the Herrington suite.

Eloise pursed her mouth in thought. "As I said before, Milady and I were having our tea on the balcony, looking our over the water. There wasn't a sound to be heard. Then, I heard a scream, followed by a muffled boom. Then another scream. It took us a second to have it register, right Milady?"

"Yes, dear. But that's how I remember it, too. Pity we weren't looking over there; although I can't imagine we could have called out in time to be of any use. Such a terrible thing to have happened to newlyweds on their first day married."

"Eloise, Dame Edith, is that how you both remember it?" Alex asked, excitedly. "A scream, the thud, and then another scream?"

Both ladies looked at one another, nodding. Eloise spoke up. "Yes. It all happened so fast, but we think there was a scream almost at the same time as a thud. Then another scream."

"Well, then, I have an idea I might know who it was," Alex said, looking pointedly at Arlie Tate.

Chapter 17

"OKAY, WE'RE HERE on the Sun Deck and I'm sitting down like you asked," Arlie observed. Alex was sitting next to him at an umbrella-shaded table. "Now, what was all that about with Eloise and Dame Edith? You told them you 'might know who it was' who pushed the pot over the railing to allegedly try to kill Victor or Jasmine. Why don't we go check out the security cameras first— or should I just go and arrest someone on your hunch?

"By the way, I heard all the same things you did, and I wouldn't hazard a guess as to who the guilty party was at this point. I could maybe get the list down to ten or twelve people who had a grudge against Garza, but I must not have the same finely-tuned detecting skills you have," he finished, rolling up his eyes.

Alex had her elbows up on the table; her chin resting on her hands. When Arlie finished speaking, she sat back in her chair to respond. "That could be, but fortunately I'm here to help you. By the way, I did check out the nearest security camera to where the pot went over, and I don't think we're going to have much luck there. But, anyway, I'm happy to share my epiphany with you."

"Oh, yeah? Thanks for sharing. Let's hear it."

"All right. So, what are the facts?" Alex asked. "We know that Victor and Jasmine were out on the balcony, side by side, equally visible from the Sun Deck, one floor above."

"Right so far," Arlie agreed.

"Okay," Alex continued. "then, according to Jasmine, just before the pot came crashing down, Victor had stood up to leave. But *he didn't leave* because Jasmine had said something that he hadn't heard, so he paused and turned back towards her. That's when the pot came flying through the air."

"Yeah, also right. But I'm still waiting for the revelation, Alex."

"All in good time, my friend. So, let's see, Victor stood up to leave, but didn't and then the pot came down and crashed. Now, put that together with what Eloise and Dame Edith said. They heard a high-pitched scream at the same time or maybe *just before* they heard the thud of the pot landing, and then they heard another scream. So what does that say to you?"

"Not much," Arlie said. "What does it say to you, Sherlock?"

"It says," Alex said, and then paused, "that *two different women* screamed."

"Why two different women? Couldn't Jasmine have screamed twice?"

"I believe it was *two*, because the first scream came before Jasmine could have been aware of the falling missile. She hadn't been looking up. According to her, she was turned towards Victor to repeat that she needed a fresh cup, or whatever."

"Okay, let's go with that," Arlie said. "Now what?"

"My point is," Alex said, slowly, "if Jasmine didn't emit the first scream that Eloise and Dame Edith heard because she hadn't yet become aware of the falling object, then the perpetrator was the one who screamed."

"Why would the perpetrator scream?" Arlie asked, genuinely bewildered.

"Aha!" Alex crowed. "That's where we come to the identification of the assailant. My epiphany. The only reason that the perpetrator would scream was if *something went terribly wrong* — if someone other than the intended target would be hit...and killed. Who was the one who made an unexpected move that put him back into target range? Victor. Who was the one who remained in the same position? Jasmine. Who is the only person we know who would not want to hurt Victor but would want to harm Jasmine? Hint— there's only one person."

"You're thinking of Sunny Giovanni," he answered, "because she's jealous of Jasmine. Is that a motive to kill? Did anyone see Sunny up here at the time of the incident?"

"No, not anyone we know. As for motive, people have been killed for less, right, Arlie?"

"Psychopaths kill for the fun of it. So far there's no actual evidence pointing to Sunny, but it is an interesting theory. You're assuming that the perpetrator was a woman, number one, and that no other woman would want to kill Jasmine, number two. And, may I throw in a third theory — a second person's scream could indicate that it had been an accident all along; that some stranger was setting the plant down on the railing, maybe to take a picture or whatever, and had bumped into it and it fell. If that were the case, it would be a normal reaction to scream and to flee the scene."

Alex was staring out to sea, considering. "Okay. Plausible, but not likely."

"Look, let's investigate what we can," Arlie said. "We need to ask Victor's attorney Morrie Feldman what he told Carlo and

Sunny last night, and what the meeting is about today. But, before that, let's check out the camera tapes."

Chapter 18

"SHOULD WE GO THROUGH IT one more time?" Alex asked, doubtfully.

"I don't think it's going to change." Arlie gave her a wan smile. "The camera shot didn't cover that section of the deck. And unless you think that waiter who walked by is a hired assassin, I think we're done here."

They had just spent the last hour meeting with Security and reviewing tape from the camera that was mounted nearest the spot where the potted palm had fallen to the Garza's balcony.

"Well, Alex, you called it right. You said the camera wasn't in the right place, so it was always a long shot. Literally. Let's get this tape back to Security and go see Morrie Feldman. Victor Garza has given him 'permission' to talk to me. I don't know if Feldman will assert attorney-client privilege over some matters or not, but he knows what I'm looking into. We're supposed to meet with him at his suite at two o'clock for a brief interview. He's meeting with Victor's family at three, so we'd better get going. Ready?"

"Did you tell him I'd be coming, too?"

"Yeah, I told him that you're assisting me since you're more familiar with the Garza family, and this isn't a formal inquiry. Trust me, Victor is making sure that I get all the help I can get with the investigation. He wants someone to pay the price. Which reminds me, I have to talk to Bruno Rasconi, to appease him."

* * *

A HALF HOUR LATER, they were seated on a sofa in the Feldman's well-appointed suite that had been decorated in watery shades of blue and green. Shirley Feldman had served them iced tea before departing for the pool on the Sun Deck, saying she'd be gone for a couple of hours.

Arlie, who had begun asking questions of the high-powered attorney, was already frustrated that the lawyer was being cagey and guarded in his responses. "Look, Feldman, I was just asking how well you knew the other members of the Garza family. I haven't accused anyone of anything at this point. I merely want to know if you've been around them enough to have formed an opinion of their characters and their regard for Victor."

"I've been Victor Garza's attorney for fifteen years. I've known his children since they were young teenagers. There's nothing wrong with them that isn't wrong with all children of very wealthy people. They're basically irresponsible with money, and expect to be taken care of, but they're not bad kids, and neither one of them would hurt their father."

Arlie leaned forward, fixing the attorney with a penetrating look. "Okay, I appreciate your point of view. But let me get right to the point. I know you're meeting with the family to discuss something that will affect Sunny and her husband, Count Carlo, and I'd like to know what it is."

"Personally, I don't think that it's any of your business," Feldman scoffed. "There's no reason to investigate the Garzas. You should be looking into motives of people who don't have a close personal relationship with Victor."

"I'll be doing that, too. Right now, I'm looking at the family. They have the most to gain or lose, depending on the financial arrangements."

* * *

THE LAWYER LOOKED OUT to the water, drumming his fingers on the arm of his chair. After a minute he turned back to Arlie with a scowl on his face. "As I already indicated, I consider this matter to be protected by attorney-client privilege, but Mr. Garza has instructed me to answer your inquiries about the family members. What I'm about to tell you should be held in the strictness confidence by you as an extension of my fiduciary duty to my client. And that goes for both of you, understood.?"

Alex nodded, solemnly, as Arlie said, "I protect any information I obtain in my investigations. Ms. Trotter is my confidante in this special situation, and I can vouch for her integrity."

"Okay, well, that'll have to do, I suppose," Feldman said. "The fact of the matter is that Victor does plan on making some revisions to his will for various reasons that I won't go into here. Last night I advised Sunny and Carlo that there would be some adverse changes in their financial positions relevant to the estate, and I invited them to today's meeting to hear the particulars. And yes, I would say that they weren't happy to hear it, but they wouldn't murder Victor to prevent him from taking action. That's patently absurd. Besides, I told them that they would have the opportunity to argue their case if they felt Victor was being unfair. Maybe they can convince him otherwise."

"Whoever dropped the pot," Arlie said, "might not have wanted to *kill* Victor Garza. It didn't hit anyone, as you know. It could have been just a warning."

"I'm sure I don't know," Detective. "If you'll excuse me, the Garzas will be coming along any minute now, so I'll wish you both a good day"

* * *

WHEN THEY WERE outside in the hallway Alex said, "Well, his legalese made him a bit fuzzy but he was very clear about showing us the door."

"I agree with you on both counts. However, he did reveal a motive for Sunny and Carlo to drop a pot on Victor's deck. I think at this point we'll wait to get to Bermuda where I'll run the prints on the pottery pieces, if there are any. Oh, but I have to first talk to Bruno Rasconi.. Do you want to go do some shopping while I check him out?

"Sure. Let's meet back at the staterooms. I won't be more than an hour."

"Okay, fine." He took out his wallet, thumbed through his bills and handed her one. "Take this with you."

"What's this?" she asked.

"It's a fifty-dollar bill."

"I know that. What's it for?"

"Buy yourself a little something, as a gift from me. Buy a sunhat. You'd look great in one of those with a wide brim. I want to buy you some real gifts in Bermuda, but I know you're just looking for sundries on board."

"Gee, thanks, Arlie. I'm stunned."

"That I would buy you something?"

"No. That you would use the word 'sundries.' Seriously, that's nice of you. I really appreciate it. And good luck with Bruno, but after we both get back, the only mystery we have to solve is where we're going to have dinner tonight."

Chapter 19

TWO HOURS LATER Arlie and Alex sat across from each other in a cozy booth in the Italian restaurant on Deck Six called, "In Mare"— at sea. As it was early, the room was not yet filled and was relatively quiet. The intimate atmosphere was enhanced by its deep-toned decor, as well as the bronze-toned shaded lamps that spilled a circle of golden light on each table.

"So tell me, what happened when you talked to Bruno Rasconi?" Alex asked after they had ordered. their pasta entrees. "Did he 'sing like a canary'?"

"Hardly. Not surprisingly, he denied having pushed over the pot and said that he had been with Roman Gregg for at least twenty minutes before Victor came charging up to their table. He said he felt like he'd been caught 'having an affair' — his words. I can believe that he looked shocked to see Garza because he was sitting with Victor's rival; not because he had just tried to *murder* the guy. Maybe he and Gregg were planning to screw him, but it wouldn't be necessary to kill him."

"Don't look now," Alex said under her breath, "but Victor and Jasmine are just coming into the restaurant. I really don't want to ask them to join us and have to eat with Victor."

"Alex, we're sitting at a table for two."

"Oh. Right. They've caught my eye. Wave at them. Isn't that a beautiful scarf Jasmine has on? But she doesn't look too happy, does she? Of course, that could be because someone tried to kill one of them this morning."

"That would do it. Or it could be that the family conference about the will went badly," Arlie suggested, pulling apart his roll and buttering a piece.

"Oh, my God!" Alex said behind her dark linen napkin. "Don't look now but Sunny, the Count, and Tony are over in that corner." As a reflex, Arlie started to turn his head to the right. "I said don't look!" Alex held her napkin up to just under her eyes. "I can just imagine what they're talking about. I wonder if they're joining forces because they're all going to lose their allowances.

"Okay, Arlie, you can look now— they seem engrossed in conversation. I just didn't want them to know we were talking about them. As a matter of fact, let's not talk about the 'dropped pot' incident and the Garzas for the rest of the evening, okay?"

"Fine with me," Arlie said. "You're the one talking about them. And you can take that napkin off your face. You look like you're going to rob the place." Alex patted her mouth and dropped it to her lap.

Arlie nodded. "Okay. That's better. On another topic, let's get to the gallery before the auction so we can take some time to look at the other paintings, besides the Dali prints, okay?"

"Sure. I had no idea that you were so interested in art."

"I could use a little culture. Besides, Horatio Krumm is expecting me. Remember how he lectured me about Dali when we were there?"

"I'm sure he's counting on you, Arlie. I want to take another look at the Dalis, though. I keep trying to remember what I learned about how to authenticate them."

"Maybe I can help you. Horatio thought I had made a brilliant choice with *Original Perfection.*"

"Oh, brother!" Alex groaned. "I hope you're kidding. I'm sure that Horatio says that to every customer about every painting they stop to look at."

Noticing that Arlie had suddenly glanced up, she followed his eyes to see the two set designers from New York approaching their table. "'Uh, hi..." she started, searching for their names. "Randolph?"

"Close. Rudolph," the one with the frosted hair said. "And this is Damien.. Don't mean to disturb you, but did you find out any more about whoever almost killed Victor with the potted tree? You told us this morning up on the Sun Deck, remember?"

Rudolph, who Alex recalled had worn a cape for the wedding, was now dressed in a puffy-sleeved white shirt and fitted purple pants. The wide leather belt that cinched his small waist seemed unnecessary to hold up what looked like tights. His friend, Damien, was only slightly less flamboyant in his lavender shirt accessorized with a heavy silver cross on a long chain.

Before Alex could think of an answer, Rudolph turned towards Arlie. "Oh, my Gawd! Wait a minute! You're a detective, right?"

Arlie nodded. "Right. And it was a ceramic pot that *fell,* and it might have been an accident. I'm looking into it. No need to speculate."

"It's verys exciting, though! You must be busy interrogating people. Don't worry, Damien and I will fully cooperate with your investigation."

"Thanks, but that probably won't be necessary. Excuse us, but I think our server is coming with our dinners."

"Oh, right. Well, good luck tracking down the fiend. Ta ta now!"

After their plates were put in front of them, Arlie regarded Alex with a probing gaze. "What? she asked, raising her chin defiantly. "I didn't put it that way — that a tree *'nearly killed Victor.'* I'm not dramatic like Rudolph, you know."

"Yes, right. Remember, you have to be careful what you say— partner. We don't want to let on if we find out anything." He took a small bite of his pasta Al Fredo. "Meantime, this is delicious. Do you like it?" She nodded, chewing on a mouthful of food. "Good. We have plenty of time to enjoy our dinner and head over to the art gallery to look around."

Alex swallowed hard. "Don't forget, there'll be free champagne. Should be entertaining, if not too exciting since we won't be buying anything. But then, I think we've had enough excitement for one day."

Chapter 20

THE GALLERY WAS ALREADY CROWDED when Arlie and Alex arrived about a half hour before the auction was set to start. As they entered, they had to stand back as people were filling the walkway, elbowing one another to get in front of the artwork. As they sipped from flutes of champagne, they stood and made observations to their companions.

Alex suggested they might as well start at the refreshments table, and then look at the paintings. As they picked their way through the group they overheard some of the commentary covering a range of opinions and concerns. One yuppie-type in a navy blazer said, airily, "The artist is obviously making a statement that there are two separate planes of existence, and life is our struggle to keep them in balance."

A young woman, wearing a shiny new wedding-ring set asked her husband, uncertainly, "How high do you think we should bid on this one?"

A silver-haired matron remarked to her bored-looking spouse, "Ernie, I asked you if you think this one will go with the rug in the den. I think it has just the right shade of green in it, don't you?"

Rounding the corner into the assembly room, Arlie spotted the refreshment table over against a wall and nudged Alex. "Over there," he said, pointing. En route, they were focusing on the dark green magnums cooling in an ice chest so they didn't notice the foppish man in a pinstripe suit hustling after them.

"Hallo! Yoo hoo!"

Turning towards the speaker, they found themselves again facing the tawny visage of Horatio Krumm and his blinding neon teeth. "I thought I saw you two fighting your way through the crowd!" the art dealer enthused. "I'm so pleased to see you've come back for the auction. I knew *Original Perfection* had won your heart," he confided, winking at Arlie who stepped back as if he'd been splashed with cold water.

"I think we'll just be observers tonight, Mr. Krumm," Alex said, coming to Arlie's rescue.

"Oh, you'll see," Krumm said, smugly. "The lure of the auction entices everyone to get in the game. You wouldn't go to the races and not place a bet, or sit at a slot machine and not pull the handle. I can tell that you're both prepared for battle and I, for one, am anxious to see how well you play." He looked around, his eyes ablaze against his orangey complexion. "Oh, we should have glorious competition tonight with all these eager contestants vying to take home a masterpiece.

"I wouldn't tell anyone else," he confided to Arlie, but *Original Perfection* is the finest woodcut lithograph we've ever had at the Gallery, and I want *you* to have it."

Arlie waved off the notion. "Thanks, Krumm, but I don't think..."

"No, I'm serious. You deserve having such a special piece. Don't miss out on the opportunity.

"Well, anyway, I've taken up enough of your time. And I'm keeping you from enjoying the champagne. And it is *real* champagne — from France."

Turning, he called out, "There's plenty more champagne, folks! Be sure to get refills before the auction begins. You've got twenty minutes." After one more ghastly grin at Arlie and Alex, he disappeared into the crowd.

"Oh my God, Arlie!" Alex whispered. "I felt like we were talking to the Devil. Didn't it feel like he was sucking our souls right out of us? I'm almost *afraid* to stay. We'll be lucky if we can escape in one piece, let alone leave without a painting."

Arlie poured her a glass of champagne. "Here, Alex. Relax. Actually, I'm flattered that he remembered that I liked that print. I think I should at least bid on it. It'd be nice to have a piece of real art. It shouldn't surprise you to learn that it would be my first."

"Arlie. Krumm is a salesman. You had only stopped to *look* at that painting yesterday when he *told you* that you liked it. I mean, bid on it if you want to, of course, but you might be surprised at how high the bidding goes. If there's certification that it's one of the prints from the original woodcuts, it'll go into the thousands."

"Okay, Alex. How about if I set a ceiling at $1,500. Would it be worth at least that?"

"I would think it would be worth more, if it's genuine. Let's take another look at the certification on it. I want to look at some of the other prints, too. There are quite a few Miros, Picassos, Klees, Kandinskys. Some original paintings, too."

After refilling their champagne glasses, they moved back into the gallery area and started working their way around the space. In front of the Picasso print of *Le Clown,* Alex spotted a familiar young family. "Toby!"

The little boy looked up, grinning, as he yanked on his mother's skirt to get her attention. "Oh, hi!" the woman said, seeing Alex. "I remember you from the cruise terminal. I'm

Kathy Wilson. And this is my husband, Darrin. You made quite an impression on Toby... Miss Trotter, isn't it?"

"Alex. And this is Arlie Tate. He met Toby there, too. It's nice to run into you. Are you interested in this Picasso? I think it's quite charming."

"We're going to bid on it as an anniversary gift to ourselves. It reminds me of Toby. Same bright eyes and impish look. I don't have any idea what it's worth, but we'll only go as high as we want to spend on it."

"Yeah, that's sensible. Arlie was just deciding on his limit for a Dali print. I'm going to sit this one out and enjoy the show. Well, we want to look around more. Nice seeing you again, and good luck with your print. Hope to see you later, Toby."

As they walked away, Alex tugged on Arlie's sleeve. "Look over there. It's Jasmine and Victor. I wonder what *they're* doing here?"

"He's an *art dealer*, Alex. Why wouldn't he be here?"

"He wouldn't buy from another dealer, that's why. Oh, good, Victor's gone over to talk to Horatio Krumm. I haven't had a chance to speak to Jasmine alone. She's waving to us. Let's go over and say 'hi.'"

"Hey, Jaz. How're you doin'?" Alex asked as they approached. "Love your scarf."

"Oh, thanks— and I'm okay. I'm tagging along to try to distract myself from thinking about the incident this morning, and, uh, other things. I'm not sure *why* Victor wanted to come to the auction. I know he stopped down here yesterday before the wedding to check out the artwork — can't keep his mind off business, you know. That's most important. Not that he would ever bid on anything in a public auction. Maybe he's checking out the auctioneer's technique to get some tips. Strange *looking* fellow, isn't he?"

"That he is. But quite persuasive. He's convinced Arlie that he needs a Dali print."

"Only up to a certain price," Arlie put in. "Uh, I'm sorry to interrupt, Alex, but we've only got a few minutes before the auction." He tapped his watch.

"Right. Please excuse us, Jasmine. We haven't been around to the prints we want to see. We'll talk later."

Making their way over to *Original Perfection* Alex said, "Well, that was strange, don't you think?"

"What? That she seemed ticked off with Victor who was almost killed this morning? Maybe. Could just be nerves. But let's take care of our business, now. What do you think of the print?"

"Okay, let me see. Well, the penciled signature on the print looks like Dali's — a squiggle and a coat hangar, as I'd describe it; not that I'd know a forgery. It's dated 1982. Dali died in 1989, so that checks out. Let's look at the certification hanging here." She pulled up the plastic sleeve. "It says that the print was originally included in the Hearst estate. I guess that gives it some credibility. I don't know, Arlie. Maybe you should ask Victor."

"No, that's not necessary. Besides, if it's anything like evaluating evidence, you'd have to run tests on it to establish authenticity. I'm not going to spend a fortune. Really, I just want to know if you like the print. I particularly like the image of the couple in the foreground."

"Arlie — that 'couple' is Adam and Eve. Listen, if you want to buy it, I hope you get it. I really do. And yes, I think it's a lovely painting. It's very soft, ephemeral..."

"All right, everybody!" the now-familiar high-pitched voice called out. "Pour yourself a last flute of champagne before you take your seats. The auction will begin in five minutes."

Chapter 21

HORATIO KRUMM STOOD AT THE LECTERN with a frozen smile on his face waiting for the crowd to quiet down, but the chatter continued. Losing the smile, he banged his gavel three times and called out, "Your attention, please! Attention, please!" The room finally hushed and he began.

"That's better. Ladies and Gentlemen, I'm about to offer for sale some of the world's finest artwork painted by such immortalized artists as Picasso, Miro, Dali, Kandinsky and others. I hope that you've picked out several pieces, because you don't want to lose out on acquiring at least one masterpiece, and there will be competition for all of them. Fortunately, there are plenty to choose from.

"But, remember, you can only buy one if you're the highest bidder, so don't be shy or too cautious and lose out. I don't want anyone to leave here disappointed because they're leaving empty-handed.

"Let me assure you that these paintings are all museum-quality, like those hanging in the Guggenheim, or Louvre, including the framing that has been professionally done with archival materials to prevent fading or deterioration of any kind, for very many years. All those that are originals or signed reproductions, are authenticated with COAs, or Certificates of Authenticity, so that you may be confident of their quality and value.

"But the most important reason you should buy tonight is that your purchase will be worth at least *twenty percent more* after you get home. At least. How significant is that? That means that you're investing in something that will beautify your home while appreciating at a higher rate than any other investment you have. What does your money earn in a savings account? In stocks and bonds? And you know how much your car *depreciated* when you drove it out of the dealership.

"How can I guarantee that kind of appreciation? I can because the price is ultimately determined by you, based on the appraised valuation I'll provide you. There is no profit added for middlemen or overhead. This is the ultimate marketplace where the price becomes what a buyer is willing and able to pay. No gallery can compete with that. Now, are you ready to get started?"

The filled room broke out into applause and cheers. Horatio Krumm had them now. He was ready for show time. Pulling a handkerchief out of his pocket with a flourish, he patted his brow, then drew back his lips to show his mouthful of phosphorescent teeth.

"My two assistants, Danny and Frank, will take care of the paintings and process the sales. May we have the first work of art, gentlemen?"

"Ah! We start off with a little jewel by Spanish painter, Joan Miro i Ferra, known as Joan Miro. You will notice that I pronounce his first name using *two* syllables that sound more like 'Ju-añ' and not like Joan as in Joan Crawford, eh? A prolific painter, Miro lived longer than any other famous artist:

one hundred years, which is saying something when you consider that he was born in 1893, before the advent of modern medicine. In fact, after surviving typhus, which killed most people, he dedicated his life to becoming a master painter, studying in the best art school in Barcelona.

"This original lithograph, titled *Ronde de Nuit*, or *Night Watch*, dates from 1970 and was originally done for the magazine, *Derriere le Miroir,* which we can all translate, no? Though it's small, at eleven by fifteen inches, it makes a powerful statement. This work combines his several influences: the colors and line work of Fauvism, the shapes of Cubism and the folklore of early Catalan art.

"As you can plainly see, it is signed in pencil right here on the image, which is a limited edition print on vellum, and is marked 'three of seventy-five.' Only seventy-five of these in the whole world, folks. The others are probably in European galleries and in the homes of celebrities. The appraised valuation is eight thousand dollars." He paused, moving his gaze from left to right to make eye contact with everyone in the room. "But I'm going to open the bidding at...seventeen hundred dollars."

Arlie leaned in towards Alex and whispered, "It's already too rich for my blood and they haven't even started. *And* it's an ugly painting."

"Ah, I have a bid of two thousand already!" Krumm called out, as everyone looked around in confusion not having seen a raised hand nor heard a spoken bid. "Two thousand." he repeated. "Do I hear twenty-five hundred?"

A middle-aged woman sitting in front of Alex poked her husband in the ribs. Taking a note out of the pocket of his plaid shirt, he showed it to his wife, then pointed at the painting, shaking his head.

"Yes, I have twenty-five hundred from the man in the plaid shirt," said Horatio Krumm, causing the man's mouth to drop open.

With the bidding seemingly ramping up, a man in the back called out, "Three thousand!" followed quickly by "Thirty-five hundred!" from the front left side. Bids continued until fifty-five hundred dollars had been offered, without a response.

"Are you done, then?" the auctioneer asked, taking one last look around. "All right. The winning bid is fifty-five hundred dollars from the gentleman on my left in the blue suit. If my math is correct, that is more than thirty percent lower than the appraised valuation. Well, done, sir!" The dark-haired muscular assistant named Danny hurried over to the dazed-looking senior with a pad of sales slips, and crouched down next to him to ask for a credit card and signature.

* * *

THE EVENING CONTINUED in this manner for another hour and a half: Horatio Krumm always announcing a mysterious opening bid that drew others in, and the highest bidders always appearing to be surprised that they had made the final bid, and were buying a print for several thousand dollars. Sandwiched in between the auctioning of expensive artwork, Horatio Krumm offered up several unsigned framed prints for modest amounts, some even under a hundred dollars.

When a ten-minute break was called, Alex turned around and searched the crowd. "I'm not surprised to see that the Wilsons have gone with their clown print, but I wonder when Jasmine and Victor left. I know they sat down when the auction began."

"They probably left after that first ugly print went for fifty-five hundred," Arlie offered. "Speaking of that, Alex, the Dali prints have gone for way too much. I don't have a chance of getting *Original Perfection* for fifteen hundred."

Alex looked down the Auction Schedule. "Oh, I don't know. It looks like most of the ones from the *Divine Comedy* series have been sold, so you might luck out. Maybe everyone else who wanted one has bought one by now. Plus, a lot of people have left, so there's less competition. And, frankly, the people who are still here look like they're half in the bag from all the champagne. Well, here comes Horatio Krumm, so we'll soon find out."

"Ladies and Gentlemen, welcome back!" the auctioneer announced with forced enthusiasm. "I hope the break revived you to be able to concentrate on the last paintings that will be made available to you this evening. We still have some fine pieces for those of you who haven't been successful bidders, yet. Now is your time. Let me have the next painting, Frank."

The assistant carried out a framed piece with the back facing out. As he set it on the easel, the print was revealed: it was *Original Perfection.*

Alex whispered, "Okay, now, be cool." Arlie nodded.

Horatio Krumm ran his fingers through his blond pompadour and massaged his temples for a few moments. "Excuse me, folks. I seem to have gotten a headache from all this excitement. I've auctioned off over fifty fine pieces, thanks to you good people.

"Anyway, where are we? Oh, yes, here we have a limited print from an original woodblock engraving. I believe that this is the last one we have from Dali's *Divine Comedy* series. It's titled *Original Perfection.* Edition thirty-nine hundred. It's COA will inform you that it's from the Hearst estate, so you know it's valuable. It measures twenty-two by twenty-six inches, framed. A magnificent piece.

This is a good example of a dream-like image that the artist summoned up from his subconscious mind. We've already talked about the eccentric Dali, who was influenced by fellow Spaniards, Picasso and Miro, as is evident in this print. It bears the artist's signature on the image, as you can see. I value this piece at four thousand dollars. Who will start the bidding at seven hundred dollars?"

Alex flicked her hand back and forth down by her side for Arlie to see. The room remained silent. As Alex gazed around, she noted that the spectators all appeared now to be drowsy and inattentive, some with their heads down and their eyes closed.

"Anyone?" Krumm asked, pleadingly. "Ah, yes, I see a hand up for seven hundred dollars. Now, do I hear a thousand?"

A muffled voice was heard up front, "One thousand."

Alex leaned over to whisper, "That bid came from Danny, the assistant! There's nobody bidding!"

"Well, why don't I, then?" Arlie asked out of the side of his mouth.

"Because, you don't want to bid against yourself. Let someone else set a price."

After several more seconds, a woman spoke up from the back, "I'll give ya'...what wuz it again?"

"The house has a bid of one thousand dollars," Krumm replied, wearily. "Would you like to go to fifteen hundred, madam?"

"No, I bid one thouzen, one hunnert," the woman said, slowly blinking.

"Okay, Arlie — now!" Alex said in his ear.

"One thousand, *five* hundred," Arlie called out.

Horatio glanced back at the woman who was now slumped over the empty chair in front of her. His eyes darted back to Arlie. "Sold! For one thousand, five hundred dollars to the gentleman in the navy blazer!" he shouted, sharply banging his gavel on the lectern.

After the next several prints received a lukewarm reception, and most people had slid down into their chairs, nodding their heads, Horatio Krumm mercifully called an end to the rapidly-disintegrating sale, reminding people to pick up their paintings or make shipping arrangements.

* * *

AS ARLIE WAS CARRYING out his wrapped print, Alex patted him on the back. "You did it! Good job!"

Arlie shrugged off the compliment. "I was the only bidder left who was sober. And you kept me from bidding first to drive up the price. Let's take this upstairs. Then you wanna come back down and go to the casino?"

"Oh, the print is protected. Why don't we just stop by the casino now. I don't want to stay long, though. To be honest, I'm not too sober myself, and the ship's movement is making me a little queasy. If you want to stay later, that's fine with me."

"I'll go up with you whenever you're ready."

"No, really, Arlie. Do what you'd like to do."

"That *is* what I'd like to do."

Chapter 22

WALKING INTO THE CASINO, Arlie and Alex found themselves in a noisy, lively atmosphere that was in sharp contrast to the somber, slow-paced auction they had just left. Adding to the gaiety of the scene were hundreds of tiny clear bulbs glittering overhead like stars. In addition, bright white and colored lights emanated from the many slot machines and arcade games that were lined up on the patterned carpet, while soft lights illuminated the gaming tables from low-hanging fixtures.

The spacious room was comfortably filled with people gathered around tables playing games of chance or watching others play. The players appeared engrossed in the action, while the spectators stood silently by, only offering polite applause at the end of the contests.

Several middle-aged women had planted themselves in front of slot machines and were continuously pulling down on the handle, robotically, while they kept feeding the 'one-armed bandits' with quarters and nickels from their plastic cups. Every so often a machine would erupt with blinking lights and clanging bells, and disgorge an ear-jangling cascade of coins, after which the player would scoop up the winnings, redeposit them into the cup and resume pulling the handle. From their grim expressions, few players appeared to enjoy the activity, although no one was seen to leave for another activity.

Alex and Arlie had stood for several minutes taking in the scene, debating what to play when Alex said, "Look over there by the cashier area. Victor seems to be having an animated conversation with a couple security guards. I wonder if something's happened. Let's just head over there and see what's going on."

Crossing the room they were soon within earshot of Victor's voice that was raised in anger. "I don't give a fuck that you're all under contract with the cruise line! You must have regular hours so that half of you are off when the others are on the job. I'll hire the guards who are on their own time. I'm telling you my life has been threatened, and you're telling me you have to stand around doing nothing. I need private security and I'm willing to pay for it. Do you understand? I'll pay you real money— not the chicken-shit you're getting!"

One of the guards who had been up in the Garza's suite that morning held his ground, and looked the art dealer in the eye. "That doesn't change the fact that security on this ship will not be breached by interference from our guests, sir."

"I noticed the cruise line had no problem prohibiting firearms on board for self-protection!" Victor shot back. "One would think that if we were to be left on our own and hunted down by murderous predators, we could at least have some way to defend ourselves!"

"We are protecting all of our guests, sir!" the other guard answered. "That's why we're here, to offer protection to everyone; not just you."

"You can't even investigate a crime when it does happen!"

"That's mostly true, sir," said the first guard. "As you are aware, these are international waters where not any one country has jurisdiction. That's been the case since the beginning of time. That doesn't mean, however, that we aren't on duty to serve and protect our guests. You'll just have to be satisfied with the security level that has been found to be adequate by the rules of the International Maritime Organization. If it makes you feel more comfortable, we'll schedule spot checks on your end of Deck Fourteen."

"Oh, that makes me feel safe as a baby in its mother's arms," Victor scoffed. "The *Bermuda Queen* will be hearing from my attorney who, fortunately, is traveling with me."

Arlie whispered to Alex, "Have you heard enough? Can we move along?"

"Yeah, sure. I really don't want to get embroiled in this fight. Where do you suppose Jasmine is?"

"Probably as far away from Victor as possible."

Alex's squinted to better focus as she peered into the semi-darkness, looking for her friend. "There she is— over in the corner with Tony." She nudged Arlie to look. "They seem to be engrossed in a serious conversation. Maybe this isn't a good time to go over and say, 'hi.'"

"That's never stopped you before," Arlie mused. "Anyway, I see some of our other 'buddies' at the blackjack table."

"Where? Oh, I see. Oh, no! Not Carlo and Sunny!"

"C'mon, Alex. They'll have to behave themselves at the table. There are strict rules of etiquette. Besides, I'd like to see how Carlo plays. He should be the 'high roller' in the group."

"All right, all right. But we'll just watch, okay? At least at first. I have to practice counting up to twenty-one in different combinations for a while. And then, the ace is either one or eleven, isn't it?"

"Or seven, in some games. And the face cards are always ten," Arlie added.

As they approached the arc-shaped table, Sunny, standing behind Carlo, nodded curtly in their direction. Finding space to stand in back of the other players, Alex pointed out to Arlie the placard sitting in one corner of the table: "BLACKJACK. $5 to $2,000. Split any pair three times. Double on any two cards" And another sign, "Dealer must stand on all 17."

"Oh, yeah — it's just counting up to twenty-one," she said, disparagingly, under her breath.

"I'll explain later," Arlie murmured. "Just watch."

The dealer waited until the players had stacked their plastic chips in front of them before starting play. Then, sliding one card at a time out of a wooden tray, according to the rules of "shoe" blackjack, he dealt two cards to each player, face-up, and then to himself. The dealer showed the queen of hearts and the five of spades, encouraging the players to wager higher because, according to the rules, he would have to draw another card.

Going around the table, the dealer paused for each player to decide on how to play his hand, either by pointing at the top card, asking to be "hit" with another card, or holding out a hand, palm down over the cards, indicating he would "stand."

Carlo had been dealt two face cards and, on his turn, announced to the dealer that he would "double-down." Adding another $2,000 pile of chips in his betting square, he was dealt a five of clubs to put on one of the tens. Pointing to the second card, he was then dealt a four of spades, giving him nineteen. He put his hand out to signal he was 'staying'. On his other ten he was dealt a four of diamonds. After pointing to it for a hit, he was dealt an ace of spades, giving him twenty, or eleven. He hesitated, and then pointed to the ace. He was next dealt a six of hearts. Twenty-one. The slightest smile crossed his face. Sunny, standing behind him gave his shoulder a little squeeze as she glanced over at Alex and Arlie with a smug look on her face. When the dealer drew another card for his hand, it was the eight of clubs. Twenty-three. Carlo and three others were winners.

The game continued for another five rounds with Carlo coming up with a Blackjack once, a "push" twice, and two "busts." He stood at three thousand dollars to the good.

The dealer signaled the start of the seventh hand in the round when Carlo stacked his two thousand in chips. His first card was the ace of clubs, and his second card was the six of hearts, totaling sixteen. The dealer's draw showed the king of hearts and the seven of spades, to total seventeen, when he'd have to "stand" according to house rules.

Carlo pointed to his cards for a third hit. The other players looked over with interest. Sunny, chewing on a fingernail, stared at her husband's cards over his shoulder. The dealer laid down another card— the five of clubs: twenty-two, if the ace was counted as eleven; twelve, if the ace was counted for one.

Carlo sucked in his lower lip and pulled at his chin. He paused. Then said, "Hit me." Sonny put a hand on his shoulder. The nearby players drew in a breath and waited. The dealer dealt another card from the shoe: the king of spades. Twenty-two. Carlo was now one thousand dollars in the hole. He had made and lost six thousand dollars in less than fifteen minutes.

Grabbing up his unspent chips, he swung around and slid off his stool mumbling that he had to find a "hotter" table. But before he could walk away, Sunny held onto his arm. "Wait a minute, babe. Maybe that's enough for tonight."

Carlo bore down on her, his face tightened into hard planes. "I can't quit. Not tonight. Not any night, thanks to your father. By tomorrow we'll be basically disinherited. Then what? Have you thought about that?"

Alex and Arlie turned and started moving away from the group. "I think it's time to go up, now, Arlie — before we run into any more irate Garzas. Victor could be right, though, that he needs his own security guard."

Chapter 23

IN THE MORNING Alex got up early and dressed to go down to the buffet to pick up breakfast before Arlie got out of bed. Riding down in the elevator she was feeling pretty smug about doing the chore, choosing not to admit that she was just hungry and had nothing better to do. Thinking of what lay ahead for the day, she reminded herself that this was Monday and would be their last full day at sea. The *Bermuda Queen* was scheduled to arrive at King's Wharf in Bermuda at eight o'clock the next morning.

    A half hour later she was back upstairs entering her stateroom by using her foot to hold open the door while she squeezed through balancing a covered tray of sweetbreads, yogurt, oranges, and bananas. Managing the maneuver without spilling anything, she put down the tray on the dresser, and noticed the sound of running water in Arlie's shower next door. Good. He should be out soon so she could eat. With that in mind, she quickly straightened up the bed and pulled open the draperies. The early light made the waves glisten like silver. After changing her sweatpants and t-shirt for a halter-top yellow sundress, she impulsively plopped on the wide-brimmed sunhat she had just bought with Arlie's money. It was a great cover for her hair that already was starting to expand from the sea air. After finishing up her makeup. she padded down the hall to get the coffee service.

A few minutes later Arlie came out onto the balcony, his hair still wet, wearing khaki slacks and a light blue sports shirt. Alex was sitting at the table, looking out to sea, lost in thought, as she nibbled on a piece of blueberry muffin.

Leaning over her from behind, he squeezed her shoulders, startling her. "I knew you'd look great in a hat like that. And I have to admit I'm impressed that you got our breakfast," he said. "But why do I have the feeling that you only went down because you couldn't wait to get your hands on a blueberry muffin?" He eyed her stealthily breaking off another piece and buttering it.

She dropped the cake on her plate and looked up, wide-eyed. "I could only find one blueberry muffin downstairs, and I gave you the only one yesterday when you went down and got our breakfast!"

"Okay. Relax, Alex. We don't have to fight over muffins. I'm *glad* that you have it. I'm just as happy with the cranberry bread, all right?

"Now, what do you want to do today? It's our last day on the ship for a while. We never made it to the pool yesterday, so maybe..." He poured himself a cup of coffee and took a sip. "Whatever you want to do," he finished, picking up a slice of bread and taking a bite.

"Thanks. I *was* a little touchy, but it's not about muffins. I didn't sleep well last night. I think it was because of all that's been going on with the Garzas. There were bad vibes with those people in the casino last night, didn't you think?

"Oh, do you like yogurt? I brought you one. I've never seen you eat yogurt, but then, I haven't seen you eat a lot of things."

Arlie shook his head. "I'm pretty basic in my diet. You'll have it down in no time. Mostly, for breakfast, I like blueberry muffins." Alex fixed him with a stare and swatted him with her napkin.

"Wait— did you hear that?" Arlie asked. "Is that someone knocking?"

Alex cocked her head towards the opening into her cabin. "It's too early for the cleaning staff, but I do hear some tapping somewhere. Not at *my* door, I don't think."

Arlie stood up. "I'll go check. I might not have put out a 'Do Not Disturb' card. Be right back."

Alex stayed seated at the table, listening. A few moments later she heard Arlie's voice and another man's that sounded more muffled. She couldn't make out any words from either of them.

Arlie returned shortly, looking flushed. "That was security. You felt uneasy about the Garzas? You must have had a premonition. Victor's body was just found in a laundry room on Deck Seven. He's been murdered."

"What?! Oh my God, Arlie, no! Murdered?! Who would have wanted to murder... oh, yeah..."

"Exactly. We know of s*everal* people who might have wanted to kill him. And there could be others we don't even know about."

"Are you sure he was *murdered?* People have heart attacks, accidents . . ."

"Alex. His body was found in a hamper in a laundry."

"Right. Right. Victor wouldn't be caught dead in a laundry room. I mean. . . oh, you know what I mean."

Arlie had to bite his lip not to smile. "Yes, I know what you mean, Alex. Like I said, where he was found proves that he was murdered. Listen, I'm going to have to get down there and take charge of the scene and start the investigation. That's why security came up to tell me. They've called the ship's doctor, but he'll have to wait there for me to view the body before he can disturb it. Security said they couldn't see much, but there wasn't any visible blood, so he probably wasn't shot or stabbed. They left a guard at the scene and put up some kind of tape. Probably, 'washroom being cleaned.'"

"I have to go up and see Jasmine!" Alex cried out, with sudden realization.

"No, I don't want you talking to Jasmine just yet. I need to interrogate her. It'll be hard enough to work on the case without any resources, but I'm going to follow procedures, anyway. I'm sorry, but right now your friend looks good as a suspect."

"No! That's crazy, Arlie! She just married the man the night before last! I don't think she wanted to kill him *last* night!"

"Maybe not, maybe so. Grooms have been murdered in less time than that. I'll tell you what. If you'd like to help out, you can come down and assist me at the scene. On the way there, I'll give you a list of items you can find for me. Oh, and grab your camera. Now, when you're in the laundry room you have to promise me that you won't touch anything."

"Oh, I don't know, Arlie. Who wouldn't like to get up real close to a corpse and put their hands on everything? Are you kidding me?! I'm not really crazy about even *seeing* the body. It's probably all stiff and blue by now. After you've taken any evidence, can you at least cover him with a sheet and have him taken down to the morgue right away?"

"Actually, he's probably already covered by a sheet since he's in a laundry basket. I shouldn't joke. Sure, we'll have him taken down to refrigeration as soon as possible. My guess is that the body will have more colors than blue in different places, depending on where the blood settled. Most likely he'll be white and waxy on top, blue in the extremities, and red where there's a pooling."

"Sounds real patriotic, Arlie. All right, I'll go with you. Just let me get a pad of paper to write things down. I know you don't want to take time for me to change, so I'll just have to show up to work a murder scene wearing a yellow sundress. Fine." Catching sight of herself walking by the dresser mirror, she pulled off her hat and flung it onto the bed.

Chapter 24

WALKING DOWN THE HALLWAY to the elevator Arlie said, "Okay, I'll tell you the items I need to process the scene, but I want you to stop by the scene with me first to see what the doctor has that you won't have to get. You should be able to find everything else on the ship."

Alex shrugged. "I'll see about that. Our elevator's here. Tell me while we're going down."

As they boarded an empty car, Alex opened her pad of paper and rested it on the brass rail. "Okay, shoot."

"Right. Let's see, security said that there aren't any fingerprint kits on the ship, so they probably don't have anything for blood analysis, either. I'll have to work with just bare essentials that you can get outside of a crime lab."

"Okay. Like what?"

"Well, like disposable tweezers...biohazard bags."

"Biohazard bags. Oh, yeah, I can get *those* in any of the gift shops."

"The doctor will have them, as well as disposable gloves, booties and swabs. You can find plastic and paper bags, permanent markers, razor blades...uh, a magnifying glass, a tape measure, chalk..."

Alex stopped writing and looked up. "Chalk? Really? You're going to draw a chalk outline around the body? Isn't that a little 'Hollywood'? That's something they'd do on a CSI show."

"Where do you think they got the idea? But you're right. I don't need chalk —the body's not on the floor and I don't think he was killed where he was found, anyway. Okay, we're here on seven, and that's all I can think of. You ready? You know you can be a big help to me, Alex. Oh, and give me the camera before I forget."

"I was thinking *I* could take the pictures, Arlie. That's sort of my specialty. Not photos of corpses, but I take a lot of candids of my tour members for mementos, so that's about the same thing. And they're as good as those," she argued, pointing at the walls of pictures in the photo studio they were passing.

"We'll see. First, I'd like you to find those items I gave you. Look, there's a guard standing outside a door down the hall. That must be the laundry room, Alex. Alex? He turned around. "Are you coming?"

"I am. I was just checking out these photos. There's a cute one of us."

"Will you come along now?"

Arlie waited while she caught up. "Are you sure you're ready for this? You look a little uncomfortable."

"I'll be fine. I just need to get used to the idea. I never liked the guy, but I didn't want to see him murdered."

"Well that's very nice of you. Hey, there's a guy in a medical coat coming towards us. Must be the doctor. See what a detective I am? C'mon. We need to talk to him."

Alex looked down the hallway at a stocky man with thinning grey hair and dark-framed glasses approaching, carrying a shopping bag. As they were about the come together, Arlie put out his hand. "Detective Arlie Tate. I guess security told you I'd be here."

"Right. I'm Doctor Jonas Briggs, head physician on the *Bermuda Queen*," he said, shaking hands. "And this young woman is...?" he asked, looking Alex over, taking in her halter-style dress and her sandaled feet.

"Oh, sorry," Arlie said, putting his arm around Alex's shoulder. "This is Alex Trotter. She's the tour operator for the deceased's wedding party. She's also my companion, and she'll be assisting me in the investigation. Actually, she's had some experience in this sort of thing," he added, giving Alex a knowing look. She lightly elbowed him in the ribs while smiling at the doctor.

"I see," the doctor said, doubtfully. "Yes, well, this is a terrible business. Quite shocking, really. I'm accustomed to treating seasickness, not determining the cause and manner of death of a passenger. And I understand you knew Mr. Garza."

"Not well," Arlie replied, "but I was aware of hostilities toward him and, perhaps, an earlier attempt on his life. Let's just say that I already have a solid list of suspects. Right now, I want to inspect the body with you, but, of course, we need a few items to protect the scene before we can go in. What did you bring with you?"

The doctor reached into his paper bag. "Well, I assumed that you would need these booties and plastic gloves. And I've got some swabs, of course, and a bottle of distilled water." He looked down into the bag, while holding onto the items he had already taken out. "And here's a few pairs of tweezers, razor blades and some biohazard bags. I guess that's it," he said, as he held up the paper sack to peer into its depths.

"All right, good. That's enough to get started," Arlie said. "Alex, why don't you get going and find the other items."

Alex looked over her list, crossing out some things. "Okay. I'm sure I can find these other things. I should be able to be back here in a few minutes, in fact. I'll just go down to Deck Six for most of this. I think I need some sort of identification if I have to borrow some things they don't sell on board, like the magnifying glass."

"I think I've got a department card here. Yeah. Here. Take that. Now you're not deputized, but for purposes of borrowing a couple pieces of office equipment, I don't mind that you show this. Oh, and Alex, I'll have to take the pictures of the body. You can take more of the scene when you get back."

Alex mumbled, "Okay, fine," and took off for the elevator to go down the one floor. Once she stepped out into the main atrium, she hurried over to the Customer Service Desk where several tourists were lined up to ask their questions.

"Excuse me," she said to the last couple in line, "but can I get ahead of you? I'm on police business."

"Yeah, right," the man scoffed, giving her the once-over. "Nice uniform. Sorry, but you'll just have to wait your turn. You in a rush to get to your pedicure— er, Sergeant?"

"No, seriously. Oh, yoohoo! Excuse me!" she called out to get the attention of the neatly-groomed young man at the desk who looked back at her and smiled.

"I'll be right with you, miss. Just four or five parties ahead of you," he said, pleasantly.

Alex shook her head in frustration and pushed her way past everyone to sidle up to the counter. "Listen, this is an emergency! I need a couple of items you might have, or you can tell me where to go." Stretching forward over the counter she whispered to the startled clerk, "Don't say anything, but there's been a murder on Deck Seven and I'm assisting the detective."

The clerk stepped back, staring at her. "What?! Who *are* you?" He looked around for help from the female clerk came rushing over.

"What's the problem, Curt?

Alex waved the Sheriff's Department card in front of them. "Look for yourselves!" she demanded in a harsh whisper. "I don't want anyone to hear me, but I'm helping investigate a murder. Just tell me if you have a magnifying glass, a measuring tape and plastic and paper bags." She checked her list. "Oh, and a Magic Marker."

The female clerk, whose name card read 'Sally Watkins' said, "Is this for some kind of scavenger hunt or something?" Seeing Alex's murderous look, she said, "Okay, I'll get you what we have, but you'll have to sign a form with your stateroom number and you'll be charged a twenty dollar deposit, okay?" She glanced over at her male counterpart, pointed at her head and made a couple of circles in the air with her index finger. He nodded in agreement. Rolling her eyes, she turned and disappeared through a doorway into a small office.

While waiting for the clerk to return, Alex avoided the penetrating stare of the male clerk by looking out across the atrium. Patting down her hair and squaring her shoulders she reminded herself that she was a "nearly deputized" police professional and must act like one.

A couple minutes later, Ms. Watkins reappeared with a logo-imprinted plastic bag and a form. "Here you are. I got everything for you. Just sign this. And return these as soon as the game is over, okay?"

"Thanks," Alex said, tersely. "But this is *no game*. You're just lucky you finally cooperated and didn't obstruct justice or... interfere with a police investigation or. . . or something," she added, running out of charges. With one last scowl, she snatched the bag off the counter and turned on her heel which caused her to skid a little in her thin-soled sandals.

* * *

BACK UPSTAIRS, she walked down the hallway with a bounce in her step, pleased that she was able to get everything Arlie needed, and at her first stop. Nearing the laundry room she saw that the guard was still there. "Excuse me," she said. "I'm here to see Arlie Tate. He's expecting me." The guard looked doubtful.

"Just tell him that Ms. Trotter is here with his CSI kit." The guard raised his eyebrows before reluctantly opening the door to go inside. Moments later, Arlie emerged from the room.

"CSI kit, Alex? Just tell me — did you get it all? Are those the things in that bag?"

"Yes, everything you asked for is here. It was one-stop shopping. Anyway, how's it going? Do you know how he was murdered? Is there any evidence of who did it?"

"Yes, to both. But you're not going to like it, Alex. The doctor and I agree that it was death by asphyxiation. In layman's terms— he was strangled. And not manually. Do you remember Jasmine's scarf that you thought was so pretty?"

"Jasmine's scarf that she wore last night? Sure, I remember. What does that have to do with this?"

"Plenty. I just saw it again, in there." He nodded towards the laundry room. "Although it doesn't look quite so pretty under a dead body. That's what was used to choke Victor to death. I'm afraid that your friend Jasmine just moved up to being the prime suspect."

Chapter 25

"ARLIE, YOU CAN'T BE SERIOUS! How can you think that Jasmine murdered Victor?"

"I'm just telling you that he was strangled with *her scarf*. Did you see anyone else with that scarf last night?"

"Arlie, if Jasmine had done what you say, do you think she's dumb enough to have left it behind like a calling card? No. The fact that the scarf was there *eliminates* her as a suspect, as far as I'm concerned."

"Maybe that's just what she thought," Arlie countered. "Since a murderer tries not to leave any clues behind, wouldn't it be clever to leave evidence like that on purpose so that it would be discounted as being *too* obvious?"

Alex shook her head, looked up at the ceiling and took a deep breath. "No, because she couldn't depend on the authorities to use that reasoning. It's far more likely that the killer planted the scarf on the body to implicate Jasmine. It's still not too clever, I grant you, but there might not have been time to come up with anything better."

Arlie crossed his arms and calmly regarded her. "Look, Alex, I don't want Jasmine to be guilty of this any more than you do, and there are plenty of unanswered questions like, how could a person of her size overpower someone who outweighed her by fifty, sixty pounds and was several inches taller? Nevertheless, she's the first suspect we need to eliminate, if we can."

"We?"

"I know that you're going to make yourself a part of this investigation, so I might as well agree to include you. Right now, if you still want to, you can go in and take pictures. I got everything I wanted. It's pointless going over the body since it's contaminated by the dirty laundry. Hairs and skin cells must have transferred from other people. Let me get you a pair of booties and some gloves."

* * *

AS ALEX WAS WAITING, she asked herself why she was so willing to get involved in this gruesome situation. The answer came easily that she didn't have a choice: the victim was her client and her friend's husband. She couldn't, in good conscience, not try to help bring his murderer to justice, and exonerate every innocent person.

"Okay, Alex, here you go," Arlie said, handing her the shoe and hand covers.

Stepping just inside the room, the sight of the deceased's body stuffed into the hamper along with an overpowering stench made her stomach heave and her throat gag. The once-handsome face was grey and covered with a waxy sheen. Sunken black eyes stared out as though still unwilling to submit to death. Below the swollen head, was the bloated torso and stiff legs that were buckled at the knees, leaving his shoed feet suspended in the air.

"We replaced the body in the position that we found it," Arlie said, matter-of-factly, noticing her shocked look. "Of course, he wasn't killed in the basket. The rolling cart was simply a means of transporting the body from somewhere on this deck, I assume.

As you see, the only piece of evidence is the scarf. We'll try to find DNA on it when we get to Bermuda, but it's a long shot. In that we're inside in a dry area, there aren't any shoe impressions on the tile floor. We might get some latents off that bar on the hamper, so don't touch it."

Alex rolled her eyes at being told the obvious. Turning her attention back to the body she sniffed at the air. "I just got a whiff of a sharp smell mixed in with that stench."

Dr. Briggs moved closer, audibly drawing in air. "Could be bleach or spot cleaner. Detective Tate and I have gotten used to all the odors, so we don't smell anything, even the bowel evacuation. Fortunately, the body hasn't started to putrefy yet. That's a lot worse."

"Oka-a-y, then," Alex said, stepping back, recoiling from the odor of an emptied bowel and the image of a rotting body. "I think that I'll just take a few pictures and get out of here." Gingerly walking around the laundry cart, she quickly took a few shots of the room with its row of commercial machines, shelving units and piles of soiled sheets and towels.

Arlie turned to the doctor. "I'm done here, Briggs. You can have security take the body down to your morgue."

"Are you ready, Alex?" She nodded and headed for the door. Once outside, he said, "I'd like you to assemble all the wedding guests in a couple of hours in that lounge next to the casino. I'll have security close it off to the public, but I don't think it even opens till later in the afternoon. Anyway, don't give anyone any details, even it they ask. They'll have heard that he was murdered, but don't give specifics— not about the manner, or time of death. Just say that I need to ask them some routine questions."

"Got it. Does that include Jasmine and the family?"

"No. I'm going to conduct preliminary interviews with them right after I leave here. I'll see Jasmine first, then Sunny and Carlo, and finally, Tony. Security has informed them of the death and has someone posted outside their staterooms."

"Sure you don't need me to come with you?"

"No, I think I can manage, Alex." His seeming sincerity was betrayed by a small smile.

"Are you mocking me?"

"Maybe a little, but you are being helpful. Don't worry, I'll keep you in the loop, okay?" She nodded, uncertainly. "Make sure you catch up with everyone and tell them it's a police order that they show up, even the aunts —everyone." She nodded, again. "Good. I'm glad I can count on you. See you in the lounge at about one."

Chapter 26

JASMINE OPENED THE DOOR barefooted, wearing a bathrobe, just as she had done a few hours before her wedding. This time, rather than looking pale without makeup, her eyes were red-rimmed and her face was blotchy.

"Arlie."

"I'm afraid I'm here as 'Detective Tate,' Jasmine."

"Oh." She looked down and opened the door wider to let him in. "I'm sorry I'm not dressed. Security came to tell be about Victor before I was even up and I haven't felt like getting ready for the day and whatever lies ahead. I had room service for breakfast, and I think I'll stay in for the rest of the day. I really don't want to face anyone if I don't have to.

"Of course I understand that you have questions for me. Here, have a seat." She took a seat on the sofa across from him.

"Damn it, Arlie. Or, 'Detective.' I just can't believe Victor's dead! This is crazy! We were only married for what— 36 hours? And who would want to murder him?"

"That's what I'm here to find out."

"Well, I know you don't think *I* did it."

"I want to hear everything you can tell me about Victor's last evening —his movements, who he talked to— anything you can think of that might be significant. Also, I want an accounting of your own movements."

"Okay. Of course, I've been thinking about all of that, myself. Shall I start with dinner?" Arlie shrugged.

"Come to think of it," Jasmine said, "you and Alex were eating at In Mare at about the same time we were. And then, as you know, we all went on to the Gallery to preview the paintings before the auction."

"Did anything happen at the auction that upset Victor?" Arlie asked. "I noticed that he was having a serious conversation with Horatio Krumm. What was he talking to him about?"

"Oh, I don't know. Victor didn't tell me. Of course, I was a little out of sorts because he wanted to spend time there when we certainly weren't in the market for overpriced artwork from a cruise ship's gallery."

"I bought a print," Arlie said.

"Oh, I didn't mean that no one should buy from there...just that Victor has his own sources. You know."

"Yeah. So, how long did you stay at the auction? We didn't see you leave."

"We were there for only the first couple of pieces — Miro's *Night Watch,* I think, and another Miro, as I remember. Then we left and went to the casino. We ran into Sunny and Carlo first, and then Tony showed up. It was very uncomfortable for all of us as we weren't on good terms following our meeting with Victor's attorney in the afternoon when we discussed the will."

"They were being disinherited," Arlie suggested.

"No, but Victor had decided to discontinue paying out anything to Sunny and Tony against their future inheritances and, also, to make me an equal beneficiary to the estate. I wasn't crazy about seeing all of them so soon, myself. You can imagine how they felt about me, too."

"I don't imagine anything. Did Sunny or Tony threaten either or both of you?"

"No, of course not. But they had been very unhappy when they learned they were about to lose a great deal of money. Both of them had tried to make the case that they shouldn't be penalized just because their father got married, since there was plenty of money to go around. Tony argued that he could actually make money for his father if Victor invested in some of his businesses. He's only asked for loans. Sunny needs money because her husband doesn't want to work and gambles away what he does have. I can't believe that either of them or Carlo would hurt Victor, though. That's just too monstrous."

"You were seen talking to Tony at the casino. What were you talking about?"

"What? Oh, I guess I was just sympathizing with him. I don't remember our conversation. I think that I just wanted him to know that I was still in his corner."

"Do you know why Victor asked the security guards at the casino for a private detail?"

"He did? No, but I know that he was pretty upset about someone trying to drop a pot on his head. Look, Victor has always known that some people have had grievances against him because of some of his business decisions. To my knowledge, there's never been a real threat to his life. Until now." She choked back tears.

"Did you leave the casino with Victor?" Arlie continued.

"No, I was tired and told him that I wanted to leave at about ten o'clock. He said he wasn't ready to go upstairs, which was understandable. He kissed me on the cheek and I left."

"Didn't you worry when he never came up? Did you call security?"

"I didn't wait up for him. I told you I was tired. I watched a little TV in bed, and then I fell asleep. I didn't know that Victor hadn't come up to bed until the security guard woke me knocking on the door this morning and told me that he was dead. That he had been murdered." She visibly shuddered.

"Did anyone see you leave alone?"

"Obviously people saw me leave, but we weren't with anyone I know so I guess I can't prove it. Arlie, you can't believe that *I* had anything to do with Victor's death. My God! I only just married the man! Why would I kill him?"

"I just have to learn all that I can about the circumstances that led up to the murder, Jasmine. Nothing personal. Oh, one other thing. Alex commented on what a pretty scarf you were wearing last night. Could I see it? I think she'd like to have one similar to it."

"What? Oh, that's right. I'd forgotten about the scarf. I remember I was playing an arcade game, like table shuffleboard, I think you call it. But the scarf was hanging down where I wanted to look, so I took it off. I must have left it in the casino. Now that you mention it, I'm sure I didn't have it on when I got undressed. Maybe I can get it back from 'lost and found' if they have such a thing in the casino. It was a Gucci scarf in lavenders and blues. It was pretty. I hope I can retrieve it."

Arlie made a show of reading over his notes before he looked up, again. "How long have you known that you're pregnant?"

"What?! Pregnant? Why would you ask that? I'm not pregnant."

"Jasmine, if *I* know you're pregnant, surely *you* do. What bothers me is that you haven't admitted it. When Alex and I stopped by your suite the afternoon of your wedding, I could see that you were nauseous and dizzy— two early signs. Several times since then you've claimed to be tired, when most people would have been energized, like at your wedding reception, where, by the way, you refrained from having even a sip of wine. You were drinking water. Not celebrating with a little champagne or wine at your own wedding reception? Then there's your coloring..."

"Oh, all right! I'm pregnant. I didn't think I had to tell everybody. Can't I keep that to myself without being accused of murder?"

"I'm not accusing you of murder right now. But it is suspicious that you wouldn't tell even close family or your friends about your condition. We live in a time when unmarried celebrities are congratulated for having 'baby bumps,' so your silence isn't due to social taboos. Did you tell Victor?"

"Uh, yes, sure. I told him."

"You're not a very good liar, Jasmine, so let's cut to the chase — whose baby is it?"

"I can't believe you're asking me that! It's Victor's, of course."

"A man with a legendary ego who was so proud to be marrying a much younger woman, and you didn't tell him?"

"Look, Arlie, this has nothing to do with Victor's murder. Please don't pry into my personal affairs."

"You affair is what makes this pertinent to the investigation of Victor's murder."

"I'm sorry. but this interview is over, Detective. I know my rights and I won't speak to you again without my attorney being present."

"Suit yourself, Jasmine. Just know that I will get to the bottom of this. The best way you can prove to me that it has nothing to do with Victor's murder is to come clean and tell me the whole story. Until then, it puts you at the top of the suspects' list. Oh, and by the way, I found your scarf under Victor's dead body. It was used to strangle the life out of him."

Chapter 27

"WHY ARE WE BEING LOCKED UP in here like prisoners?!" Sunny groused as she opened the stateroom door to Arlie Tate "This is *your* order? What happened to our civil rights? As if I haven't suffered enough by having my father murdered by some fiend, now I have to be treated as a common criminal!" Arlie looked past her at the luxury suite with its tasteful appointments and expansive view of the Atlantic Ocean just beyond the balcony.

Count Carlo appeared by her side. "Sunny, my darling, don't let yourself get overwrought," he cooed, wrapping an arm around her. "You have to forgive my wife, Detective. She's a very passionate woman who dearly loved her father. Really, this has been devastating for both of us. We're in a state of shock, but I understand that you need to talk to us as a matter of course."

"I don't think *I* understand," Sunny sniffed. "I think you should be out looking for my father's killer, Detective. He certainly isn't *here*."

"Yes, well, I'm sure it was hard having to stay in this suite for a couple of hours, Countess, but I need you to answer some questions to help me in my investigation," Arlie Tate said, without betraying any satire.

Sunny's features softened at the use of her title. "Oh, all right. Come in. Might as well get it over with. Have a seat. We'll sit on the sofa."

Arlie entered and claimed the closest chair. After flipping open his notebook he glanced over at the couple, noting Sunny's carefully-applied makeup and Carlo's European-tailored clothes. Sunny still appeared irritated, while Carlo was smiling broadly, like a genial host.

"So," Arlie started, "I'm interested in your movements yesterday and last evening, as well as any interactions with Victor Garza. Let's start with yesterday afternoon— your meeting with Morrie Feldman. How'd that go?"

Arlie was amused to see the color drain from their faces as they looked at each other. "It went well enough," Sunny offered, cautiously. "Father was adamant about keeping us in his will. You'll probably be talking to Morrie who'll tell you that Father made a revision in his gifting policy, so I'll tell you about that from our point of view. Father decided, because it was in our best interests, that he would retain our inheritance in investments rather than making regular disbursements to us. We were shocked at first, but then we agreed that it was for the best. Isn't that right, Carlo?"

"Yes, that's just how I remember it," Carlo said, nodding with conviction. "Of course, Morrie might have misread our reaction as being negative because we had been caught off guard." He cast a sideways look at Sunny who glared back at him. "Uh, maybe I'd say that we 'questioned' it before we came around to accepting it. You know how it is, Detective; people find change difficult at first."

"Yes, I do, especially when the change is from having money to not having money. Just so I know how big of a 'change' it was for you, how much money are we talking about?"

"Not that much," Sunny responded.

"How much is 'not that much'?" Arlie persisted.

"Oh, a couple hundred thousand a year. Just enough to keep the lights on — you know."

"Yeah, right. That'd keep the lights on in Times Square. So, will Mr. Feldman corroborate your version of events— that your father did this only because it was in your best interests, and not that he was upset with either of you. Or that it was due to Jasmine being an additional dependent. And when was this 'change' going to go into effect?"

The Giovannis again locked eyes and stayed frozen in place.

"Anyone?" Arlie prompted, looking from one to the other.

Sunny twisted her mouth around before responding. "Morrie might have gotten the impression that my father was angry with us but, as his daughter, I knew that his bark was worse than his bite. I'm not even sure that he wasn't just bluffing." She waved her hand in dismissal. "Father was chagrined that Carlo had come late to the reception when he couldn't break away from a high-stakes poker game. My husband just didn't want to ask my father for money after he had a run of bad luck."

"I bet he didn't. So when was your allowance going to be terminated?"

"There was mention of drawing up some paperwork— when was that again, Sunny?" Carlo looked at his wife for help.

"If Morrie got around to it...maybe today," she replied, "but I don't think that anyone thought it was a drop-dead date. I mean..."

Arlie remained straight-faced. "Okay, why don't we talk about last night. Of course, Alex and I saw you both at the blackjack table just before we left. How long did you stay there?"

"It was pretty late, wasn't it Sunny?" Carlo asked.

"I know we didn't get up here until after midnight," she answered.

"Where did you go after the casino?" Arlie asked, noticing the subterfuge.

Her face reddened. "We stopped at the bar next to the casino for a drink. That's all."

"Did you *see* anyone at the bar?"

"There were several people there...oh, all right. You'll probably interrogate the bartender, anyway. My father was there and we talked to him for a while."

"Had you followed him in?"

"No. It happens that we wanted a drink just when we noticed that he was going into the bar."

Arlie clenched his jaw and slapped down his pen. "Do you remember me telling you that I needed some answers to try and find your father's killer? All of this 'beating around the bush' gives me the impression that you don't want to cooperate with this investigation. What do you have to say about that?"

Sunny looked up at the ceiling, took a deep breath and slowly exhaled. "Look, I know how it sounds — my father wanted to discontinue my allowance, we met with him and his lawyer to change his will, and we saw him late last night, but none of that has anything to do with who murdered him."

Arlie broke into her discourse. "So you thought you'd help me out by holding back the details about your meetings with your father so I wouldn't 'misinterpret' anything that could be seen as pointing to your guilt. How am I doing?"

"That's it exactly!" Sunny exclaimed, her face clearing. "*I* know that we would never harm my father and that we have no knowledge of who murdered him, but certain coincidences could give *you* the wrong impression."

"Well, thanks for trying to make my job easier, but evasive tactics usually make me think of a 'consciousness of guilt.' Now that we understand each other, tell me exactly what transpired between you and your father in the bar, and when did you leave him?"

Sunny appeared to be defeated. "Honest to God, we didn't kill my father. We left him in the bar just before midnight and I don't know where he went after that. And no, he wasn't too happy with us and still intended to change his will, but we didn't kill him."

Arlie stroked his chin, considering. "At least that sounds more truthful than anything else I've heard here today, but I'm not taking it for gospel, in case you're wondering. By the way, did your father happen to have Jasmine's scarf with him?"

"What? Jasmine's scarf? No, I didn't see it, did you, Carlo?" Carlo, who appeared totally bewildered only shrugged and held up his hands in mute response.

"Okay," Arlie said, closing his notebook, "I guess that's all for now. As you surmised, I will be interviewing others to corroborate your testimony. Oh, and you should also know that I'm not crossing your names off my list of suspects."

Chapter 28

"HI, ARLIE, if i can still call you that," Tony greeted as he opened the door of his stateroom. "Please come in. Security told me to not leave, that you'd be coming by to talk to me about...well...about my father's murder." He visibly shuddered. "I hadn't said that before just now. I've never personally known of *anybody's* murder, much less someone close to me. I can't quite even grasp it. Anyway, please have a seat. I don't know how I can be of help, but I'll answer any questions you have."

Arlie noted, again, how handsome the man was with his trim muscular physique and his exotic dark coloring. "Good," he said in response. "I'll just take this chair, and if you'll sit there, that'll be fine." He had indicated a pair of upholstered chairs in front of the sofa that were facing each other.

"So, you were 'close' to your father?"

"No, it would have been more accurate to say someone *'closely related'* to me. My father and I have never been close.

While I was growing up, he had to spend much of his time away, in Europe, and elsewhere. Also, he and my mother divorced when I was a teenager, so I didn't live with him after that and rarely saw him. As an adult, he was often critical of me, especially of my business ventures which he considered to be all pipe dreams; unworthy of serious consideration."

Arlie studied the relaxed demeanor of the younger man. "That must have been upsetting to you. Especially since your father started out selling poster art. Not exactly an inspired business plan."

"No, you're right, there, but in time he made it big, and all on his own. Dad's family didn't have any money to give him, so he expected Sunny and me to make it on our own, too, without any financial help from him. Maybe we have been too comfortable knowing the resources are there if we're ever in real trouble. I don't know. Right now I just wish he were still here to debate it.

"Arlie, can you tell me how my father died? I was told it was murder. I mean, did he suffer?"

"You're the first one to ask that, Tony. For now, let's just say that he didn't have any defensive wounds, so I think he was taken by surprise and died quickly."

Tony lowered his head and stared at the floor for several seconds. When he looked up, his dark eyes were glassy with tears. "He was a decent man, Arlie. I know he could be difficult, but he had his principles. He had a strong work ethic and he helped many talented people he thought were deserving and had enough ambition. He will be missed, even by the people who didn't like him. I can't imagine who could have done this terrible thing."

"Well, in order to eliminate you from the list, tell me about your movements last night, and the last time you saw your father."

"Oh, sure. I understand." He gazed out at the sea. "Um, I had dinner with Sunny and Carlo. Wait — we saw you and Alex there in the fish restaurant."

"That's right," Arlie agreed. "And I noticed that you didn't talk to your father. Weren't you on speaking terms?"

"'Speaking,' maybe, but we weren't on 'easy' terms. I'm sure you know about the changes in my father's will. He had made it official that we wouldn't get any more 'advances' from the estate, but that really didn't affect me, since I never did, anyway. I guess the formality and the finality of it created fresh hard feelings for all of us. I was just afraid that Sunny might hold it against Jasmine, since Sunny has never warmed up to her, anyway. It's such a shame since they're both great people. Sunny is very clever and Jasmine is a loving, giving person."

"What did you talk about at dinner?"

"What did we talk about? Well, I know what you're getting at, so I won't even try to claim that we weren't talking about Dad closing off access to his money. But no one was being openly hostile. Matter of fact, we were kinda joking about it. Sort of black humor, you know. Like, that our inheritance will come in handy to pay for our nursing homes and our funerals.

"Carlo joked that it gave new meaning to 'dead money.' He uses a lot of poker terms. I think that's an expression for the money that's left in the pot from players who have folded. He said he'd have to give up being a high-roller and become a 'grinder'— someone who makes small profits over a long time. Quite a come-down for him.

"Even Sunny found some humor in the situation, like telling Carlo that they'd be the only Count and Countess on food stamps.

"Of course, we didn't find the situation funny, but we tried to laugh about it to get through the disappointment. I can tell you this. Neither Sunny nor Carlo would ever think about hurting Dad, much less killing him. Neither would I, of course."

Arlie nodded without conviction. "Where did you go after dinner?" He flipped over a page in his notebook and continued writing.

"We debated going to the theatre for the show, but ended up going to the casino. I think Carlo felt he needed to have a big night. I'm sure he thought he could outplay anyone there but, of course, there's always an element of luck you have to count on. I don't think he did too well last night, in fact."

"What did *you* do? Did you gamble?"

"Me? No, I'm not much of a gambler. I can never even remember the last hand that was played. I fed a slot machine for a few minutes and then watched Carlo."

"Who did you talk to?"

"Sunny and Carlo."

"Oh, yeah? I saw you talking to Jasmine."

Tony looked uncomfortable and rearranged himself in his chair, crossing one leg over the other. Running his fingers through his hair, he pursed his lips and looked up at the ceiling before answering. "Yes. That's right. Later, I saw Jasmine and we talked for a while. Why? We're friends. I'm very fond of her."

"I think you're *in love* with her."

"What?! You make it sound improper. I *love* her as a family member and as a great friend. She was my father's wife and I respected that."

"Really? Before you say anything else, you should know that she told me about her pregnancy," Arlie said, looking up from his notebook.

Tony slumped down in his chair and rested his chin on his balled fists. After a moment he sighed, and looked over at the detective with heavy-lidded eyes. "I see." His voice was thick.

"It's your child, isn't it." Arlie posed the question as a statement.

"It's possible," he answered, hoarsely. "I'd rather not explain my answer. It doesn't have anything to do with my father's death. It's a personal matter between Jasmine and me."

"From where I sit, it could have a great deal to do with your father's death. I'm sure you were prepared to do most anything to prevent him from knowing you fathered a child with his wife. And I'm equally sure you'd do most anything to protect Jasmine from being exposed as being unfaithful with his own son."

"It wasn't like that! We didn't sneak around having an affair or anything. Jasmine and I have a special understanding and care about each other. I only just found out about the pregnancy, and I don't even know that it's my child."

Arlie slowly shook his head. "If Jasmine believes that it's not her husband's baby, eventually your father would have come to the same conclusion with the same set of facts. And the list of candidates would have been very short.

"Those are a lot of deductions, Detective. All I know for sure is that I didn't have anything to do with my father's murder. Frankly, I can't believe that I actually have to defend my innocence. Obviously, you don't have any evidence against me."

"Well, so far you have motive. Let's talk about opportunity. Where did you go after you talked to Jasmine? By the way, did you buy her that scarf that she was wearing last night? She had told Alex that it was a special gift."

"Scarf? No, I never bought her a scarf. I think she did have something silky in light blue around her face, but I don't really remember what it was. But, you asked where I went after we talked in the casino. I left and went up to my stateroom where I stayed the rest of the evening. I didn't feel like socializing with anyone after our conversation. Jaz had been very upset— about the attempt on my father's life that morning, her pregnancy; maybe even her marriage. Anyway, she was pretty down, and I'm afraid I couldn't cheer her up much. I just told her that I'd be close by and see her through it all."

Tony suddenly sat up straighter, looking more alert. "Hey, speaking of whoever threw that pot down on their balcony, that must be who murdered Dad! There couldn't have been *two* people who tried to kill him on the same day. Oh my God, what am I saying? This is all crazy!"

"Did anyone see you come up to your stateroom?" Arlie asked, without commenting on Tony's epiphany.

"No, I don't think so," Tony said, glumly. "But I had room service yesterday morning that can establish where I was when someone dropped the pot. That's the best I can do.

"Look, I don't mean to be impolite, Arlie, but there's nothing else I can tell you and I'd like to be able to leave and go see my sister and Carlo— and Jasmine, if I'm allowed."

"Sure, you can see anyone you want," Arlie said, closing his notebook. "I'm ready to terminate this interview. I've got everything I need for the time being, but I'll probably want to talk to you again, soon."

"All right, Arlie, but next time I think I'd better have my lawyer present."

Chapter 29

AS ALEX WALKED INTO THE LOUNGE, she wrinkled her nose at the odor of stale beer and whiskey that hung in the air. The dark decor and the low lighting were additional indicators, if any were needed, that the room was used only at nighttime: The carpeting was a deep blue with multi-colored speckles that resembled confetti, and the ceiling had been painted black and outfitted with tiny clear spot lights to resemble stars. The sofas were low-slung with fitted covers in a durable taupe fabric. Round pedestal tables were set about to accommodate drinks.

Waiting for her group, she had time to think about the events of the night before. How was it possible that such a virile, strong-willed man was killed by someone's hands and in a public place? Arlie said that Victor wasn't murdered in the laundry room, which seemed obvious, but where was he killed? Was he lured to some secluded place? By what means? For what reason? Of course, the ship was a maze of a nearly unlimited number of rooms and corridors so that it wouldn't be too difficult to find a place away from public view. More curious was how it was possible for a highly intelligent man to have allowed himself to be put in such a vulnerable position, considering that he was already on high-alert after someone had made an attempt on his life earlier in the day.

And who had a motive to kill him? Alex had plenty of answers to that question: Sunny, Carlo, and Tony had all been financially cut-off; ex-partner Roman Gregg and artists Bruno Rasconi, Lydia Corbin, and Frances Maria Lazaro Marquez had all felt cheated by him. Maybe even Jasmine had a motive. She had seemed so stressed and unhappy since marrying the man. And then, there could be others in the group who had motives that Alex wasn't aware of. Someone who had felt slighted by him or was jealous of his success. Maybe the only person she could confidently cross off the list of suspects was Dame Edith Herrington, who was over eighty and could barely walk.

Voices from outside the lounge brought Alex back to the present. Looking over at the doorway, she saw Jasmine's aunts Lola and Alaana entering. Both ladies were dressed similarly in floral print blouses and beige slacks.

"Halloo, dear!" the one in the blue flowers called out, causing Alex to wonder, *Who is who, again?* "Of course, you're the first one here!" the same lady said. *Oh, of course, that was Lola!* she chuckled to herself remembering the woman's constant use of the phrase.

"I still can't believe this is real!" Alaana exclaimed, her hands flapping. "We've just seen poor Jasmine. The dear girl is trying to be strong, but we could see that she's devastated. She looks so pale and unhealthy. Not at all like herself."

"That's right," Lola said. "Of course it's to be expected when your husband is killed on the second day of your honeymoon, don't you think, dear?"

"Well . . . " Alex managed, stalling to formulate a suitable reply. "We're all in shock," she ventured, hoping that that also explained the aunt's bizarre remark. "You two ladies just have a seat. I need to greet the others who are coming in."

"Certainly, dear," Alaana said. "Lola shouldn't be holding you up. Will you be giving us information about our excursions tomorrow?"

"Not right now, Alaana. Detective Tate has called this meeting to ask a few questions of everyone. He's investigating Victor's murder, you know."

"Oh, yes. That's a good idea, isn't it?"

Alex just rolled her eyes and turned in response to hearing the voices of others coming into the room. The first ones to enter were the theatre designers, Rudolph Perino and Damien Loren.

"Oh, my God!" Rudolph exclaimed to Alex, wide-eyed, his hands clamped over his cheeks. "We got your message, so here we are! Isn't this too outrageous! We just saw the man last night and he was looking so well!"

"He was," Damien chimed in. "I loved his jacket. I swear it looked like he was wearing Phillip Lim. Not many guys his age can wear that edgy vibe and cut. Rudy, did you notice it had a ticket pocket? I guess in our business we look for that," he explained to Alex who was looking puzzled.

"You know that Victor didn't die from natural causes," she said, slowly, looking for a sign of understanding.

"Oh, we know," Rudolph broke in. "I think Damien just meant that it's even more shocking when a man is cut down at his sartorial best."

"Well, his clothes didn't hold up too well during his murder," Alex remarked, conjuring up the sight and smell of the corpse's defecation in its pants.

"Well, anyway, we should have a lovely funeral service for Victor," Rudoph continued, not dwelling on an image of designer clothing losing its finish. "And you know what I'm thinking?"

"I'm sure I don't," Alex responded without hesitation. "What are you thinking?"

"You remember that we talked about the fabulous wedding floral pieces with the mostly authentic Hawaiian flowers, right?" Alex nodded. "Well, they should still be in good enough shape for the funeral! I mean, it's been only a couple of days. Wouldn't that be marvelous?"

"Uh, yeah," agreed Alex, "that'd be like the best repurposing, ever. Now, would you excuse me?"

Alex looked about wildly for someone else to talk to. She noticed the art critic Walter Sneed standing alone just outside the lounge.

"Mr. Sneed, please come in and find a seat. Detective Tate will be down shortly," she said to the man beaming at her.

"Quite a fascinating turn of events, isn't it Miss uh ... "

"Trotter. Alex Trotter. Yes, it's unbelievable, really. I mean, the poor man—"

"Yes, yes. But, what a story this will make! And to think that no one else in the art world even knows that Victor Garza is dead. This is the scoop of a lifetime for me, I'll tell you that." He smiled broadly, again, looking off in the distance as though imaging the story in print with his byline. "Did you see the body? Can you give me any details about how he met his end? Just anything you can tell me would be great. Was it a bloody scene? Do you think he looked his killer in the eye before he died? Oh, my God, This is such big news I can hardly take it in. This could be the column that becomes my legacy, that's what this is. Just give me something descriptive about the body. Was he blue? Oh, of course he was blue."

"Mr. Sneed, please! I'm not authorized to give out any details about Mr. Garza's murder. Detective Tate will be conducting a thorough investigation, and will release details at some point, I would imagine. I know that right now he's interested in obtaining everyone's whereabouts last evening, so you should be prepared to tell him about your movements."

"Oh, of course. To think that I am a suspect! Oh, this is more than I could have hoped for."

Alex shook her head and glanced around, recognizing Victor's ex-partner Roman Gregg, and his wife in the doorway. Walking over to the couple she said, "Excuse me, I'm Detective Tate's assistant. Also, your tour director, Alex Trotter. I know you're Victor Garza's former partner."

Roman Gregg sighed. "Look, Miss, I've got nothing to hide. Vic and I weren't on the best of terms but I had nothing to do with this, so I don't know why you've asked me to come down here."

"*All* of the wedding guests have been asked to meet with Detective Tate. I'm not sure of the time of Mr. Garza's death, but if you can account for your movements last evening, you have nothing to worry about."

"Well, I should hope not. If you're looking for a suspect, you might ask the artists who had exclusive deals with Garza. They haven't been happy with the man."

"Aren't those the same people *you* have been encouraging to end their contracts with Mr. Garza and have their work sold in your gallery?"

"What? How do you know that? I mean, that's not even true."

"Excuse me, Mr. and Mrs. Gregg, but I need to talk to some of the others. Just have a seat."

Alex wanted to move them along as she spotted several of the artists coming down the hallway led by Bruno Rasconi, who gave her a little wave. As they approached, Bruno said, "Hi, Alex. This is really terrible, isn't it? I want you to know that all of us were shocked to hear about Victor's violent death. It's true that we've had our problems with the guy, but I can't believe that anyone wanted *this*. I just hope that Detective Tate realizes that we had *business* disagreements with Garza, and didn't hate him, personally. I mean, no one would kill a person over a financial dispute."

"Bruno, all I can tell you is that Detective Tate wants to eliminate as many suspects as he can. If any of you can account for where you were when Victor Garza was killed last night, I'm sure he'll be happy to cross you off the list. There is only one person who has any reason to be nervous about being questioned. And he or she won't be able to escape detection for long."

Francesca Marquez appeared from behind Bruno, her face creased in concern. "I want you to know, Mees Trotter, that I never pushed Walter Sneed into the fountain on purpose. I simply tripped and fell into the group and he was knocked over."

"O-k-a-a-y," said Alex, "but why are you telling *me* and why *now*?"

"I know you're Detective Tate's friend, so I wanted you to know that I'm not a violent person. When I heard about Victor I was afraid he thought I did it. I went up early to my room last night, so I don't even have a good story!"

"Relax, Francesca. I know for a fact that Detective Tate doesn't think that you 'did it.' Just tell him the truth and you won't have anything to worry about. You go in and have a seat, okay? The detective should be along any minute now. Oh, here come the others. Everyone should be here by now."

Alex faced down the hallway and called out, "Would all of you take a seat in the lounge as soon as you can? There are some folding chairs stacked up against the far wall if there aren't enough places to sit."

The hallway started to clear. The last people to go in were Cindy Carmody and her husband Michael, Edmund and Juliana Devers, Dame Edith Herrington and Eloise Brown, and lastly, attorney Morrie Feldman and Shirley.

Alex hoped that she hadn't lost count and that that was everyone. It would take Arlie a while to get around the room to ask each one anything at all, much less to get enough information to be able to eliminate anyone as a suspect.

Just as she was thinking about Arlie and his interviews, he materialized at the end of the hallway. Waving to get his attention, she pointed to the lounge and then made the OK sign. Peeking inside the room again, she was struck by how normal they all appeared to be. Just a group of vacationers sitting around quietly talking— but was one of them a murderer?

Chapter 30

"WHAT'S WITH THE HAND SIGNALS, Alex?" Arlie asked as he walked up. "Did someone score a goal?"

Alex made a face. "I was trying to tell you that I got everyone in the lounge and they're all there waiting for you. Twenty-two of them."

"Yeah, well, I'll be able to quickly eliminate quite a few of them. I had security run a report on when everyone last used their electronic key cards to their rooms last night. The computer makes a record when every stateroom door is opened and when it's closed, so I know when everyone last went into their cabins without coming back out. Here, I've got the printout," he added, holding up a couple sheets of paper.

"That's pretty good Arlie, if you know the exact time of death. Do you?"

"Briggs estimated that Garza had been dead about eight hours when he first saw the body this morning. It wasn't in full rigor, which is completed after 12 hours. So, from the amount of stiffening and blood pooling there was, we can say that Garza was killed between midnight and one a.m. Briggs didn't do an autopsy— he's no surgeon— so he couldn't take the temperature of the liver."

"We can do without that, can't we?" Alex asked, wrinkling up her nose.

"Oh, that upsets you? You were poking around a corpse with a sunken waxy face that had turned blotchy purple in the nether regions and had pooped in his pants, but you don't want his liver cut into."

Alex's eyes widened. "Oh, Arlie, I just remembered— those guys from the theatre were talking about having a funeral service for Victor, but the body can't be embalmed, can it?"

"No, and you wouldn't want anyone to see the body as it decomposes. By tonight the head and neck will be a greenish-blue, and by tomorrow the whole body will be that color. About the color of the drapes in our stateroom."

Alex rolled her eyes up to the ceiling. "Thanks for that mental picture, Arlie, and for spoiling the room decor for me in the process. This is getting a little too morbid for me. Anyway, if you're ready to start interviewing, what can I do?"

"Well, I thought you would have figured out who the murderer was by now and I could just go in there and arrest someone. Don't you know who did it yet?"

"I do have a few ideas, as a matter of fact," she answered, smugly. "Not that I'd tell *you* so that you can mock me. Go ahead. Have your fun. I'll just wait until you admit that you're stumped and need my help."

"I could use your help right now," he said, ignoring her ploy. "Why don't you go in and start bringing them out, one at a time. The order doesn't matter. I'll talk to them in the casino, okay? And I'm always open to your ideas, smart ass." He tapped her on the nose with his papers.

Chapter 31

MORRIE FELDMAN CAME HUFFING into the arcade game area, and threw up his hands when he spotted Arlie Tate. "Are you serious, Detective, that you need to interview me? Do you really think that I had a motive to kill my most lucrative client? Wouldn't that be like killing the goose who laid the golden egg?"

"There's some logic there," Arlie admitted. "Sit down, Feldman. Actually, I'll ease your mind right off the bat. You and your wife are pretty much off the hook. Your room card key was last swiped in your door lock just before eleven o'clock last night." The attorney's jaw dropped. "I know, technology has probably surpassed any criminal mind."

The detective looked down at his notebook and flipped back a few pages and read before he looked up again. "As you recall, I talked to you earlier about Garza's son and daughter— after the 'dropped pot' incident. I wonder if you're ready to be more candid now that the man has actually been murdered. You know— to show your last respects for the dearly departed. Tony, Sunny, and Carlo didn't go up to their staterooms until after midnight, so they're still suspects."

"Really?" The attorney stretched his neck out of his shirt collar a couple of times, rotated his shoulders before leaning in towards Arlie. "To tell you the truth, any of the three of them could have perpetrated this crime," he said out of the side of his mouth. "Especially Sunny and Carlo. They were both parasites about to lose their host. Mind you, this is strictly off the record. I wouldn't want this to come back to me. I'm taking great liberties with my clients, here, speaking of them this way, but—"

Arlie winked. "I get it. I never heard it from you.'"

"Exactly. But, if you're looking for motive, they're your guys. Now, I wouldn't say the same thing about Tony. Victor has been very tightfisted with that young man all along, so the revision didn't change his circumstances." The attorney rubbed his hand over his bald head. "Hmm. You know, that's not really relevant, when I think about it. The changes in the will just leveled the playing field and put Sunny and Carlo in the same position as Tony. Tony's position didn't improve, of course. But Tony's a nice guy."

"And Sunny and Carlo aren't *nice*?"

The attorney stuck out his lower lip and lowered his head before answering in a low voice, "You didn't hear that from me."

Arlie spent the next hour questioning other wedding guests about where they had been the evening before and when they had last seen Victor Garza. The ones who had retired early were relieved to hear that they had been eliminated as suspects. Unfortunately, none of them had any useful information to contribute concerning Victor's movements or knowledge of any enemies who were previously unknown to Arlie.

Looking over the list of the people questioned, the only names that remained were: sculptor Bruno Rasconi, art critic Walter Sneed, artist Lydia Corbin and her husband Craig, and none of them was very promising as a perpetrator. Bruno Rasconi had wanted to be released from his contract with Garza, but no sane person would murder someone rather than just violate the terms of an agreement. Walter Sneed was so delighted to be involved in a murder investigation it was hard to believe that he had any guilty knowledge. Lydia Corbin was a petite, soft-spoken artist, and her husband didn't even know the victim. All of them claimed to be in public places until midnight and could probably find witnesses to support their alibis, if that were needed.

Only two of the guests he had yet to question seemed like good candidates: Victor Garza's former partner Roman Gregg and his wife Monica. Arlie had personal knowledge that they both had hated the victim and were out for revenge. The others on the list were hopeless as suspects: the Devers were refined upper class Brits who were only grateful to Garza for finding them fine artwork for their collection, and Dame Edith Herrington and her assistant Eloise Brown were both unimaginable as being murderers. Dame Edith couldn't have managed the deed, physically, and Eloise Brown was too sensible to resort to murder for any reason, in his mind. And both of them were in their suite at the time of the pot-dropping incident, he reminded himself, if that perpetrator and the murderer were one and the same.

As he was wrapping up his ruminations, Alex came around the corner followed by Roman and Monica Gregg. Arlie nodded to Alex and showed the Greggs a pair of chairs. "Sit down, please."

Roman Gregg lowered himself into a chair, blinked a couple of times and swallowed hard. "I just want to tell you how shocked Monica and I were to hear about this tragedy. Weren't we, Mon?"

His wife nodded vigorously and seemed to choke back tears. "Oh, it's terrible to think that the poor man was so brutally killed, and just one day after he was married!" She put her hands over her face and produced sobs and moans that Arlie thought were really Oscar-worthy.

"I didn't say that he was 'brutally' murdered."

The suddenly-composed Monica looked up, wide-eyed in surprise. "You didn't? No, of course you didn't. You didn't say anything. We *heard* that Victor was murdered and, considering what a strong and virile man he was, we *assumed* it had to be a forceful attack. Wasn't it?" she asked, managing a tone of innocence.

"We don't need to discuss the specifics of the attack," Arlie said, crossing his arms. "Suffice it to say that Victor Garza was murdered. By the way, before we go any further, tell me if these words sound familiar: 'How does he have the balls to even invite us on this cruise?' And, 'he cheated me after we broke up the business and I'll talk to the artists he stole from me.'"

Both of the Gregg's mouths dropped open. Roman was the first to find his voice. Snapping his head back and forth a couple of times, as though to clear his mind he said, "Whoever told you I said that that is a damned liar! Where did you get that?!"

"From you. I was sitting at the next table during the cocktail reception."

"Well, then, you know we were drinking pretty heavy," Roman shot back, drops of moisture appearing on his high forehead. "We were just letting off steam. You know how it is. Look, I'll freely admit that Victor stole from me and it made me mad. That doesn't mean I killed him! How would that benefit me?"

"I guess, with him out of the way, you'd be able to get back the artists you lost," said Arlie.

"I had already talked to them about leaving Victor and letting me represent them. You can ask them. Please, ask them! I'm not saying that Victor would have let them go without a fight, but that was between them and Victor. I didn't have nothin' to do with their agreements with him."

"You just wanted to have those agreements broken and everyone would go on their merry way," Arlie said.

"You're making me sound craven and sneaky."

"Oh, I wouldn't want to do that," Arlie said, straight-faced. "I was just trying to be accurate."

"Okay. I mean— no. I *suggested* to Victor's artists..."

"All of them?"

"Uh, yes. Well, I didn't want to play favorites. Anyway, I let them know that I would be happy to represent them again. Nothing wrong with that. They seemed pleased with the prospect. At any rate, I'm only telling you this so you see that I had no reason to kill Victor."

"How about because he had stolen from you and was 'rubbing your nose in his success?'"

"I wasn't in his will so I wouldn't gain, monetarily. And, anyway, I'm not a savage, Detective. I don't go around killing people who take advantage of me."

"That's right!" Monica put in. "Roman just wanted to take back what had been stolen from him." A light came into her heavily-outlined green eyes. "Like when OJ Simpson took back memorabilia that had been taken from him!" she enthused, evidently pleased with the comparison.

"OJ's doing a minimum of nine years for kidnapping and armed robbery," Arlie deadpanned.

"Monica, for God's sake!" Roman hissed. "Never mind her, Detective. She's upset. We both are. Honestly, we didn't murder Victor! That's the truth."

"You got back to your room after midnight. Where were you?"

"Oh, that's right! You need for us to account for where we were. Is that when Victor was murdered? Midnight?"

"Just tell me where you were up to the time you retired to your room."

"Okay, sure. Let's see, we ate dinner in the seafood restaurant —what was it called, 'Good Catch!' or something, then we went to the show. After it let out, about 10:30 or so, we slowly made our way up to the Sun Deck and had a couple of drinks at the bar. It was a beautiful night there under the stars. The bartender would probably remember us. I mean, Monica's a flashy blonde. Ask him. We left the bar after midnight, like you said, and went down to our room on Deck Five. That's it."

"Okay, folks." Arlie stifled a yawn. "Let's call it a day. I'll check out your story. If necessary, you'll be hearing from me. For now, you're free to go. Let Ms. Trotter know to send in the next person. Thank you."

"Sure will. Bye." With that, Monica and Roman Gregg jumped out of their seats and made for the door.

A minute later Eloise Brown came in, waving. She was followed by Alex. "The only ones left are the Devers and Dame Edith," Alex said as she turned to leave."

"I'll see Dame Edith next, then the Devers, together. Tell them it'll be just a few more minutes. Thanks."

Arlie turned to regard Eloise Brown. "Well, Miss Brown. Nice to see you again. How are you doing?"

Eloise had settled her solid figure into a chair. Arlie smiled at the woman's sturdy brogue shoes and thought that they were likely the only pair of their kind on the cruise ship.

"Of course, this business has got me knickers in a twist, same as everybody else, Constable," Eloise responded. "All I can think is that there must be some nutter runnin' around loose. Sure can't be any of our people. Least ways, I never noticed any one of us who looked too dodgy. A couple of benders, but they're in the theatre so it's to be expected. Very nice to talk to, really.

"I can't say that I actually knew Mr. Garza, but he appeared to be a nice enough bloke, although he and Jasmine seemed like chalk and cheese to me."

"Chalk and cheese? You mean, that they didn't get along?" Arlie inserted.

"I don't know about that. I mean that they didn't seem to have much in common. Age difference and all that. Beautiful girl, though."

"Miss Brown, do you know of anyone who had it in for Mr. Garza? You strike me as someone who's pretty observant. Maybe you heard something or saw something?"

"Nope. Sorry. He seemed to be a nobby no-mates to me— you know, didn't have friends— but I never heard him threatened by anyone. He musta been conked on the head by a stranger for a few quid, is all I can say."

Arlie hid his smile behind his hand at Eloise Brown's expressions. "Miss Brown, just tell me where you were late last night. I know you and Dame Edith didn't retire to your suite until after midnight."

"Oh, why didn't you ask me, Constable? Milady and I were playing Auction Partnership pinochle with the Devers in the lounge after the show. We went up too late, do you mean? I told Lady Edith that, but we were having lively games, so I let it go. Lady Edith and the Devers will tell you the same."

"I'm sure they will, Miss Brown. I'm sure they will"

Chapter 32

LATER, IN THE STATEROOM, Arlie was leaning back against the sofa with his hands intertwined behind his head, while Alex sat on the edge of the chair across from him.

"Don't keep me in suspense, Arlie. You've talked to everyone who could possibly be the murderer, so— who was it?"

"You know that's not how it works, Alex, especially with so little evidence. I can tell you that, outside of the family, the only people who had the opportunity to kill Garza were the Greggs, the Devers, Dame Edith and Eloise Brown. Now, of that group, who would you bet on as being a killer? Dame Edith doesn't have the strength for it, Eloise Brown doesn't have the stomach for it, and the Devers don't have a motive," he summarized, ticking them off on his fingers. "That leaves only Roman Gregg and his wife, and they don't benefit from Garza's death. Besides, they have a reasonable alibi that can easily be verified if it's true, and nearly impossible to disprove if it's a lie.

"The way I see it, it's one of the three family members who murdered Victor. Follow the money. They're the only ones who would profit if the man died, and they're the only ones whose alibis aren't worth shit. Tony and Jasmine lied outright. They both told me that they went up to their suites early, but I know that their key cards weren't used until after twelve-thirty. At least Sunny and Carlo were honest about seeing Victor late in the casino bar."

Alex cocked her head. "Wait a minute, Arlie. Jasmine hadn't been added to the will when Victor was killed! She would only have inherited as his wife if he died *intestate*. The way it is, she gets nothing! I hadn't thought about that before now. But that proves that she's innocent— not that she's capable of killing anyone, anyway; and especially not her husband of two days."

"Alex, I need to tell you something about Jasmine that you don't know— about her relationship with Tony."

"Her relationship with Tony? I know that they're close friends. Why? What are you implying?" She looked cross.

"I'm not 'implying' anything, Alex. You should know that Jasmine is pregnant and Tony is most certainly the father."

"What?! How could you even say such a thing?! First of all, I don't think Jasmine is pregnant, or she would have told me. Secondly, if by some remote chance she is, Victor would have to be the father. They had been living together for months." She shook her head. "Sometimes I wonder about you, Arlie Tate. Where do you get these crazy ideas?"

"Alex, Jasmine admitted to me that she's pregnant when I confronted her with all the signs I had noticed."

"What would *you* notice? What signs?"

"Her being dizzy and nauseous that she didn't want to acknowledge; the fact that she was drinking only water at her wedding; that she seemed depressed whenever we saw her. Anyway, she owned up to her pregnancy, and couldn't hide the fact that Victor didn't know. Then it wasn't too big of a leap to figure Tony as the father."

"I can't believe this! Maybe she just agreed with you because she didn't want to name the real father, for some reason."

"No, Alex. She finally came clean. I don't think she wanted to admit it to herself for a long time. I believe Tony when he says that he only learned of the pregnancy on the cruise. Actually, just before Victor was killed."

"Tony has admitted being the father? Well, I don't care— maybe they conceived a baby together, which is shocking, I grant you. But I still think they're decent people. And they certainly didn't murder Victor!"

"What makes you so sure?"

"Because Jasmine really cared about Victor. Apparently she wasn't faithful to him, but she loved him— in her way."

"And how do you know that?"

"I had dinner with them at his house and she was very nice to him, very protective. Like, she did her best to try to cover up that he was screaming and cursing out someone on the phone."

"Oh, I see," Arlie said. "So, in your book, a good hostess would never kill her husband. Who was Victor swearing at? That might be more revealing."

"Bruno Rasconi. I remember, because I thought it was funny that Victor accused him of being a 'chiseler' — and the guy is a sculptor."

Arlie shook his head. "Alex, Alex. Back to the business at hand, the one piece of evidence I have is Jasmine's scarf — the murder weapon. A weapon of 'opportunity' that the person had at hand, which says to me that it was a crime of passion. No one goes out to murder someone with a silk scarf. I need to find out more about Jasmine's and Tony's movements last night, but now they've lawyered up: Morrie Feldman — the same guy who gave up Sunny and Carlo for having motives.

"Anyway, I told you about the pregnancy because maybe you can get Jasmine to talk. That could help her. I actually don't like her for the murder: She's too small to overpower Victor, unless he was drugged. She's smart enough to know that she'd be the prime suspect, and it would be colossally stupid of her to leave her scarf behind. But, she's decided to clam up. She may be trying to protect Tony, with or without knowledge of his guilt."

"Oh, Arlie. This is so awful! I didn't like Victor Garza, but he was my client and now the only good people in his family are the prime suspects in his murder. What about Sunny and Carlo? I could easily believe that either one of them is capable of murder. Sunny has murder in her heart every time she *looks* at me just because I'm a friend of Jasmine's. She's always hated Jasmine as a rival for her father's affections and his money. Why aren't you going after her?"

"Don't worry— she's still in the running. So's Carlo. But they helped themselves by telling me that they met Victor around midnight in the bar next to the casino, which is something I might not have found out about otherwise. And how could they have gotten Jasmine's scarf without her being aware of it?"

Alex chewed on her lower lip. "I don't know, but I'm going to assume that Jasmine is innocent and go from there. To respond to your suggestion, yes, I'll try to talk to her. I don't know what she's willing to tell me, since she hasn't confided in me about her pregnancy or her relationship with Tony, but she may want to talk to someone besides the police— sorry, but that's who you are to her.

"By the way, are you the only one investigating this? What if you weren't on this cruise? Then, no one would even look into it? If that's the case, anyone who wants to kill someone else should go on a cruise with them. Hell, they should invite them!"

Arlie allowed a little smile to cross his lips. "It's not quite that bad, although you're not too far off, either. The law states that any serious crime against an American citizen on the high seas must be reported to the FBI— by ship-to-shore phone. Also, it's a requirement to email the Coast Guard and the Department of Homeland Security.

"Those are the reporting procedures, but do you see any FBI suits around here? No. The FBI doesn't get involved until the ship returns to the port of embarkation on home soil. Until then, a cruise ship's security officers are the only ones who conduct an investigation and it's usually pretty superficial They figure agencies from the passenger's own country will follow up. Theoretically, the country of registry has responsibility, but don't look for anyone coming from Norway, either. So, I guess the answer to your question is— yeah, I'm it for now. And I'm deputizing you to interrogate Jasmine, if you want to."

Alex slid back in her chair and gazed out to sea. "Oh, brother!" she huffed, mostly to herself. "Now it's up to *me* to vindicate Jasmine and Tony since they won't talk to you, and I have to pretend that you didn't talk to me. Well, God help me— I can only try to pull this off. I just hope that she'll trust me enough to give me the whole story, sordid as it may be. Whatever it is, I believe it'll clear her. I'm just afraid that she'll smell a rat because I'm with you— no offense."

"None taken. I'll just stay here and eat cheese while you put on the charm. Good luck."

Chapter 33

"OH, HI, ALEX." Jasmine's voice was flat as she opened her door. "I'm not really dressed, but you can come in if you want to."

Alex was shocked at her friend's appearance. Wearing a baggy terry robe, Jasmine's hair was a tangled mess with some strands hanging over her face making her look like she had just rolled out of bed, except that her splotchy complexion and reddened eyes indicated that she had just been crying. *Tears of guilt, of regret, of loss?*

"Jasmine, my God! You look terrible!"

"Thanks." Jasmine smiled, wanly.

"I'm sorry, but you look really bad. I know you've suffered a terrible shock and loss, but you look like you've been living under a viaduct. I hesitated to come up here and bother you, but now I'm glad I did. Not that I bothered you . . . but . . . whatever," she ended, helplessly.

"Why don't you go take a nice hot shower, wash your hair, and get dressed while I call room service and get a snack for us. How does that sound"

"Okay, I guess."

"C'mon, Jaz. It'll do you good. How about a pot of hot tea and something sweet to munch on? Or would you like something more substantial?"

"Oh, just the tea, I think. I had breakfast in the room."

"Oh, yeah? Well, it's after four. You missed lunch. I'll order you a cup of soup, too. You'll need to have a decent dinner, but right now let's just get some nourishment in you. Now go."

* * *

TWENTY MINUTES LATER Jasmine emerged from the steamy bathroom dressed in a pale green shift with her glossy hair neatly twisted into a chignon. To complete her makeover she had applied foundation to even out her skin tone, dabbed on mascara to brighten her eyes, and added a touch of gloss to freshen her lips.

"Jasmine! Look at you— you look positively revitalized! How do you feel?"

"Not as well as I look, apparently," she answered, glumly. "Listen, I appreciate what you're trying to do for me, Alex, but I have problems that I can't just wash away or hide under a clean dress.

"In fact, there's not much that's *right* in my life right now. To begin with, it was so shocking that Victor was murdered. And then I find out that he was choked to death with my scarf, so I'm suspected of killing him." She sank down onto the sofa and covered her face with her hands, moaning softly.

Alex moved over and wrapped an arm around her shoulder. "Jasmine, I *know* you didn't murder Victor. *Arlie* doesn't believe you murdered Victor. Anyone who *knows you* can't believe you murdered Victor. You and I can figure out how your scarf was found at the scene, and maybe think of something else that'll help in the investigation." A knock was heard at the door.

"There's our food," Alex said, standing up. "I'll set the tray on your dining table over there, okay?"

Jasmine nodded slowly and gave Alex a weak smile. "Sure. Thanks."

* * *

AFTER POURING TWO CUPS OF TEA, Alex placed the hot tomato soup in front of Jasmine and reached for a chocolate chip cookie for herself. "Go ahead— eat. You must be weak after not having had anything since breakfast, which was probably just coffee. I'll nibble on a cookie or two while you finish. Take your time.

"This is a beautiful room, isn't it?" Alex commented, to lighten the mood. "I love the contemporary dark wood against the cream-colored walls and carpeting. And the artwork is surprisingly good for ship decor."

Jasmine raised her head, holding her spoon in midair. "Even Victor liked it and he's hard to please. I mean— he *was* hard to please," she added, miserably.

"Listen, Jasmine. When you're done with your soup, we'll talk this through. I want you to feel free to tell me anything in confidence. You know I consider you to be a good friend." Jasmine managed a small smile.

After a couple of minutes, she finished her soup and laid down her spoon. "That was just what I needed, Alex. I actually do feel a little better, in spite of the fact that nothing's changed."

Alex patted her arm. "It just shows you that you need to take care of yourself, especially now when you're under a lot of stress and dealing with a crisis. More tea?" Jasmine nodded, and Alex filled her cup.

"So— let's first figure out how your scarf ended up under the, uh . . . under Victor." Alex said. "Do you think it fell off someplace and you didn't realize it?

"No. As I told Detective Tate — Arlie— I took off the scarf when I was playing table shuffleboard in the casino. It was in my way when I bent over to shove the puck, so I just took it off."

"Okay, good. Then where did you put it?"

"That's what I'm not sure of. I think I hung it over the back of a nearby chair. Then I forgot about it when I left the casino."

"Which was when?"

"Sometime around eleven o'clock. I was tired and wanted to go to bed early. It had been a long, difficult day, as you know. The pot incident is less important now, but we had been upset all day over that. Of course, we must have been right that it was attempted murder, since poor Victor was killed hours later by that same person, no doubt. You would think that irrefutable logic would eliminate me as a suspect, wouldn't you?"

"Right, but let's stay focused on the scarf. We can't get away from the fact that it was used to strangle Victor. Where was Victor when you left the casino? Didn't he want to go up with you, even if it was early?"

"No. He was all keyed up. When I told him I was going to bed he said he wanted to check something out and he'd be up later. But I didn't think he was in any danger." Her lower lip started to quiver.

"Of course you didn't! There were dozens of people around, including security. He *should* have been perfectly safe. But— wait a minute. Did you say you left him right after your shuffleboard game?"

"Yes. He had just come over when I finished playing a game. I didn't do that well so I was ready to go up to the room."

"Jasmine, *Victor must have picked up your scarf!* He would have known it was yours and just stuffed it into his jacket pocket. Unfortunately, we might not be able to prove it, but it's a logical explanation of how the scarf was available to the killer.

"Okay, *now* we're getting somewhere," Alex said "So did you go right up to your room at eleven?"

"Yes. Of course it takes a few minutes to get there."

"Right. So, then your key card will record the time as eleven-fifteen, or close to that."

"The key card records the time?"

"Yeah. Arlie's gotten a printout of everyone's key card swipes and has eliminated the people who went up well before midnight. The others will have to get corroboration for their whereabouts after midnight; and I feel sorry for anyone who lied to him about what time they turned in."

While Alex was explaining the key card system, she noticed that Jasmine had been shredding her napkin into small pieces and wadding them up into balls. When she finished, she spread her hands out on the table, and took a deep breath.

"Alex, I can't go on like this any longer — I've lied to Arlie; I've lied to you; I've lied to everybody."

"Jaz, what are you talking about? You didn't have anything to do with Victor's murder, did you?"

"No, of course not. But I need to tell you about my situation. I just hope you won't hate me." She dabbed at her eyes with a couple balls of shredded napkin.

"I promise you, Jasmine, you aren't capable of doing something that would make me hate you. Feel free to tell me whatever." Alex reached into her pocket. "Here's a clean tissue. Looks like you need it."

"Thanks. Okay. Well, here goes. Might as well just come out with it— I'm pregnant. Three months along. Actually, Arlie guessed it so he would probably tell you, eventually. The hardest part about it is that it's not possible that Victor is the father."

"Are you sure? I mean — oh, never mind. I guess you should know. Do you want to tell me who the father is?"

"Tony is. My 'step-son.' How sick is that? No, I don't mean that at all. I love Tony and he loves me, but I don't consider this a proper way to conceive and bear a child. Okay, let me start from the beginning. Remember when you came over to Victor's house and we talked to Tony about his ideas for a chain of tea rooms?"

"Yes, of course." Alex quickly did a mental calculation that her visit had been three months earlier, and felt her stomach lurch.

"Well, I was very upset with how Victor treated Tony that day, especially in front of you."

Alex squirmed in her chair and tried not to show her anxiety. Surely, her visit hadn't provoked Jasmine's outpouring of affection for Tony, had it? Alex tried to think back to that day. She *had* stuck up for Tony to Victor, telling him that she had asked Tony about his business plan for the shops he wanted to call 'Tea Leaves.'

"I remember thinking that it was a private concern of your family's," Alex said, "and none of my business."

"You're right. The argument had nothing to do with you," Jasmine said.

Alex felt her shoulders relax a little. "But that day was significant?"

"Yes. That was the day that I decided to tell Tony a family secret that he needed to know. And that was the day that I stopped sleeping with Victor."

"Okay, then," Alex rushed in before more was said. "You don't have to tell me all this. Really—"

"No, now that I'm opening up I want you to know everything," Jasmine responded. "Where was I? Oh, after you left, I left, too. . .with Tony. I didn't want to be alone with Victor. I was fed up with the abusive way he treated Tony, and I was the only one who knew why he was so hard on him. That's what I shared with Tony that night. And that's what led to my expressing my love for him and what led to our intimacy.

"You see, Victor had real doubts that Tony was his son. After Tony's birth, Victor's first wife Marguerite admitted to having an affair with a playboy Italian count named Gregorio Rossi. Victor had been in Europe a lot at the time, so there was plenty of opportunity. Of course, there weren't DNA tests at the time, and nothing was ever verified.

"But, as Tony grew up and became so charming and handsome, Victor's suspicions grew. From pictures I've seen of Rossi, Tony is his spitting image. When Tony exhibited creative ideas, instead of wanting to get a nine to five job to work for advancement, Victor saw this as further evidence that he wasn't his son.

"I would have respected Victor more if he had had blood tests done to determine paternity; but he seemed to prefer, instead, to mistreat Tony; to taunt him and cut him off from his money. It was cruel. That's what I finally saw that day, what a bully Victor was.

"Weeks later, when I realized that I was pregnant, I felt trapped. The invitations had been sent out and you had reserved all the staterooms. I had made a sort of truce with Victor, because I couldn't see breaking off my engagement.

"To be honest, I was afraid of him. I knew how he had cheated business contacts and had mistreated people who worked for him. I couldn't imagine what he would do to me if he learned that I was carrying Tony's child. And, no, I didn't tell Tony, either. I became an actress, just playing my role as happy fiancée. I didn't really have an 'end game.' I just figured, at some point, I would confide in Tony and we would come up with a plan.

"On the cruise, I've had to hide my morning sickness, and dizziness— even that I'm showing a little. I bought a special girdle for the wedding dress. It hasn't been easy." She dabbed at her eyes again. "It's funny, but Arlie Tate is the only one who wasn't fooled. That I know of."

Alex nodded. "Arlie's a smart guy. He's hard to fool— believe me. Jaz, I just want you to know that I'm not judging you. I had worried about you being married to Victor because I knew he could be ruthless. And I knew you had special feelings for Tony. But what about last night? You didn't go up to your room? Where did you go? Do you know where Tony was after midnight?"

"Oh, that's right. The key card times. That's what started this whole 'confession.' I didn't go up to my room at eleven o'clock. I'm sure Tony lied, too. When we were in the casino we arranged to meet up on the Sun Deck at eleven. We needed a place to talk in private. I had just told him in the casino that I was pregnant with his child. It was the first chance I had to talk to him without someone else being right there, and I couldn't keep it to myself any longer."

"What was his reaction?"

"Not surprisingly, knowing Tony, he was only concerned about me. He said that he'd support me in whatever I wanted to do: If I decided to stay in my marriage, he'd remain in the background and pretend that the baby was Victor's; or, he'd stand with me to tell Victor that he had fathered my child. Of course, I couldn't have fooled Victor that he was the father once he knew about the baby. He might have let people assume the child was his to save face, as he would have been humiliated if people discovered the truth. Most likely, he would have thrown me out and made sure I didn't get a dime after he divorced me. But I didn't care about the money. He couldn't hold that over me."

Alex peered into the pot. "We've finished the tea and I think you're exhausted. I should get going, anyway. Let me just thank you again for confiding in me, Jaz. I personally think your story exonerates you as a murder suspect, but your alibi isn't corroborated by anyone except Tony, and his testimony would be seen as being self-serving."

"That's right, it would be," Jasmine agreed. "It's too bad that we didn't let Monica and Roman Gregg see us."

"What?!" Alex sat up straight in her chair. "You saw the Greggs? Where?"

"They were sitting having drinks at the bar on the Sun Deck. They had their backs to us, so I'm sure they didn't see us. Besides, there were a lot of people in the bar area."

"Jasmine, you and Tony need to tell Arlie about seeing the Greggs on the Sun Deck at midnight, as soon as possible. That's almost as good as if they had seen *you*, since no one told you they were there, and you haven't been around them since then.

"Nothing's more important right now than establishing your alibis because, well . . . you and Tony are prime suspects in Victor's murder."

Chapter 34

GOOD JOB!" Arlie sounded impressed with Alex's account of her interview with Jasmine as they sat on their balcony having a glass of wine.

"Of course, she and Tony aren't off the hook," he added.

Alex put down her glass. "What? Why not?"

"Why not? Because we don't have an accounting of their movements after midnight until twelve-thirty when they used their key cards. I'll admit Jasmine volunteering that they saw the Greggs at midnight puts them in a better light, but they still had time to kill Garza. Let's say they came upon him right after they left the Sun Deck. Don't you think they could have acted in the heat of the moment to choke the life out of him? And we only have Jasmine's story about leaving her scarf behind."

"Oh, geez, Arlie. How is anyone supposed to prove what they've done and where they've been every minute of the day and night? No one videotapes everything they do."

"I'm not talking about every minute of the day and night. Just an hour either way of the estimated time of death. *You're* accounted for."

"Yeah, well, that's one advantage of being with you all the time— you can't accuse me of murder. Let me think if there's another one..." She looked off into space with a furrowed brow. "No, that's it."

"Very funny, Alex. Listen, I think we should put aside the murder inquiry for tonight and relax with a romantic dinner at that French restaurant and maybe go listen to some music for a while.'"

"I'd love to, but first I have to call everyone and tell them about the land excursions tomorrow in Bermuda, okay?"

"Sure. Take all the time you need. I have to go up to get Jasmine's revised statement. Tony's too. I'm assuming they won't lawyer up now that you've wrung the truth out of Jasmine."

"You make it sound like I water boarded her."

"No, your 'enhanced interrogation technique' is more verbal. I liked the way you withheld information to set a trap."

"I learned that from you."

"Yeah? Well, I guess that's why I liked it."

* * *

TWO HOURS LATER, they were seated in a cozy booth at Le Francais scanning the French-language menu with English translations. The soft lighting cast a flattering glow on Alex's face and made her eyes sparkle. Alex, in her blue cocktail dress, and Arlie in his tan linen blazer and open-collared shirt, they appeared to be just another carefree couple on vacation.

Looking over the bill of fare Alex mused, "French makes everything sound exotic, doesn't it? I mean, you wouldn't guess that 'La tarte flambeé' was pizza, would you?"

"Hell, I was going to order it for dessert," Arlie responded. "Anyway, for dinner I'm looking at the filet mignon a la Bordelaise. What about you?"

"Yeah, I think I'm ready for a steak, and it's served with potatoes au gratin. Perfect indulgences after the day we've had. Actually, doesn't it seem like it's been *three* days since we were told about the murder this morning?" She put her head back against the upholstery and blew out a long breath of air.

Arlie patted her hand. "You were a real trouper today. You had a couple of moments but came through and showed a lot of toughness under very unpleasant circumstances. I'm proud of you, partner."

"Really?" Alex sat up straighter. "I felt like I was just hanging in there. You were the one who interviewed twenty-two suspects — make that twenty-six, with the family."

"That's my job — although, not usually when I'm on vacation." He gave her a little smirk and chucked her under the chin. "And you promised me this trip would be 'smooth sailing' — your words. I should have known better. Are you sure you don't attract this kind of thing? It's getting to be the norm with you"

Alex looked wide-eyed and innocent. "I thought it would be a sure thing. What could be safer than escorting a group of artists on a honeymoon cruise?"

"That's one way to describe them. I'd say they're a bunch of neurotics fighting over the fortune of a tyrant who married a woman impregnated by his own son. I mean, what could go wrong with that?"

"Tony may not be his son," she answered, weakly.

"Right. That makes all the difference. Anyway, I'm not upset with you — but you're lucky you're cute. Also, you've worked hard to help me out. Thanks to you, I got my revised statements from Jasmine and Tony. How did you do with your excursion plans? Did you reach everyone?"

"I did. Most people have signed up for the five-hour bus tour of the island to get an overall view and see the highlights—

Somerset Village, the lighthouse, a coastal drive up to the Botanical Gardens, and ending at St. Georges. Of course, I've divided people up and assigned them to the two mini buses to avoid conflict. Artists on one bus; collectors, critic, and attorney on another; and the aunts filling in where there's more room.

"Some guests are opting to just walk around the malls and visit the museums at Kings Wharf where we dock. Of course, the theatre guys, Rudolph and Damien, are going off on their own to shop, taking the ferry to Hamilton.

The waiter arrived at the table and took their dinner orders and promised to return soon with rolls and salads.

After he departed, Alex continued. "Oh, I called Jasmine after you were there. She told me that Tony, Sunny, Carlo and she are accompanying Victor's body to a crematorium in Bermuda tomorrow morning. Did you know that?

"Yes. She asked me if that was all right, and I told her it was."

Alex nodded and went on. "She also told me that she's decided to announce her pregnancy. She figures that it'll be good for her to come out in the open on that, at least, and that everyone will assume that Victor is the father."

Arlie shook his head. "I don't think that's a good idea."

Alex took a sip of her Bordeaux as the waiter set down the roll basket and salads. "Why not? It's going to be obvious soon enough."

"Well, I'd rather it not be on my time. You think that Sunny has been unwelcoming to Jasmine before? How welcoming do you think she'll be to a new heir that keeps Jasmine tied to the family and its wealth? Tony better stay close although, from the look of things, that shouldn't be a problem."

"You think Sunny would try to hurt Jasmine?"

"I think she's capable of that, yes. I'm sure she's thinking that Jasmine will be out of the way, but the baby changes everything. Of course, if she were to find out that the baby is her brother's child, she'd be thrilled. But that could remain a secret forever."

Alex ate a forkful of salad. "I think Jasmine will want to have the paternity determined with a DNA test, and be only too happy to stay clear of Sunny and Carlo, no matter what the results are. The inheritance question is interesting since the baby is either Victor's child, his grandchild or is totally unrelated."

Arlie touched his napkin to his mouth. "Jasmine should protect her interests and have a tissue sample taken tomorrow. You're right— the baby could still be Victor's."

"Oh good, here comes our food. Let's put the Garza family's troubles to rest and enjoy our dinners."

"Okay, Arlie. Just tell me if you're going with the family tomorrow, or with me, or what."

Arlie cut into his steak to check the doneness. Satisfied, he carved out a small piece and stabbed it with his fork. "I have to take the pieces of that ceramic pot to the crime lab in Hamilton and have it swabbed for latents. I'll call you when I'm done and meet you. Now that's the last word about the investigation. Let's just enjoy the rest of the evening, okay?"

Chapter 35

THE NEXT MORNING Alex dressed in a crisp white shirt and khaki Bermuda shorts, and went up to the Sun Deck to meet with everyone who would be going ashore.

Approaching the group she observed that the artists were conversing among themselves, sitting as far away from Walter Sneed as they could manage; while the Greggs were sitting by themselves behind the English contingency who were three seats down from Morrie and Shirley Feldman.

Only Rudolph and Damien and Jasmine's two aunts were becoming acquainted, sitting together.

Alex recalled that the last time they had all been in the same room was the day before when they had waited in the casino lounge to be questioned as murder suspects. And not all of them had been eliminated. A chill went up her spine at the thought.

Handing out packets of maps and descriptions of places of interest on the island, she made eye contact with Lola and Alaana, who waved cheerfully in greeting. Alex lingered on them for a moment to try to figure out who was who, again; a task complicated by the fact that they were dressed in similar floral prints, again.

Clearing her throat to get everyone's attention, she still had to raise her voice to talk over the continuing conversations. "Welcome to Bermuda," she started. A smattering of applause followed. Not many smiled.

She forged ahead. "We're here on King's Wharf at the Royal Dockyard, which is furthest east on the island that's shaped like a fishhook, as you probably know. We're at what would be the sharp point.

"We won't be staying together today since you have opted for different activities and means of touring the island." Several smiled and nodded at this news.

"There's a lot to see and different modes of transportation. I'll be joining those of you who have signed up to take the five-hour tour on mini buses. Since Bermuda is just twenty-two miles long and only one mile wide, we'll be able to cover all the highlights and have lunch as well. There will be a local guide on both buses to describe what you'll be seeing and the history of Bermuda.

"Does anyone plan on renting a scooter?"

Cindy Carmody called out, "Michael and I are!" as she and her husband raised their hands.

"Oh, good! I'm sure you'll like that. Some others of you might like to try them, too. They're a very popular, fun way to get around. Just be sure that you're always riding on the *left side* of the road. Remember, Bermuda is a British Overseas Territory.

"What does that mean, dear?" one of the aunts asked. "Isn't it a colony?"

"Of course it is," her sister answered, allowing Alex to identify her as Lola and making a mental note that she was the one in the *pink* flowered dress.

"It's basically the same thing," Alex said, mediating the issue. "'Overseas Territory' is more modern, I think. I guess *crown colony* sounded too repressive."

Edmund Devers spoke up. "Quite right. But Bermuda is essentially self-governing. The Queen appoints the Governor, but he invites the majority party to form a government from elected parliament members."

"Thank you," Alex said, amused at his defense of his homeland. "You'll see the British influence everywhere," she continued, as the English people nodded with approval. "They play both soccer and cricket, sell British-made products, are a financial center for British banks, and most of the buildings reflect British colonial architecture. The Bermudian accent is unique, though. It sounds like a mix of Caribbean and British. Very lyrical. Lots of other things are their own, too — like their shorts, their grass..."

"Bermuda Green!" Damien Loren called out.

"What's that?" asked Alaana, turning to face him.

"Oh, it's the most delicious shade of bluish-green. You'd love it. It's the color of the ocean around the island. And it goes with everything. I'll probably be buying something in the color. I'll show you."

"That reminds me," Alex broke in. "I know you and Rudolph are going to Hamilton to shop. As you probably are aware — but the others might not be — the ferry is only three blocks from the ship and makes regular trips back and forth to the capital city. Each crossing takes about 20 minutes, but they're about three hours apart, so take note.

"The ferry also services St. George, Paget, Somerset and Warwick parishes. I've put their schedule in your packets.

"Also, I've put in a directory of everything on King's Wharf. For those of you who will be staying on the pier you'll see that there are lots of activities, like those at the snorkel park.

"If you want to shop here, there's the Clock Tower Mall that's a covered arcade. You'll find good buys there on things like china, crystal, silverware, Harris Tweed jackets, and Scottish wool. Also, there are local handcrafts sold there like banana dolls, baskets, jewelry. Lots of gift items."

"This is the best place for locally-made pieces," Rudolph Perino added.

"I agree," Alex said. "There are also the Glassworks and the Clayworks here on the pier. If you go to the Art Center you can see local artwork and talk to the artists.

"Some of you may be interested in the National Museum that has exhibits on archeology, historical architecture and furnishings.

"So, there are lots to see and do within walking distance."

Morrie Feldman raised his hand and Alex nodded for him to speak. "How would we manage to take the local buses? Are the routes posted? Are there 'on-off' privileges?"

"Good questions," Alex commented. "If you think you want to do your sightseeing and shopping by bus, you'll want to buy a two pass from the Visitors Center here. They have color-coded routing, and every bus allows you to get on and off continuously. Thank you for asking about that."

Alex turned to speak to the whole group. "Remember, tonight at eight-thirty is the Bermuda Triangle Cruise from this dock. It's very popular because of the guide's narration about the legend of the Triangle and the fantastic marine life you'll see illuminated through the glass bottom boat.

"That's about all I have for now. How does everything sound?"

"Jolly good, I'd say!" Eloise Brown called out.

* * *

AN HOUR LATER ALEX WAS READY to board the mini bus with Edmund and Juliana Devers, Dame Edith Herrington, Eloise Brown, and Lola and Alaana. Seeing Walter Sneed start to edge over to the other bus, she quickly took hold of his arm, steering him toward hers.

"Here you go, Mr. Sneed," she whispered. You'll be able to get a better seat on *this* bus.

On the other bus were the artists: Bruno Rasconi; Lydia Corbin and her husband Craig; Marcel Longine; and Jonathan Welles and his wife Christine.

Going off on their own were the Spanish artist Francesca Lazaro, the Carmodys, the Greggs, and the Feldmans.

* * *

THE MINI BUSES STARTED UP past crowds of tourists that were seen pressing their way into the square of shops and restaurants, and outward to the park and the manmade beach.

The buses continued southward across bridges onto small islands that were just rocky spits of land where the turquoise water and its foamy edge could be seen from both sides of the vehicles.

After a few minutes the road sloped downwards to the old Village of Somerset. Henry, the guide on Alex's bus, described the history of the seventeenth-century settlement that had retained its simple charm. Its poky downtown consisted of a police station, library, post office, and a few shops and restaurants. By contrast, just outside of town they passed by many luxurious resorts, some clinging to the cliffs.

Leaving the area and traveling further south, the buses drove along Middle Road, so named for its central location on the narrow strip of land. Coming to a fork, they took South Road that ran along the cliffs that bordered the ocean until they came to Gibbs' Hill Lighthouse where the bus pulled into the parking lot.

"You'll notice that the lighthouse isn't right on the water," Henry informed them after they had come to a stop. "This hill is 245 feet high. That puts the top of the 117 foot tower at 362 feet above sea level. Ships can see the 1,000 watt light from 40 miles away and planes from 120 miles away.

"We'll be here for about 20 minutes. I would encourage you try to climb up to the top as you'll be rewarded with the best view of the island. You can take your time and there are eight different levels with places to rest along the way, each with a window to check on the view.

"It's really not that hard a climb at 185 steps. For comparison, the Washington Monument is 555' high and has five times the number of steps."

Everyone from both buses, except Dame Edith, got off and took the dozen steps up to the white painted tower, while debating the merits of climbing to the top.

Alaana and Lola opted to have a cup of tea with Eloise Brown in the first floor tea room. Eloise explained, "You'd have to be daft to go up there without a lift."

The others remarked that they would probably begin to make the climb, since they could stop at lower levels and still enjoy a view out the windows along the way.

Alex was the first to start up the stairs setting a reasonable pace, encouraging the others to follow. "We'll just take our time. I've been up to the top before and it is a spectacular view. You decide where and when you want to stop. We'll be here another fifteen minutes so don't push yourselves."

After four flights, Juliana Devers said to her husband, "This is far enough for me, luv. I just can't give it the welly to make it any higher. You can go on." Edmund waved off her suggestion, saying he was content to stay at that level, and to prove it he looked out the nearby window to admire the long-distance view.

Six people made it up to the observation deck: Bruno Rasconi, Lydia and Craig Corbin, Marcel Longine, Walter Sneed and Alex. Sneed was the last one up, stumbling over the last step. Once on deck he stood bent over, gasping for air.

"Guess you don't have any wisecracks to make now, do ya, old man?" Bruno taunted. "I'm not even breathing hard. That's because I'm always doing physical work, chipping stone, while you're sitting on your ass criticizing me and the others who are doing real work with their hands. So look who comes out on top — literally."

"All right, all right," Alex broke in. "It was a long, hard climb. I'm sure we're all feeling a little out of sorts. Let's just enjoy the view for a couple of minutes and go back down, okay?"

After grumbling under his breath, Bruno circled the deck with the other artists and looked out at the sights.

* * *

FIVE MINUTES LATER they all started down the stairs, with Alex trailing the group. Arriving on the seventh floor landing she heard a man's voice below cry out, "Ugh!" and then, "You son of a bitch!" She recognized the voice as belonging to Walter Sneed.

Alex took the stairs two at a time down to the next level where she found him lying flat on his back with his legs splayed out over the stair below.

"What happened? Are you hurt?"

Looking up at Alex, his face contorted — *in pain? In anger?*— he bellowed, "That third-rate sculptor tripped me! I was just lucky to catch myself!"

"Mr. Sneed, can you move?" Alex persisted. "Where does it hurt?"

"I'm all right!" he groused, pulling himself up to a sitting position. "I guess I'm tougher than he thinks."

"Mr. Sneed, did you actually *see* Bruno Rasconi trip you?"

"I didn't have to. I felt it. That's all right. I can ruin him in my column. I'll make sure that he's never taken seriously in the art world again. Mark my words — he's finished."

Chapter 36

AS PEOPLE STARTED COMING OUT of the lighthouse, Alex sidled up to Bruno Rasconi and spoke in a low voice. "Do you know how Walter Sneed fell down the stairs? Did you see anything?"

"I wasn't anywhere near him," Bruno scoffed. "He was behind all four of us. You can ask them. He must have tripped over his own feet. I didn't realize he had even fallen until I heard him cursing me out. I don't like the guy, but I'm not going to push him down a flight of stairs."

"Okay. Okay. Sorry I had to ask, but he was sure that you had tripped him. I guess I'm a little jumpy about anyone else getting hurt since Victor Garza was murdered."

"Yeah, well, that's understandable — for you. I can't say it's been much on my mind."

"Oh. Anyway, it might be a good idea for you to steer clear of Mr. Sneed to avoid any other accusations."

"Sure. Fine with me."

* * *

LEAVING THE LIGHTHOUSE, the mini buses rolled over a few steep hills before they followed hairpin curves down towards the shore line. In a few minutes they arrived at Horseshoe Beach.

"This is the most famous beach on the island," Henry advised. "It's known for its pink-colored sand, its turquoise water and its protected coves. We'll have our picnic lunch here in one of the coves where we can be out of the wind. Our driver Ted and I will bring the food, if you'll all make your own way around. Dame Edith, do you need some help?"

"Oh, thanks Henry, but Eloise can manage, can't you El?"

"Piece of cake, ma'am. It's not too big a place. Nice and flat. We'll just walk along the water, make our way back in front of those concession stands to the break between the rocks, and then, 'Bob's your uncle,' we're there in the cove."

Edmund Devers chimed in, "Juliana and I will follow behind." He looked out the bus window. "Blimey, look at this place! Gorgeous!"

"The beach looks pretty crowded," Walter Sneed groused. "Let's just hope we can find our own space and not be bothered by other people."

"No doubt we can find a nice quiet place in the cove," Alex said, biting her tongue not to say more.

* * *

AFTER FINISHING THEIR SANDWICHES, the group made its way back to the small bus and boarded again to continue the tour. Back on South Road, the route took them over more hills and around more sharp curves. Being on high ground following the shore line, the road afforded spectacular ocean views most of the way to the Botanical Gardens, their next stop.

"We'll stop here for about twenty minutes," Henry announced as they pulled into the parking lot. "Not too difficult to walk around. This is the largest public garden in Bermuda, by far. It's a combination of woodlands, greenhouses, agricultural buildings and horticultural collections. Some of you may be particularly interested in the numerous orchid varieties. There's also a lovely rock garden, and many plumeria, hibiscus, and other ornamental plants.

"Okay, let's go. Browse on your own. All of the plants are tagged to identify them. See you in a few minutes."

* * *

BACK ON THE ROAD, they headed toward their last stop, the historic Town of St. George. Approaching the most northern point of Bermuda, they first crossed over narrow islands that bordered onto Hamilton Harbour and Castle Harbour, then took an indirect route to stop briefly at Carter House, Bermuda's oldest residence, and St. Catherine's Fort and Museum.

As they came into town, passing by low pastel-colored homes with white roofs, Henry said, "We're now in the City proper. St George was named for Sir George Somers who landed here with his men in 1609 after his ship, the *Sea Venture*, was wrecked on a nearby reef. Some of them continued on to Jamestown in America, while a few men stayed behind to claim the island for Britain. Three years later Bermuda became an official British settlement."

"Righto and three cheers!" Eloise Brown called out.

"So," Henry continued, "St. George was the first capital for nearly a hundred years until Hamilton became the center of the government.

"You'll notice that this town retains the look of its early beginnings with roads that are only wide enough to accommodate horses and carriages. Many have their original names — like Aunt Peggy's Lane and Printers Alley, named for local people.

"Our first stop will be King's Square at the waterfront. This is the town center where you can wander around on your own. We'll be here for an hour to give you time to visit a couple of shops, the British National Trust Museum, maybe the Town Hall, or an old church — there are many historical places. Or you can just walk around to take in the flavor of the place. I have some printed maps of places located in the surrounding blocks for your convenience."

Within a few minutes the mini bus had parked by a curb next to a salmon pink two-story building with a Colonial-style facade.

* * *

GETTING OFF THE BUS, Alex heard her cell phone's tone and answered it. It was Arlie. Checking her watch she suggested they hook up in Hamilton, at the ferry terminal, in an hour, saying. "We can explore for a while and have dinner before the evening cruise. I know a special place to eat, if you'd like that."

"By 'explore,' do you mean, shop?" He chuckled. "No, that's fine. Whatever you want."

"Thanks, Arlie. Oh, I almost forgot. Were you able to get something from the crime lab?"

"It'll take at least forty-eight hours for DNA results from the scarf. The good news is that we were able to get one print and a partial from the pottery. Ran them on the NCIC data base, but there wasn't a match. Must be a novice who's new at trying to kill people."

"Geez, that's sick," Alex groaned. "Though I'm not surprised that it was someone who doesn't have a record. I mean, they don't let murderers on cruise ships."

"Oh, yeah? Well they did this time."

Chapter 37

HAMILTON'S BUSY DOWNTOWN sits across from the City's harbor, bordered by Front Street. This commercial area of the capital city is renowned for its many upscale businesses and tourist attractions. Pastel-tinted buildings, ornamented with scalloped awnings and deep pillared porticoes, house numerous designer boutiques, souvenir shops, salons, and trendy restaurants. Green spaces, like Par-La-Ville Gardens on Queen Street, beautify the area while offering visitors cool retreats and places to rest.

On the other side of Front Street, the bustling harbor services not only commercial vessels, like the commuting ferry, cargo boats, and cruise ships, but many pleasure craft and yachts are buoyed there as well, making for a picturesque scene as they bob on the turquoise water.

That afternoon, as was usually the case, a cruise ship was seen tied up to the dock next to the street, its upturned bow looming over the smaller boats as though affecting a snobbish attitude. Many of its passengers had likely joined the hundreds of other tourists, fanning out through the downtown streets and into the various commercial attractions.

By six o'clock, Alex and Arlie had slowed their pace as they made their way along Front Street weighed down with bulging plastic bags. They were discussing their options for dinner, having been in and out of shops for the previous two hours.

"Here's Burnaby Hill." Alex sounded relieved. "This is where the Barracuda Grill is. Frankly, I can't go much further. I need to sit down."

"Well, God knows you've earned it, Alex. You did some hard shopping. If you recall, I was ready to stop for a drink an hour ago."

Alex rearranged a couple of her parcels. "I know, I know. But this is probably my only chance to buy souvenirs. Tomorrow, I thought you'd like to do other things, like snorkeling at one of the beaches, or touring museums, like the Verdmont."

They rounded the corner passing a constable in traditional shorts directing traffic. "Here's the restaurant coming up on our left. See what you think. How does it look to you?"

Arlie shaded his eyes to peer into the glass-fronted bulletin board attached to the front of the building. "I think the menu looks great, Alex. Come in here closer so you can read it. Make sure there's something you'd like." He pulled her over to him, keeping his arm around her.

"Ooh." Alex puckered her mouth in concern as she scanned the bill of fare. "It's more expensive than I remembered. We'll go Dutch, okay?"

"Of course not. You're treating me to the entire cruise. I'll take care of the extras. It's the least I can do." He gave her a little squeeze. "Don't worry about it."

Alex put down her bags. "But you just bought me these fresh water pearls, too. Besides, this hasn't been much of a vacation for you. You've spent most of the past two days investigating a murder."

He shrugged. "Well, that's not your fault — let's go in and get a table. We can talk about how great I am over dinner."

Alex grinned, picked up her bags, and headed for the door.

Inside, they were shown to a comfortable booth by the maitre d' who lit the candle in the centerpiece on the white linen cloth as he announced that their server would be 'Anthony.'

* * *

OVER THEIR MEALS of grilled fresh red snapper and Bermuda rockfish, two of the specialties of the house, Arlie related his visit to the police lab earlier in the day.

"It's fantastic that there were usable prints on those shards of ceramic," Alex enthused. "Don't you think they'll identify Victor's killer? All you have to do is get everyone's prints, right?"

"I'd say that's an optimistic view," Arlie responded. "First, people don't have to submit to being printed. Second, whoever pushed the pot over the ledge isn't necessarily the person who ended up strangling the man. And I don't hold out much hope that there will be useful DNA information on the scarf."

Alex frowned, pushing roasted potatoes around her plate. "That never seems right to me – that people don't have to cooperate with a police investigation. But, if the prints weren't made by the murderer, then what's the use in identifying whose they are? You can't accuse someone of the 'attempted murder' of a person who's been *actually* murdered by someone else, can you?"

"Of course I can. Each person's act is judged independently. It doesn't exonerate the first guy if a second guy was more successful. It's a little unusual, I grant you, but not unprecedented."

Alex shook her head and looked at the ceiling. "So right now it's more likely that you'll discover the person who *tried* to kill Victor, rather than the one who *actually* did. Geesh. Let's hope you get some DNA from the scarf; that's all I have to say."

Arlie touched his napkin to his mouth. "The problem with the scarf is, if Jasmine's DNA can be lifted, it's an exemplar— it's expected to be on her own scarf. So, if she's the murderer, you can't prove it with that piece of evidence by itself. What you don't know is whether the DNA was transferred when she looped it around her neck or when she pulled it tightly around Victor's."

"But if some *other* DNA is on the scarf, it would eliminate Jasmine as a suspect, right?" Alex argued.

Arlie puckered his chin. "It would help. It's just not that easy to obtain *any* DNA from fabric that has only skin cells and oils and doesn't contain any other body fluids."

"Okay, let's not talk about body fluids over dinner," Alex said.

"Fine with me," Arlie responded, taking a sip of wine. "Just one more thing. I forgot to tell you that I got saliva swabs from the family members yesterday. That's a start. Maybe everyone will be cooperative about the prints. Of course, Sunny felt it necessary to claim 'invasion of privacy' and 'harassment' before she'd deign to put the Q-tip inside her cheek."

Alex shook her head, sympathetically. "I still say there should be some penalty for not fully cooperating with the police."

She checked her watch. "Look, I hate to end this scintillating conversation, but we just have time to split a dessert, if you want, before heading back to the ship. We need to be on the King's Wharf dock before eight-thirty for the Bermuda Triangle Cruise."

"They still use that term?"

"They do, but legends about ships mysteriously disappearing in the area have long since been put to rest. The Triangle is comprised of the most traveled shipping lanes in the world. Of course, there'll be accidents, and some boats will capsize in storms or hitting shoals, or whatever.

"Believe me, Arlie, you have nothing to fear. We'll be getting back at ten o'clock and nothing bad will have happened."

Chapter 38

JUST AS ALEX HAD PREDICTED, the Bermuda Triangle Cruise boat returned to the dock at ten o'clock without incident. It had been a most pleasurable evening out on the water under the stars with the passengers enjoying the spectacle of the lighted marine life over the sunken shipwreck.

But the excursion had turned into a party when the crew started serving rum swizzles and played a Beach Boys CD.

Eloise Brown began calling everyone "Duckie" as she moved about the boat, chatting and hugging people.

Aunt Lola and Aunt Alaana danced on deck while singing off-key to the California group's biggest hits like, "Kokomo," prompting others to join in on the familiar refrains, lustily: "...to Bermuda. Bahama. Come on, pretty mama. Key Largo. Montego. Baby, why don't we go?"

By the time the boat pulled up to the dock, everyone appeared to be the best of friends, taking pictures with one another before getting off the boat, so they could remember the special evening.

Arlie and Alex held hands as they disembarked and started strolling up the dock, making their way past two other cruise ships on the way back to their own. "I don't know," Alex said, "but there did seem to be a little magic in the Triangle."

Arlie cocked his head towards her. "I don't think it was in the Triangle. I think it was in the Bacardi; but it worked, either way. Are you ready to go up to the room, or did you want to do something else?"

"Oh, I don't want to go anywhere. I was thinking we could sit out on the balcony for a little while since it's such a nice night. Not too long — I need to get up early and meet with everyone again about their excursions."

"Really? That'll be a good opportunity for me to take their prints."

"Oh, swell. We'll make a good team. I'll talk up all the fun they'll have, and you come around and ink their fingers and arrest one of them for attempted murder. Here we are at the brow for our ship. Let's go in."

* * *

THEY HAD BEEN SITTING OUTSIDE for only a few minutes when they heard a knock on Alex's door.

Arlie turned toward the sound, scowling. "Who the hell could that be at this hour?"

Putting a hand on his arm Alex started to get up. "I'll go. It's probably someone who doesn't know what excursion they've signed up for."

Arlie stopped her. "No, you stay here. I'll go and get rid of whoever it is."

Alex could see the door open and heard another man's voice, but couldn't make out the words. When Arlie walked back through the doorway, his forehead was creased with concern. "That was security."

"Oh no! Now what?!"

"The officer said that Walter Sneed fell down some stairs."

Alex waved her hand, dismissively. "Oh, that. That happened earlier today in Gibb's Tower. It was nothing, really. Did Walter ask security to look into it? That man is such a drama queen. He probably tripped over his own feet, anyway."

Arlie sat heavily in his chair. "He said that Walter fell down at least fifteen steps on the stairway between Deck 7 and Deck 6. He's unconscious, possibly in a coma."

"What?!" Alex sprang forward in her seat, her mouth open. "Oh my God! What's going on?! Honest, this afternoon he wasn't injured, but he was sure that he had been pushed by Bruno Rasconi. I asked Bruno about it, but he denied it and I believed him. Arlie, it's all my fault! I should have taken Walter more seriously!"

"And then what?" Arlie put a hand on her shoulder. "Don't blame yourself. You couldn't have prevented this. We don't know yet what *this* is. It could have been another accident. Stranger things have happened. Let's go down to the infirmary and check on Walter. Who knows? He might have come to by now."

"Sure. Of course," she responded in a small voice.

* * *

DOWNSTAIRS, they were again met by Dr. Briggs. "Looks like we have another situation," he said grimly, in greeting.

"Anybody see what happened?" Arlie asked. "Who found him?"

The doctor shook his head. "No one saw him fall that I know of. There weren't many people around on Deck 7 since the casino is closed while we're docked. The couple that called security said they found him on the stairs as they were walking up from Deck 6 to see if the Art gallery was open. That was at about ten-thirty. He was out cold and has remained unconscious.

"I'm stabilizing him, and giving him barbiturates by IV to try and reduce brain swelling. You know, we're not really set up here for these things." He looked at Arlie and Alex as though expecting an apology.

"We'd like to see Mr. Sneed," Arlie said.

* * *

IN AN ADJOINING ROOM the art critic was lying perfectly still, his stomach mounding under the white sheet and blanket. Alex was shocked at his grey face and his closed, sunken eyes. "He looks dead, like Victor," she breathed.

"He's not," Arlie said. "He's still breathing, although it seems to be irregular."

Dr. Briggs spoke up. "That's a symptom of coma, brought on by the brain trauma he suffered. He has all the classic signs. Pressing on a pen light with his thumb, he pulled back the patients eyelids. "See? the pupils don't get smaller with the light." He picked up an arm and dropped it. It fell like dead weight.

"Can he hear anything? Is he aware of anything?" Alex asked.

"No, he's in a deep state of unconsciousness," Briggs answered. "He could stay this way for weeks, maybe months. Who knows? I haven't seen a case like this since I was a hospital intern. He's certainly the first comatose passenger on *this* ship." He gave them a look of disapproval.

* * *

ON THEIR WAY TO THE ELEVATOR Alex tugged on Arlie's sleeve. "We need to find out if anyone saw what happened."

"We will, but don't expect to find a voluntary witness. If Sneed was pushed, the perp would have made sure that no one but a collaborator was around to see it."

"Arlie, we'd better visit Bruno Rasconi right now— see if he has an alibi for ten-thirty. He's our prime suspect."

"I'll go talk to him, Alex. You see if you can find anyone on Deck 7 who saw or heard anything unusual at that time."

Alex made a little moue. "Okay, but be sure you get something from Bruno that we can check out. I just bet he had something to do with this. Poor Walter. That's three times now that the man has taken a fall; first, when he landed in the fountain, tripping this afternoon, and now this. And Bruno was present at each incident."

Arlie nodded. "It's only circumstantial, but don't worry, I'll put the screws to him and his friends and report back to you — sergeant. By the way, how did you move up from being my assistant to being my superior?"

"I don't know. I guess I just have a knack for this kind of thing," she shrugged.

Chapter 39

AFTER LEAVING ARLIE, Alex hurried to the elevator, which arrived promptly, but the ride up was annoyingly slow as passengers got on and off at each floor. On Deck 7, she eased out from behind several people and quickly made her way to the stairs where Walter Sneed had been found.

Looking down the free-standing spiral staircase she could easily imagine how someone could slip on the bare steps. Any fall could result in an injury due to the lack of padding. But still, there were sturdy brass railings one could hold onto, and hundreds of people went up and down the stairway every day without difficulty, as far as she knew. All cruise ships had similar open staircases as centerpieces of the glass-covered public areas, going back to the first luxury ocean liners, like the Titanic. Most people were familiar with its 'grand stairway' that was a central prop in the movie about the disaster.

Her attention was then drawn to two couples who were talking and laughing as they started up the steps from Deck 6, possibly coming from a late dinner or from looking in the windows of the closed shops.

She checked her watch. It was just before midnight. They probably weren't here an hour and a half ago, but she'd ask them, anyway.

"Excuse me," she said, after they had reached the top step. "Someone in my group fell down these stairs about ten-thirty tonight. Were any of you here then, by chance, to see how it happened?"

They all shook their heads 'no.'

"Hope your friend wasn't hurt too badly," one of the women said. "We've been on Deck 6 all evening. We were just coming up to see if the art gallery was still open. Have you asked *them*? They're not too far away."

Alex took a quick look around, and seeing no other people or having any better options, said, "That's a good idea. Thank you. If you don't mind, I'll tag along with you and talk to them if they're still there."

When the five of them approached the gallery, the lights were still on. As they stepped inside, a tinkling chime sounded, followed by the sight of a harried-looking Horatio Krumm coming around the corner.

Seeing the visitors he stopped and clasped his hands against his chest, favoring them with a mirthless smile. "Oh my goodness! I couldn't imagine what set off the chimes! I mean, I didn't expect any customers now. It's our closing time, you see, but if there's something special..."

His eyes darted from face to face. "We'll be having our next auction tomorrow night after we're underway. Maybe you could come back and look, perhaps?" Sweat had beaded above his thin upper lip.

The woman who had spoken to Alex waved him off. "Oh, don't worry about us. We were just looking for something to do. The other stores haven't been open, as you know."

When the dealer looked disappointed at her response, her husband added, "Maybe we'll come back tomorrow."

The two couples turned to leave allowing Alex room to step forward. "Uh, Mr. Krumm — I don't know if you remember me, but ..."

"What? Oh, yes. You were here with your boyfriend. You're another one of those artists in that wedding party, right?" He took keys out of his pocket and started jingling them in his hand.

"Your friend bought one of the fine Dali lithographs, wasn't it? I'm sure he's very happy with it. One of a kind." He looked around, nervously, and called back, "Danny, you want to catch the lights?"

Turning to face Alex, his face tightened. "I'm sorry, but I need to close the gallery now, so . . ."

"I'm not here to talk about art. Someone in our group took a bad fall down the spiral staircase about ten-thirty tonight. I was just wondering if you or your customers heard anything about it, how it happened."

"A fall? No, I didn't hear anything. Of course, I can see how someone could lose his footing on those slippery stairs. You should sue the cruise line. Was he badly hurt?"

"We don't know the extent of his injuries, yet."

Krumm held out his arms and stepped forward to force Alex back to the door. Turning his head he called back, "Danny, how about the lights?

"Sorry I can't help you, Miss...," Krumm mumbled.

"Trotter. Alex Trotter. That's all right. I'm sorry I bothered you this late."

Several lights went off leaving one spotlight on several stacks of paintings that were leaning against the wall near the back of the space. Alex caught a glimpse of the top painting on one of the piles before the last light went out. It was Dali's *Original Perfection* — just like the one up in their stateroom.

Chapter 40

UPSTAIRS, ALONE IN THE SUITE, Alex retrieved the brown paper-wrapped package from Arlie's closet and laid it on her bed. Slitting the masking tape with a nail file, she carefully picked up the print and propped it against her headboard.

Original Perfection was a lovely painting, she had to admit, although she now doubted its authenticity. Taking a moment to look at it, she admired the looseness with which the artist had been able to capture the atmosphere and images of Adam and Eve and an angel in the Garden of Eden. But now, she reminded herself, she had to put aside her appreciation of the art to critically examine its support, or painting surface, the quality of the reproduction and framing materials.

What was it that Horatio Krumm had said when he was auctioning off the painting? That it was a 'limited-edition' print. The last one he had left from the Divine Comedy series.' Hmmph! She knew *that* was an outright lie, having just seen its double in the gallery. And she wouldn't be surprised if there weren't several other *Divine Comedy* and other 'limited-edition' prints in the foot-deep pile underneath *Original Perfection*. And there were several other stacks.

Was Horatio Krumm planning on auctioning them off on the return voyage? What if the former buyers came to the auctions and saw their 'one-of-a-kind' prints being sold? No, that didn't make sense. With so many on the floor, Horatio and his assistants must have been taking inventory and going over the record of sales, when she and the two couples had walked in on them.

The gallery manager said that he hadn't expected any more customers. After all, it was right before closing and most of the businesses had been darkened all day due to the ship's being in port. That would explain why the usually smooth manager had acted so jumpy and unnerved, especially with her. It was possible that he remembered that Arlie had bought the *Original Perfection* print. He had recalled which print Arlie was interested in when they went back to the gallery.

Feeling more confident in her theory that Krumm was dishonest, Alex began to scrutinize the print. The colors looked true and the paper seemed of good quality, although she couldn't tell its weight while it was in still in the frame. The print was dated 1982. The original had been done much earlier, but had been reproduced for several years, so that didn't seem suspicious.

The signature looked like Dali's as far as she could recall. The artist's squiggly mark was written in pencil on the image. Did that mean anything? Had Dali only signed in ink? No, she was sure she had seen his signature in pencil.

She had heard in school that there had been many forgeries of Dali prints, but how could one tell a fake print from a legitimate one? She could check in the gallery whether the same artist's signature looked exactly alike on different paintings, indicating the use of an automatic writing device. Beyond that, she'd have to go to the computer room on Deck 6 and do some research, which she should have done before the auction.

Carefully, she picked up the painting and turned it around to face the headboard. There was more brown paper glued onto the back. She considered for only a moment before slitting it at the outside edge. Pulling it off she felt sick to her stomach at what she saw: the frame in back was unstained so she could identify it as being soft pine, rather than cherry as the dark stain on the front made it appear; and the frame's sides were stapled at the corners.

The print had been sold as being in its original condition, in its original frame. A valuable signed Dali from 1982 should have been in a hardwood frame, constructed with dovetailed corners, and would have shown signs of aging after more than thirty years. She couldn't imagine that a professional framer would have put such a valuable piece in an inexpensive hobby-store frame.

It now seemed very unlikely that it was a genuine woodblock print from 1982, signed by Salvador Dali. And if not, it wasn't worth $1,500; although Arlie hadn't paid nearly as much as many of the bidders had for similar prints that were probably fakes, too.

She needed to look at the print up close to be sure, so she removed the spring-style clips holding the paper and glass in the frame and pulled the image out, turning it to face her.

She was relieved to see that the paper was of good quality, noting the Arches watermark on it with the infinity symbol underneath. She was familiar with the logo of the 100 percent cotton archival paper that was manufactured in France. This was a sign pointing to authenticity. Could it be a legitimate print, but cheaply framed?

Just then she heard Arlie's door being opened. Hurrying to cover the print with the brown paper, she called out, "Hello, Arlie? I'm in here." No response. "Arlie?"

"Yeah, it's me! Just a minute. I'm putting these fingerprint kits away. I'll be right in."

After a few moments he came through the connecting doorway. "Well, I talked to Rasconi and some of the other artists—" He stopped in his tracks; his eyes widening. "What are you doing? Is that my Dali print?"

"Uh, yes. This must look bad, but I can explain. Why don't you sit down."

After Alex related the details of her gallery visit, she finished by saying, "So, that's why I had to take your print apart — very carefully, and I can put it back together — but I wanted to see if it was a fake."

During the telling of her story, Arlie had been sitting on a corner of the bed looking back and forth between her and the print. "So, is it or isn't it?"

"I can't be positive, but I'll let you know after I've done some research. I'm concerned that all of the artwork in the gallery may be fakes or forgeries, or something. You know how weird that Horatio Krumm is."

Arlie shrugged his shoulders. "He has weird teeth, but so did George Washington. I'd just as soon you didn't find out if my print isn't from the original block, or whatever. I'm stuck with it."

"I know, 'all sales are final,' but I'm more concerned about the people who can't afford to invest their savings in what may be poster art. Your print is on fine archival paper, so it's a nice piece of artwork, at any rate. Maybe not what it was represented to be, but we'll see."

Arlie stretched and yawned. "Okay, look into it if you must. I'm more concerned about the murder. Rasconi and the others claim to have stayed in Hamilton late after your tour. I'll check out their alibis tomorrow.

"Also, I'll need to go back to the crime lab with the prints I get in the morning. If you want to do your research then, maybe we can get together and go to the beach or something in the afternoon."

Alex started putting the painting back into the frame. "I hope so, but I guess that depends on what we both find out tomorrow."

Chapter 41

THE FOLLOWING MORNING Alex dressed in a watermelon-colored knit top and a long floral skirt in an attempt to look relaxed and cheerful; a camouflage for her true feelings of anxiety and dread.

Dr. Briggs had called Arlie's room early to report that Walter Sneed was still in a coma. She would have to tell the group about his fall since Arlie had already questioned several of the people about their whereabouts at the time of the incident.

Furthermore, after her meeting, Arlie would be taking everyone's prints to compare with those on the pieces of the vase, hoping to find a match to make an arrest for attempted murder.

While he was doing that, she would be going down to the computer room to research art fraud before revisiting the gallery to inspect other artwork for deceptive practices.

But first, she had to meet with her group to hand out tickets to those with pre-paid sightseeing excursions, and to talk up attractions to the rest of them who had not signed up for anything.

As a tour director, she had to be enthusiastic and encourage exploration. even as she was distraught about the unsolved mysteries that were piling up by the minute.

Walking into the dining room, she noticed an unusual amount of chatter. Everyone appeared to be friendlier and in a better mood than the day before. Hopefully, that was because no one there was guilty of murdering anyone, or trying to.

Quickly scanning the crowd, she noted that the Garza family members were missing, again.

In front of the seated company, she managed a weak smile. "So," she started. "It's already our last day in Bermuda, but there's still time to have a lot of fun on the island. Is everyone here who planned to be, that you know of?"

Aunt Lola raised her hand. "Jasmine and Tony are at the crematorium picking up Victor's ashes, and Walter Sneed's in a coma in the infirmary."

Alex felt a tic begin under her right eye as she looked back at the shocked faces of the rest of the group. "Right. Thank you for that. Well, since you brought it up, yes, Walter Sneed took a bad fall last night down the spiral staircase between Deck 7 and Deck 6. Detective Tate is looking into that and is also working hard to solve Victor's murder so we can put the matter, and poor Victor, to rest, properly.

"And, while we're on the subject, right after our meeting Arlie Tate needs to fingerprint all of you ..." Sounds of disapproval cut her off.

"To *eliminate you as suspects* in pushing the vase off the ledge," she hurriedly added. "Just a formality to clear people of attempted murder." She winced at her unvarnished phrasing.

Victor's ex-partner Roman Gregg leapt to his feet. "What the hell's that for?! The man's already dead from being strangled. That vase business coulda been an accident, anyway.

Who knows, my prints could be similar and I'll be arrested. No way!"

Eloise Brown called out from the back, "Oh, blimey! Don't get all brassed off about it and throw a spanner in the works. It's not my cuppa tea to be fingerprinted, either, but I know from crime shows on the telly that it's a science. No constable's gonna put the clamps on ya' if you didn't do nothin."

"We don't mind, either," Edmund Devers said, cocking his head towards his wife. "Frankly, old man, it looks worse if you don't go along." He had directed his last remark to Roman Gregg who just glared back at him.

"Okay, then!" Alex jumped in. "I hope all of you will cooperate with Arlie. But, right now, we need to respectfully leave these issues behind us and talk about how you can best spend your last hours in Bermuda. Remember, you must be back on the ship by five o'clock for a six o'clock sailing. I'll run down some of the highlights, briefly, and answer any questions. Also, here are the tour tickets for those of you going to the Verdmont House Museum in St. Georges. That's a docent-guided tour on the hour there, so watch when you arrive. You'll learn a lot of interesting island history as well as seeing many of the original family's belongings.

"Oh, I see Arlie coming to take your fingerprints. So, before he gets started with his forensics, who wants to hear about beaches?"

Chapter 42

AFTER THE MEETING Alex left Arlie to fingerprint the group as she headed over to the computer room on the same deck. Approaching the communications center, she saw the spiral staircase up ahead, a grim reminder of Walter Sneed's serious condition from his fall that was just the latest in a series of tragic incidents. Maybe it wasn't so important to find out if Arlie's painting was authentic. Still, if she could prove that *his* was a fake, she might be able to expose Horatio Krumm's scam and save others from being ripped-off.

As she entered the computer room, there were a lot of people there, although the only sound was the soft tapping of keys. No one even looked up, except for the tawny-skinned woman sitting at the front desk behind a 'Check in Here' sign. She was wearing a uniform-style white blouse with a name tag reading, 'Yvonne.'

"Did you want to use a computer?" Yvonne asked, putting down her magazine.

No, I'd like to rent snorkel equipment. "Yes. Do I have to sign up in advance, or is one available now?" Alex asked, dubiously, trying to take in the whole room.

"There's one. All the way in the back." Yvonne pointed at the obvious location. "But you have only forty-five minutes before its next reserved time — and it's fifty cents a minute. Your time will start when you log in."

"Okay. I'll take it."

"Fine. Here's your password. Remember, forty-five minutes."

Geesh, I got it. Forty-five minutes; fifty cents for each one. This'll cost me — what? Twenty-two fifty!. She hurried to the back of the room to the last carrel and plopped down on the office chair, not even taking the time to adjust the seat. When she rolled the chair up to the table, she realized that it had been set for someone much shorter, so that she was typing down by her knees.

Flipping open her notepad, she glanced through her questions. After logging in and pulling up the search engine, she typed, *How to tell a fake signed Dali print.* From the looks of the numerous results, this was a popular subject, if the responses were on point.

Quickly scanning some articles, she took a few notes, but clicked to print several pages to save time, as well as having material evidence. What had been discussed in class on fake Dali prints was coming back to her. She recognized the name Albert Field, as having been the director of Dali Archives, Ltd., who had published *The Official Catalog of the Graphic Works of Salvador Dali* in 1994.

Since so many Dali forgeries had been released on the market after 1980 when Dali went into retirement, there was a lot of material on the variations: new print images never made by the artist, unauthorized prints of paintings, copies of prints sold as originals, and fake signatures. Dali forgeries were made harder to detect as the artist had habitually signed blank pieces of paper as a shortcut for printers. Therefore, the positioning of his signature on prints wasn't consistent.

Alex scrolled down a few more references before she found what she was looking for: the peculiarity about Dali's signature on the *Divine Comedy* series. She leaned back in her chair and blew out a long stream of air to consider what she had just read. *What typical tourist would know that?* she asked herself. She had sat through a lecture on the subject and hadn't remembered it.

She glanced at her watch. Only ten minutes left. She quickly typed inquiries on other artists she could recall who had paintings hanging in the gallery.

Finally, she pulled up articles of general information regarding how artwork is faked or misrepresented in various ways. There was a lot to read. She clicked on print.

Checking her watch again she saw that her time had expired, just as a pretty teenage girl was coming down the aisle to claim her computer. *Darn it! She's just going on Snapchat or Twitter, or whatever, while I'm trying to uncover a major fraud scheme.*

Alex nodded at the girl and reluctantly got up and retrieved her pages from the printer; more than she had thought. When she went over to settle up with Yvonne she found that she owed thirty dollars and fifty cents.

Walking out the door with her pile of papers, she was surprised to see Toby Wilson and his mother approaching. "Oh, Hi!" she called out. "Kathy, right? Hi, Toby. What a coincidence running into you two."

Kathy Wilson's face cleared with recognition. "Alex Trotter. Nice to see you again, too. Enjoying the cruise?"

Alex grimaced. "Well, it hasn't exactly been a *fun* cruise for my group, I'm afraid. To quote Shakespeare, it's been more like a 'sea of troubles'."

Kathy Wilson cocked her head. "Really? A couple of days ago I heard about a man being killed. He wasn't in *your* group, was he? The housekeepers were talking about how one of them had found him dead in a laundry basket."

Alex nodded. "That was Victor Garza from our group. Actually, he wasn't just one of our members, he was our *host*. This was supposed to be his wedding trip, but he ended up murdered on the second night out."

"Oh, my God! I hadn't heard the details. Oh, that's terrible!"

"Yes, it was a shock, as you can imagine. Victor was a famous art dealer — you might have noticed him at the art auction. He was tall, distinguished, with a mustache, graying at the temples. He was with a gorgeous dark-haired younger woman. She was wearing a lavender and blue print scarf."

Kathy Wilson's eyes opened wide. "Oh, I remember them! *That* was the guy who was murdered? Yeah, they were standing in the back and left early. I noticed them because, well, they were so striking. Oh, I can't believe that I saw the man before he was killed!"

Toby's face brightened. "He was the man who was mad at the auction guy!"

Alex raised her eyebrows as she looked down at the little boy. "What do you mean, Toby?"

"The man with the mustache told the auction man that the paintings were for some guy named Gerry. He pointed to one picture and then another, saying that that they were for Gerry. But he was angry. Like the auction man had *stole* them from Gerry."

Alex knelt down and put her hands on the boy's shoulders. "He said they were for Gerry. Toby, could the tall man have been saying that each of them was a *forgery*?"

"Yeah, that sounds like it, too."

Alex stood up, shaking her head and looked at Kathy. "You know, yesterday I stopped by the gallery and saw a duplicate of Arlie's Dali print that made me aware Horatio Krumm hadn't been truthful that it was the only one of its kind. When I later examined Arlie's print, I was sure we had been duped about its value. And now, I just did research and found proof that Horatio Krumm is selling other fakes." She held up her stack of papers. "Damn! I should have known that Victor would have spotted them as forgeries on sight!"

Kathy Wilson stared at her. "Do you think that Horatio Krumm murdered Victor Garza?"

"Well, that's quite a leap," Alex responded. "For one thing, Krumm could never overpower Victor to strangle him. For another, Victor was seen alive after the gallery was closed. And lastly, there are several people who had personal grudges against Victor, who either lost a lot of money to him when he was alive, or who stood to gain a fortune if he were dead."

"Oh, my gosh! This is like something you'd see on TV!"

"Kathy, could I go up to your stateroom with you and see your Picasso?"

"Uh, sure, but I don't really want to know that it's a forgery. I mean, I can't return it."

"That's what Arlie said. If we prove that it's not authentic, you sure can return it and get your money back! How much did you pay for it?"

"Five thousand. We thought we were lucky. Most of the prints went for far more."

"Yeah, I know. Let's go up and see if yours is worth five thousand . . . or considerably less."

Chapter 43

KATHY WILSON SLID HER KEY CARD through the door slot for the three of them to step inside the compact stateroom. Explaining the empty room she said, "Darrin's in Hamilton at some museum we didn't think Toby would enjoy. We're going to meet him for lunch and go from there. I'm not sure where."

Alex put her purse and papers down on the sofa. "You might try the Aquarium on North Shore Road. Toby would love the tropical fish and harbor seals. It's an easy bus ride from Hamilton."

"Oh, could we, Mom?"

"Sure. Of course. Thanks, Alex. Well, we need to get going soon, so let me get the print. It's in the back of our closet for safe keeping. Hah! Maybe we don't have to worry about someone stealing it. Oh, that isn't really funny."

Kathy disappeared into the closet and brought out a parcel wrapped in brown paper.

After staring at the package Kathy had placed on the bed, Alex said, "Well, let's open it and see what we've got."

Kathy tore off the wrapping to reveal the back of the print and its Certificate of Authenticity. Alex picked it up and said, "I was just reading what a COA has to include, like the number of the edition, the publisher and date of publication, original size, original title, and the type of paper used for the print. Let's see what yours has. It says here that it's a new edition, number 348. There's no publisher named, but the date of the signed print is 1979. Whoa!" She dropped the certificate and stared at Kathy.

"What's wrong?" Kathy asked, sounding alarmed.

Alex reached for the painting. "Let me see the front of that print and I'll tell you what's wrong."

Turning it around she pointed to the signature. "See, that's supposed to be an 'original' pencil signature by Picasso." She looked at Kathy with a wicked smile. "This may be more valuable than you thought."

Kathy's face cleared. "Really? It is?"

"Yeah, if Picasso was brought back to life to *sign* it. He died in 1973, so he couldn't have written his name in 1979.

"Furthermore, there were only 300 limited-edition prints made of this particular 'Clown' painting." Kathy jerked in surprise at Alex's knowledge.

"I just read that. I printed an article on Picasso's clown prints and I checked on this one, knowing that you bought it at the auction. I'll leave it for you to read.

"Anyway, what you have here is a silk-screening of the limited edition print. Meaning that it's a third-generation copy."

"So it isn't worth $5,000.00, I'm guessing," Kathy said, dismally.

Alex shook her head slowly. "Sadly, no. Let's check out the frame to see what it's like."

She turned the print over and pulled away a little of the back paper to expose one of the corners underneath. "See this? It's stapled, not dovetailed. They glued the paper on to cover that.

It's a cheap framing technique that many people would spot if they could see it — anyone who's bought good furniture knows that quality construction has interlocking corners for strength.

"I'm sorry, Kathy. But you were scammed —as Arlie and I were— I might add. The good news is that the paper is probably archival cotton. With that kind of paper, there's no fading under the bright gallery lights that would immediately give it away as being a fake."

"So what should we do now?" Kathy asked.

"I think you should return it and get your money back."

Kathy winced. "Could you go with me? You can explain it more knowledgeably than I can."

Alex held up her hands. "I will if you wait until I can check out the rest of the artwork in the gallery. I don't know if everything's fake, and I don't want to show my hand until I know what's what."

"Alex. I don't think you should go there by yourself. It could be dangerous. That Horatio Krumm is a weirdo. He's maybe not as strong as Victor Garza, but he might be able to take you on."

"Don't worry, I'll go during business hours when other people are around. And I wouldn't say anything to Krumm even then. If what I suspect is true, I'll go with Arlie and present my evidence. We shouldn't have a problem getting his money back, then.

"And if I find more forgeries, I'll inform the Olympus line, which will no doubt shut down the whole operation. I'm sure they don't want their reputation besmirched by one phony gallery owner. And they'll want to refund everyone's money, I would think."

"Oh, I hope it works out, Alex, although I'm disappointed that it turned out this way. I had thought it was such a special anniversary gift, since it reminded me of Toby and all." She looked fondly at her son who was obliviously reading a picture book.

Alex followed her gaze. "I owe it to Toby for repeating what Victor Garza said about the prints being forgeries."

Kathy nodded. "The little scamp was walking around that whole night eavesdropping on people talking about artwork, weren't you Toby? No one notices a little kid."

"Well, let me know what you discover in the gallery, Alex. Is security looking into Mr. Garza's murder? I hate to think that there's some homicidal maniac running around on board."

Alex started gathering up her papers. "Actually, my boyfriend happens to be a homicide detective and is investigating.

"It's kind of a long story, but on the morning of the murder someone tried to kill Victor by dropping a heavy potted tree on his deck where the Garzas were sitting. "And then, last night, someone in our group was seriously injured and is in a coma after falling down the circular stairway from Deck 7. That's what I meant by saying it's been like a 'sea of troubles' on this trip."

Toby looked up from his illustrated book. "Was it a man or woman, Miss Trotter?"

Alex turned towards the boy. "What, Toby? Was *who* a man or a woman?"

"The person who fell down the stairs. You said 'someone' fell down and was hurt real bad, but you didn't say if it was a man or a woman."

"Oh, it was a man. A Mr. Sneed. We're hopeful that he gets well, soon, though. He's getting good care in the infirmary."

* * *

ALEX HAD AN UNEASY FEELING later when she was walking down the hallway towards the elevator. Something about Toby asking if it was a man or a woman who had fallen down the stairs. However, nothing came to mind, so she shrugged it off. *I'm starting to see mysteries everywhere,* she chided herself.

She turned her mind to her mission which was to read through the rest of the material on art forgeries. If Arlie wasn't back by the time she finished, maybe she'd run down to the gallery and take a quick look around. It would be a tricky operation. She needed to examine details, but not take too much time so that she attracted attention to what she was up to. After all, Krumm knew that they were forgeries, so he'd be on the lookout for anyone who seemed to be catching on to his scheme.

As she got on the nearly empty elevator, she checked her watch and saw that it was eleven o'clock; still early in the day. Maybe if she went to the gallery around twelve-thirty, it would be a slow time and Krumm wouldn't be there. The man had to eat lunch, after all. If the assistants were the only ones there, she could take her time; even take photos and a few notes.

Chapter 44

AFTER READING THROUGH HER RESEARCH, Alex couldn't wait to go down to the gallery to see what forgeries she could spot; although, as she reminded herself, she wasn't really an expert after spending less than two hours researching the subject. Hopefully, she'd see something obvious that had been addressed in the articles she had read.

Unfortunately, she hadn't yet heard from Arlie. Since it was a quarter after twelve, she was running out of time to investigate the gallery when Horatio Krumm would probably be at lunch. Arlie must still be at the Crime Lab, or would be leaving soon. Either way, if she left now she should have time to visit the gallery and get back to the room before he returned. Too bad she couldn't call him from the ship to coordinate their movements.

Picking up a notepad, she sat down and dashed off a few lines.

Hey, Arlie—

I'm leaving now for the art gallery and should be back between 1:00 and 1:30. Then let's go to the beach, okay?
L, A
p.s. I'm pretty sure that all the paintings are fakes!

Grabbing up her papers, she closed the stateroom door behind her and headed down the hall towards the elevator. This time she had to wait for a car and it was nearly full when it arrived. Presumably, many people were going down for lunch before they went ashore for the last few hours in port.

Standing behind a family excitedly talking about their plans for the afternoon, Alex smiled grimly to herself. *I must be the only person missing out on Bermuda to stay on the ship to look for bad art.*

* * *

STEPPING INTO THE LOW-LIT, hushed gallery, the only sound she heard was the tinkling of the chime announcing her entrance. She paused, waiting to see if Krumm would come bounding around the corner like he had last night. But no one came. In fact, the place seemed empty.

Was is always so dark in here? There had certainly been more lights on before the auction. The only illumination now came from the small spotlights on the paintings, while the rest of the space was shrouded in darkness.

Standing in the gloom, she shivered. She could hear herself breathe. Maybe she should go upstairs and come back later with Arlie. No, she should take a brief look around since she was there, anyway.

While she was debating her choices, she suddenly heard the sound of voices. *Was that good or bad?* Steeling herself, she peeked around the edge of a free-standing divider. Halfway down the wall she saw the source of the conversation, and exhaled in relief. An elderly couple stood talking together in front of a Norman Rockwell print, maybe discussing how much to bid on it that evening.

That's right! The next auction was only hours away. She and Arlie would have to confront Krumm this afternoon and demand that he cancel it.

She'd better work fast to find more fakes and get out of there. Turning to look at the wall, she noted that there were several signed Miro prints hanging there The first one she looked at was an abstract that looked familiar, but she couldn't be sure. They all looked alike, anyway, she thought. *Boy, some art critic I am. I can barely identify who the painter is.*

This print was titled, "Untitled." *Not very helpful.* The center of interest was a round black object with a stem. It looked like a cartoon image of a bomb. The rest of the print contained squiggly lines of red, blue and green, typical of Miro's palette. *Looks okay. Now what? Tear the paper off the back? There must be something on the print itself that looks fishy.*

Focusing on the signature, she leaned in closer and squinted at the letters. *Wait a minute! That wasn't how Joan Miro signed his name.* He made the "M" with separate curved strokes that reminded her of Far East lettering. This "M" had connected straight lines. Of course, she couldn't be sure that Miro *never* made an "M" like that, but there was something else. She remembered that the artist always drew a line under his name that turned up a little, like a smile. This line was drawn curving downward, like a frown.

She rifled through her papers until she found a page of Miro signature exemplars. Holding it up next to each print on the wall, she became convinced that none of the gallery signatures was genuine. They weren't bold enough, black enough, sure enough. They were fakes.

Sensing a movement behind her, she jumped, causing the sheet of paper to slip out of her hands. Peering into the semi-darkness, she made out one of Krumm's assistants, the taller dark-haired man. He was wearing the clothes that he wore for the auctions — grey pants and matching short-sleeved shirt. He was apparently looking for a place to hang the large print he was carrying and he didn't seem to be paying any attention to her. However, his mere presence made her uncomfortable since she was spying on the place. She decided not to reach behind the Miros to check if they had paper glued on the backs.

"Good afternoon," the man said pleasantly, glancing over at her and then at the white-haired couple. "Any questions you folks have, you can ask me. Mr. Krumm is at lunch right now." Alex and the couple nodded.

Oh, brother! Did this guy think he was an art expert, too? He should only know that these are a bunch of fakes. She remembered him as the assistant who went around to the "successful bidders" to take their credit cards. After a moment, he moved along and she turned back to the wall.

The next grouping were prints of sentimental subjects like cozy cottages and impossibly-full gardens. Several were painted by Thomas Kincaid, and some were by lesser-known artists. The art community had been harshly critical of this type of art, but they were popular and sold well. Since Kincaid's death, his pieces undoubtedly commanded even higher prices.

A sign read that the prints were "hand-touched" signed lithographs. "Geesh," Alex muttered to herself. *The public should only know that artists ran off thousands of these and then added just a brushstroke or two. In the case of Kincaid, even those few strokes had probably been made by students in his studio. Looking over the whole array, she thought that none of these lithographs was worth much more than an ordinary print from a hobby store.*

Next, she came to a collection of Rembrandts identified as being "authentic prints" made from original woodcut masters. Alex shook her head. The reproductions were mushy, lacking in details in the deep-toned areas, and the chiaroscuro effect had been minimized, not the dramatic contrast between light and dark for which the artist was famous.

There were more than a dozen of the Rembrandts on the wall and probably many more in the storage area, belying any notion of rarity. At least there was no suggestion that these were "authentic" signatures, considering that the artist had been dead for four hundred years.

As she moved down the wall, she was close to the couple who were still looking at the Rockwell print. They both turned towards her and smiled.

"Hello, dear," the woman said. "Are you looking for something to bid on at the auction? You know, it's the last one of the cruise."

"Uh, no I'm not," Alex mumbled, not sure how much she should reveal of her activities. "Are you going to bid on that Rockwell print?"

The woman looked at her husband, questioningly. He gave a little *why not* shrug and nodded.

Her wrinkled face lit up. "Yes, I think we are! I've always loved this print of *Freedom from Want*. Such a warm, happy picture of grandparents serving the Thanksgiving turkey, don't you agree?" Before Alex could answer she leaned closer and said in a low voice, "It's *hand-signed*, you know, which makes this very valuable."

Alex bit her lower lip. "Well, it is a very nice study, and Norman Rockwell was a fine illustrator, but he didn't technically *sign* his paintings. That block printing isn't an autograph. It's really more of a *logo*. See how it's exactly the same on all his prints? You shouldn't pay more than a couple hundred dollars for this one."

The wife looked crest-fallen. "Oh, we would *never* get it for that. At the last auction everything went for well over a thousand dollars. Many paintings went for over *ten* thousand. Are you sure this isn't worth more than two hundred dollars?"

Alex shook her head. "I'm afraid not. It's a lovely decoration, but it's not an investment piece." She lowered her voice. "Nothing here is. Trust me. I'm an artist, myself, and I've done some research on these prints. I've already been able to verify many of these that don't have authentic signatures and aren't even lithographs. I'm almost sure that everything here is fake and I'm reporting this scam to the cruise line."

The husband and wife looked at each other in confusion. "Well, thanks for your advice," the man said, taking his wife's arm and starting to steer her away. "We'll be sure and give it some thought."

Alex wanted to go after them. They obviously didn't believe her and thought that she was just some kind of crazy person.

As the couple neared the door the assistant called out to them, "Horatio Krumm stands behind all of these valuable works of art and provides a Certificate of Authenticity for each piece. You have nothing to worry about, folks."

As the pair left, the assistant gave Alex a dirty look and followed them out the door, carrying a chrome stand with him. When he came back in, he closed the door behind him with a click. Alex looked up nervously.

The assistant smiled at her reassuringly "I think they'll be back for that print. The wife really liked it. It sounded like you didn't care for it, though. People have different tastes, of course." He gave a little shrug.

Alex nodded, hesitantly. "I suppose so." She really didn't want to get into a discussion with the employee about the gallery's dishonest representations. He seemed to think they were all genuine.

"Yeah, we try to have something for everybody," he continued. "I noticed you seemed quite interested in the Miros. You more of an abstract fan?"

"I like abstracts, sure." She glanced at the door hoping someone else would appear. The man continued to look at her, questioningly.

"Uh, I'm a graduate of the Chicago Art Institute so I learned to appreciate different genres. I'm pretty traditional, myself.

Landscapes and street scenes — that kind of thing." She took a deep breath and exhaled. "Well, since there aren't any other customers, I might as well leave you to your work. I'll come back later."

The man came closer, close enough that she could make out the tattoo of a hawk on his upper arm and could read his nametag: *Danny.*

"Uh, thanks for the chat, Danny."

"No problem. Oh, wait, I know who you are," he chirped. "You stopped by last night to ask if we knew anything about the guy who had fallen down the stairs. How's he doing, anyway?"

Alex gulped, her mind flashing back to something little Toby had said that morning. Almost to herself she mumbled, "I remember now. Horatio Krumm asked me how badly *the man* was hurt. But I hadn't said it was a *man*."

"Of course you did," Danny's tone was icy and his dark eyes had narrowed to pinpoints. "Or maybe we just assumed it was a man. It doesn't make any difference, now, does it?"

"What do you mean — *now*?" she snapped.

He waved a hand in the air. "Well, I mean, it's not important *at this moment*. What *is* important is what you told that nice old couple to discourage them from buying a quality piece of art."

"It *isn't* a quality piece," she answered automatically. She stared at the door. *Someone should be coming in soon.*

"Oh, no one's coming," Danny said in a cheerful voice that made her blood run cold. "I just put out the sign that says we're closed until the pre-auction viewing at six o'clock."

Alex felt wobbly on her feet and sank down onto a nearby bench. She swallowed hard. "Look, this isn't a big deal. Most people know that the lettering on a Rockwell print isn't a signature. That's all I told them."

His features became contorted with rage. "Liar! You told them that these are all fakes and you're filing a complaint with the cruise line!" His spittle sprayed out, landing on her face.

Alex shrank back in shock and disgust, pulling up the hem of her skirt to wipe off her cheek. "Excuse me, but who are *you* in this operation?! I think I'd better talk to Mister Krumm!" She stuck out her lower lip and held herself, protectively.

His face returned to normal. "And so you shall. You seem to like talking to everyone, and that's why you're a problem. You think you're pretty smart, don't you? You think you have it all figured out?" He chuffed her under the chin. She cringed and turned away.

He cocked his head toward the left. "Oh, it sounds like Horatio and Frank just came in the back way. But I think you'll be disappointed to find out that Horatio can't help you. You see, he works for *me*."

Alex blinked and stared at him. "*You're* in charge? I've been here for an auction. Horatio runs the show."

Danny made a guttural sound of contempt. "Before Horatio Krumm joined up with me he was a two-bit grifter running cons in Atlantic City. Small-time, mostly, but I could see he had potential. The man has a silver tongue, and he understands human nature. You can't teach that.

"Anyway, he needed a better gig and I needed a mouthpiece; but *I'm* the *artist* here."

"You mean *forger*," Alex muttered.

"Call me what you want. If you couldn't tell the difference between an original masterpiece and a forgery, who's the better artist?" He paused. "Huh? Don't know? The *copier* is, because he not only has to be technically proficient, he has to adopt someone else's style — *perfectly*."

Alex was feeling more wretched the longer he talked. "Why are you telling me all this?! Just let me go back to my room and we can both forget that I was even here."

He twisted his mouth into an ugly snarl. "Yeah? Nice try, kitten, but you went too far when you blabbed that you were going to the cruise line with your fraud charges. They're not fakes. They're 'expertly-done copies.' Better than you could do. You think you're an expert? You probably know just enough to be dangerous." He looked back into the darkness.

"Horatio! Come out in front and talk to our visitor!"

Alex felt her heart beating through her top. This was madness! She wanted to get out of there but, considering it was three to one and the door was locked, her only option seemed to be to keep Danny talking. Surely Arlie would come here looking for her when she didn't get back to the room when she'd said. She checked her watch. It was only a little after one. He wouldn't come for another half hour. She had to stay cool. These goons had shoved Walter Sneed down the staircase, and had maybe strangled Victor Garza.

"Helloooo!" she heard from behind her. Turning, she first saw the big white teeth. "Well, I didn't expect to see *you* back here so soon, my dear." Sensing the mood, his tone darkened. "What's going on boss? "

Danny threw up his hands. "Oh, just another fucking artist who wants to be a hero and close us down! What kind of a Mickey Mouse cruise is this, anyway?!"

He leaned over to go nose to nose with Alex. "Do *all* of you people think you're experts? At least Garza was a dealer and Sneed was a critic. Who the hell are *you*?"

He turned toward Horatio. "I caught her telling a sweet old couple that Rockwell didn't sign his prints. Brilliant, right? And then she has the gall to tell them that everything here's a fake. How does she know?" He batted his eyes and wiggled his hips. "She went to a-a-r-r-r-t school," he mocked in a sing-song voice.

Horatio smirked. "She's pretty, but she's no genius. She encouraged her boyfriend to buy one of the *Divine Comedy* prints."

Alex drew herself up, her eyes flashing. "I know now that that print is a forgery! And don't be so smug. Other artists will be able to spot your fakes better than I can. You can't get rid of all of us."

Danny sniggered. "So far you haven't said anything damaging. Why don't you tell us about all our so-called forgeries? Go on. Tell us."

Alex snuck a peek at her watch. She needed at least ten more minutes.

"Seriously. This could be fun," Danny egged her on.

Alex took a deep breath. "Okay, you asked for it. Let's see . . . I know that Dali's signature on Arlie's print is a forgery. How do I know that? Because it's *in pencil.* Big mistake. Dali never signed *any* of the *Divine Comedy* prints in pencil. Oh, and he never put his signature on the *Divine Comedy* prints in the block, itself."

Danny let out a harsh laugh. "Dali signed *blank* sheets of paper, for Chris' sakes. His signature could be *anywhere* on a print and still be genuine."

Alex raised her eyes to meet his. "He *did* sign some blank paper, but not for the *Divine Comedy* prints. And speaking of paper — you used the wrong kind."

"Okay, now I *know* you're talking out your ass! We use only archival paper. You say you've been to art school — you should know Arches and Rives."

"I *do* know their paper. Better than you do, apparently. I know that Arches didn't use the infinity watermark until 1980 — *after* Dali had signed his last print and had gone into retirement. They started using it to distinguish genuine Dali prints from the fake ones because there were so many forgeries around. Any Dali signature on Arches paper with the infinity watermark is *by definition* a forgery."

Horatio and Frank stared at Danny. "Boss, this ain't good," Frank said.

Danny waved him off. Leaning back against the wall, he coolly regarding Alex. "You just keep digging yourself in deeper, don't you? I think you figured out that we're pretty good at silencing our critics, but there you are, daring us to take care of you, too. Frank, here, has had a little practice." Frank beamed, revealing missing teeth.

"With Victor Garza and Walter Sneed," she said, flatly.

Danny stood up straighter and sneered, "They were both troublemakers. They *bragged* about being able to put us out of business and have us prosecuted for fraud. I don't know in what country, but we don't need that kind of aggravation and publicity."

Alex tried to look nonplussed. Crossing her legs, she studied her nails. Not looking up, she purred, "Well, I hate to break it to you, but my boyfriend happens to be a homicide detective. More importantly, he'll be here any minute." She glanced up at Danny. "Do you think I'm dumb enough to come here knowing what I know without a plan to protect myself?"

At that moment there was a knock on the door. Alex stiffened in shock.

"See? There he is now!" she croaked, unable to contain her excitement. "Now — if you'll just get out of my way..."

She stood up just as Danny held her from behind and clamped a hand over her mouth.

"Frank, get the turp!" he hissed.

More hands grabbed her forcing her back down on to the bench. Danny pulled his hand away for a second when a soaked cloth was mashed against her nose, making her swoon. *Turpentine.*

"Aack! I can't breathe!" she gasped, trying to wriggle away. After a few seconds, she felt woozy and collapsed just as everything went black.

Chapter 45

ARLIE WAS ANNOYED when no one came to the gallery door after he had knocked several times. He knew that someone was there. The lights had been on when he had first arrived, and had just now been turned off. Thrumming on the door several more times in rapid succession he called out, "Open up! I know you're there!"

Several more seconds passed. Finally, he heard the lock turn and the door was opened a crack. In the darkness he could make out a glowing set of teeth, and then the tanned face of Horatio Krumm.

"Oh, Arlie Tate, isn't it? Sorry if I kept you waiting but I was in the back. We're closed now, of course, but if I can be of any assistance..."

Arlie frowned with impatience. "Would you let me in, Krumm? I'd like to ask you a few questions."

The auctioneer stepped back. "Oh certainly, certainly. Come right in. I'm always glad to see a good customer."

"Yeah, right." Arlie stepped inside and looked up. "What happened to the lights? They were on just a minute ago." He craned his neck to peer into the darkness.

"I turned them off when I heard the knocking. I thought someone didn't realize that we were closed." He flashed one of his bright smiles. "But, here you are, so — what can I do for you?"

"I'm looking for my girlfriend Alex. I know she was here, and she planned to come straight back to the room afterwards. Now she's way overdue, so I'm retracing her steps."

The gallery manager's eyebrows rose in surprise. "No, as a matter of fact, I haven't seen her at all today."

"You haven't? Hmm. That's strange. I'm certain that she was here. Turn on the lights, wouldya? I'd like to take a look around."

"Okay, sure. I have to go to the back to get to the switches."

"Fine. I'll come with you."

The auctioneer walked to the rear of the space with Arlie on his heels. "Ah, here we are." He clicked on a couple of switches. A few small spotlights came on in the front of the gallery."

"*All* of them, please. So I can *see* something."

The gallery manager flicked more switches. "You're welcome to take a look around, but I really don't think she's been here."

Arlie scowled at the auctioneer. "I told you that I *know* she was here. Actually, I'll tell you why. She was pretty convinced that the Dali you sold me was not a signed print from woodcut as you claimed. She came down to investigate your other pieces." He glanced around before turning his attention back to Krumm. "And maybe she found something you didn't want her to find." He scrutinized the gallery manager's face.

Krumm's eyes widened in alarm. "Oh, my goodness! but I'm more than happy to help you any way I can. As for the Dali print, she must be mistaken. That came from a reputable source with a COA. We'll straighten that out, but right now I'm more concerned about your girlfriend. When was she supposed to have been here?"

"I know that she came down here at twelve-thirty. She should have been back in the suite," he checked his watch, "a half hour ago — at the latest. I need to find her."

Horatio Krumm patted his chest in relief. "Now I understand why I didn't see her. I go to *lunch* at twelve-thirty. Let me think, I believe I came back at one-fifteen. You can ask Frank, my assistant. He was with me. She must have already left by then."

Arlie was still frowning. "Who *was* here at twelve-thirty?"

"Well, my assistant Danny was here. But he doesn't know your girlfriend, I'm sure. Why would he?"

"Just let me talk to Danny."

"Certainly. I'll check in the back."

"I'll check with you."

Krumm put his hands up. "Never mind. I'll just call for him." He cupped his hands around his mouth. "Danny! Would you come out here, please? Someone wants to see you!"

Arlie turned to start looking around the gallery, but the assistant came through the back door within a few seconds. "Did you want me, Mr. Krumm?" he asked, glancing sideways at Arlie.

"Yes, Danny. This is Arlie Tate. He's looking for his girlfriend who was supposed to be here at around twelve-thirty."

"No — she *was* here for sure," Tate clarified for Krumm before turning his attention to Danny. "You would have noticed her. She's slim, good-looking, about thirty, with long, reddish-brown hair. She was wearing a bright pink top and a flowered skirt, I think. What can you tell me about her being here?"

Danny scratched his head. "Well, there were a lot of people here earlier, looking around. We're having an auction tonight, y'know? Anyway, there were several women wearing colorful tops like that. I dunno if your girlfriend was here or not," he shrugged.

Arlie closed in on Danny. "You would have *noticed* her, like I said. She's a real looker. Tell me what you know about her being here. Like, how long was she here, what she did, whether she talked to you."

Horatio Krumm got beside Danny. "I told you he wouldn't know who she is, Tate," he said in icy tones.

Arlie whirled on the auctioneer. "Listen to me. Your man here is lying! And that makes me real suspicious. Now, I'm going to take a *good* look around this place, and you try real hard to remember something, Danny Boy."

Arlie glowered at the assistant, waiting for a response, but he just stared back.

"No? Nothing? Well then, I'll just show myself around." Arlie turned on his heel and headed for the back door.

The auctioneer went after him. "All right, Mr. Tate. I'm happy to show you our entire space, but this is highly irregular. I assure you, we have nothing to hide. Right this way, please."

Krumm led Arlie through the door that opened onto a hallway. "The last door down there is our art storage room, next to that is our shipping and supplies room, that door leads to my office, and that one is a washroom."

"What's that other hallway, at the end?"

"Oh, that's the main hallway leading to the casino one way, and the photography studio and other rooms, the other way. So, shall we start with the storage room?"

Arlie nodded curtly.

When they got there, they both went inside. "So, there you see shelves of artwork stored vertically. Everything is organized alphabetically by the artist, starting with Bosch and ending with Wyeth, I believe. Go ahead. Look around."

"I can see there are only pictures here, Krumm. Let's move on."

Outside in the hallway, they came to the second door. Krumm went in first, followed by Arlie. Inside, a burly man was wrapping a painting on a large table. Pop music was playing in the background. The employee kept his head down and continued what he was doing.

Horatio Krumm had to raise his voice to be heard over the music. "Frank, this is Detective Tate." Frank barely nodded without raising his head.

"Turn down the fucking music," Arlie ordered. Frank responded by walking over to the shelf and turning the knob on a radio.

Krumm continued as though there had been no interruption. "Frank is busy getting a painting ready to ship. As you can see, there are several rolls of brown paper on the shelves, along with string, tape, bubble wrap, skinny cardboard boxes — everything we need to ship artwork. Also, there are some props on that side of the room: easels, clamp lights, microphones, and the like."

Arlie walked over to the shelves and looked under some bubble wrap and pieces of brown paper. After surveying the rest of the shipping materials, he walked around the room. Lastly, he bent down to look under the table.

"Everything all right, Tate?"

Arlie didn't answer the auctioneer, and looked at Frank. "Where'd you have lunch today?"

"Huh?"

"Where did you have lunch? It's a simple question."

Frank glanced over at his boss before answering. "Mr. Krumm and I went to the buffet, one deck down."

"What time did you leave here? Arlie persisted.

Frank shrugged. "The usual time. Twelve-thirty."

Arlie scowled at Krumm. "Let's go to your office next door."

The two men walked a few feet down the hallway and entered the next room. Krumm gestured towards the space. "Go ahead, look around. As you can see, there are only file cabinets. my desk and a couple of chairs. My living quarters, if you can call them that, are on a lower deck. And that's it. I really don't know what you expected to find. Alex might have changed her mind about coming down here, you know."

Arlie's eyes flashed, briefly. "I don't think so."

Krumm shrugged. "Well, then, maybe she's back up in your suite."

"No. She's not. I left a note for her to call me here if she did get back. Let's go back out front. I want to look around there."

Back in the gallery, Danny was sitting on a bench reading a magazine.

Arlie started walking around the make-shift partitions, scanning the artwork. Rounding the end of the wall that was closest to the front door, he looked at the colorful Miro prints. Glancing down that wall, he saw that there were some more realistic paintings.

He was about to leave the area when he noticed a piece of computer paper on the floor. Picking it up, he saw that it was a page of Joan Miro signatures: exemplars, apparently. Examining them, he noted that they were all a little different, one from another. Of course, no one signed their name exactly the same way every time. What was this doing here?

Arlie held up the sheet of paper to compare the signatures to those on the framed prints. Closing his eyes to concentrate, he almost slapped the side of his head when it occurred to him what this was. It must be a page of Alex's research. She evidently had been doing the same thing when she dropped the paper. Had she been interrupted by someone who maybe grabbed it away from her? Did she leave it behind on purpose?

Walking briskly to the back, Arlie waved the paper in Danny's face. "Does this help jog your memory? Alex was comparing these signatures with the ones on your Miro prints. *That* would have gotten your attention. Do you remember her now?"

Danny glared back and remained silent.

Arlie turned towards the gallery manager who stood a few feet away. "Where's your phone? I want to call Security."

Krumm stammered, "Th-the phone? It's on that desk over there, but it isn't necessary to call Security, not that we don't call them ourselves from time to time. Mr. Tate, I can vouch for both my employees' integrity. I can appreciate your concern that your girlfriend appears to be missing, but you seem to think that someone here is responsible."

Arlie walked over to the desk, picked up the phone and punched in four numbers. After a moment he said, "Security? This is Detective Tate. I want a couple of officers to report to the art gallery immediately. I need assistance with a ten-fifty-seven." He replaced the receiver in its cradle.

Horatio Krumm stared at Arlie. "*Detective* Tate? A ten-fifty-seven?"

Arlie flipped open his badge. "I'm a homicide detective in Georgia. A ten-fifty-seven is a *missing person.*

Chapter 46

WHEN ALEX CAME TO, she was horrified to find herself wrapped from head to toe, her mouth taped, and her ankles and hands tied behind her back. Panicked by the lack of oxygen, she sniffed like a coke addict to take in what little air was available.

Trying to get some circulation back in her arms and legs, she wriggled and twitched as much as her confinement would allow. Knocking into the sides of the stiff covering, she heard it crinkle. Paper. Then she recognized the smell. *Brown* paper. She had been rolled in the same paper that the gallery used to cover the backs of paintings.

She didn't have any memory of being trussed and packaged like this. The last thing she remembered was a knock on the gallery front door; then she had been grabbed from behind and then she smelled turpentine. The fumes must have been so strong that they knocked her out. She could still smell it and had a throbbing headache from it.

Some repressed memory was coming back to her. It was another time, recently, when she had smelled turpentine, but hadn't recognized it. The scene now came back to her with clarity: it was when she was standing over the dead body of Victor Garza. That must have been how he had been subdued before he was strangled.

They had probably forced Walter Sneed to inhale the fumes, too, to make him dopey before pushing him down the stairs.

At least she was alive, and her brain was still functioning. But what did those monsters plan on doing with her? Wrapped up like a package, it seemed pretty obvious: they would dump her overboard once the ship was out at sea.

She had better figure something out in a hurry. She couldn't stall for time now to wait for Arlie to come and rescue her like she had in the gallery. She thought back to how smug she had been, making a show of idly looking at her nails, waiting for him.

Her nails . . . She had fairly long fingernails that she continually strengthened with hardener and polish. Testing, she found that she could move her fingers behind her; enough to scratch against her paper prison. She couldn't tell how many layers of paper there were around her, but she only needed one hole.

* * *

Leonard Marks, the senior security officer that Arlie had worked with before, responded to his call, along with officer Joseph De Marco.

"I don't know what they've done with her, Lieutenant," Arlie was saying, "but Alex was here last, and Danny had to have seen her."

Lieutenant Marks rocked back and forth on his heels. "Well, I find it hard to believe that Horatio Krumm would kidnap your girlfriend. I've known the man for some time..."

"For five years, Lieutenant," Horatio inserted. "And I've never given you a moment's trouble."

Lieutenant Marks rubbed his chin. "Well, I wouldn't go that far, Krumm. There've been previous complaints of being ripped-off, not that I would know whether they were valid or not. And there's been some rowdiness by patrons who've imbibed too much champagne, but all in all, I'd say you run a smooth operation." He looked at Arlie. "We get more calls to the casino, I'll tell you that.

"And after all, your girlfriend's been missing for only a couple of hours. If that. It's a big ship, and we're moored in Bermuda. Do you know how many shops there are within a stone's throw of the ship?"

Arlie waved him off. "Look, Marks, you know there's been a murder on board, and —"

"A murder!" Horatio Krumm cried out. "Oh, my God! I hope you're not connecting me to any murder!" He dramatically fanned his face with his hand, throwing back his blond head.

Arlie glared at him before looking back at Lieutenant Marks. "Like I said, there's been one murder and at least one case of attempted murder. Did you hear about the man who was pushed down the spiral staircase and is in a coma?"

"I heard that someone *fell*, yes."

"Marks, I don't want to waste time arguing with you. One victim was a renowned art dealer and the other one is a New York art critic. Alex said she found evidence of fraud here, and now she's missing. I think we can start connecting the dots. Your people need to search Krumm's suite and Danny's and Frank's rooms.

"All right, all right," Lieutenant Marks said. "Hope you don't mind, Krumm."

The auctioneer rolled his eyes up to the ceiling. "Oh, go ahead, but this is totally unnecessary, not to mention embarrassing. Here's my key — it's Suite 5227."

"Good. You two guys give me your room key cards as well."

"Wait a minute, here," Danny said, jutting out his chin. "Don't you need some kind of warrant to search my room?"

"This is what they call an 'exigent circumstance,' — smartass," Arlie hissed.

Turning to the security personnel, he said, "Oh, Marks, you and your partner better search the area around the gallery, as well. Garza's body was found in a laundry room just down a hallway that connects to the one in back of the gallery. I'll stay here with The Three Stooges. They might start to remember something."

* * *

AFTER HALF AN HOUR Alex had managed to dig through only one layer of the heavy brown paper, and feared that there could be several more. If only she could get some saliva from her mouth to soften the paper. This was taking far too long. Her captors would certainly come back for her before she had been able to dig her way out. They'd certainly come back and dispose of her before the auction started. Unfortunately, she couldn't even estimate what time it was with all she'd been through.

She desperately needed water, more air, and to go to the bathroom. Of course, she could just pee where she was. This wasn't the time to be squeamish about urinating on oneself.

Wait a minute. Maybe it wasn't appealing, but it would be far more effective than saliva to soften and weaken the paper. And this was about saving her life, after all. It was worth a try.

First, she had to pull her skirt up out of the way. Ruching the material with her fingertips, she managed to crimp the garment up to her waist. Then, she simply relaxed and relieved herself.

Impatiently, she waited a couple of minutes for the paper to absorb the liquid.

Okay. It was time. She started scratching again with her fingernails and now her fingers could easily claw through the layers, one at a time, until she could grab hold and rip off pieces.

With one last thrust of her tied hands, she finally broke all the way through and her fingers felt the cold hard surface she was lying on. Sensing fresh air, she deeply inhaled.

But where was she, and what was that music? It wasn't very loud, but she could make out Daniel Powter singing "You Had a Bad Day." *No shit, Shakespeare.*

Back to the task at hand, she worked on tearing the opening wider and wider until she could push her head and shoulders out of her cocoon. Turning her head to the right, she was looking at a commercial roll of brown paper. To the left was a wall, and above her was another shelf.

She obviously was in the shipping room, which meant that Danny and the other two men were still nearby. Maybe one of them was right there wrapping paintings and listening to music. At least the radio had covered whatever noise she had made; but she would have to make a lot more noise before she got out of there.

Having had movement restored from the waist up, she squirmed forward out of the rest of her paper shell. But she couldn't reasonably escape from the room without freeing her wrists and ankles. Looking around, she couldn't see anything remotely sharp enough to cut through twine. She would just have to get down from the shelf with her feet and hands tied-up.

Turning over onto her right side, she drew up her knees and banged them against the heavy roll of paper next to her. It rocked back and forth a little, but stayed put. Determined now, she threw all of her weight at it. This time the cylinder kept rolling until it disappeared off the edge and tumbled to the floor.

Skitching over to the shelf's edge, she saw that she was about five feet off the floor. Making a rough calculation, she realized that without being able to use her hands she couldn't swing her body off the ledge so that her head would clear the shelf above.

Realizing the hopelessness of her predicament, her bottom lip started trembling under the tape. Feeling defeated, she rolled onto her left side to face the wall. Bringing up her knees into something like a fetal position, she felt a pain in her knee. Looking down, she saw that it was bleeding from being torn on a thick rusty nail in the wall. *Oh, great. Now I'll probably get tetanus.*

Glaring at the offending spike, she suddenly got an idea that might even work. Moving into position so that her wrists were directly over the nail, she caught a knot over it and experimented with pulling one way and then the other. After a few attempts, one end of the rope fell across her wrist. Encouraged, she worked faster, creating larger loops of twine until at last her hands were separated. She brought them around in front, and felt like clapping in jubilation. Instead, she pulled the tape off her mouth and gulped in air.

Then it was a simple matter to bring her feet up enough to untie her ankles. She was finally freed from all that had bound and contained her. She lay back for a moment to savor her victory.

But she still wasn't in the clear. She had to get out of that room before someone came back for her.

She turned onto her stomach, swung her body around, slid down the shelving unit and landed on her feet. Scanning the room, she saw that someone had been there but had left in the middle of wrapping a painting.

Hurrying over to the door, she opened it just a crack and listened for voices or movement. Nothing. Stepping outside the room, she found that she was in a hallway. Looking down it past a couple of closed doors, she saw that it terminated at another corridor. That had to be her best escape route.

But as she approached the next closed door, she heard voices coming from the other side. Silently she turned the handle and pulled. They were voices that she knew.

Yanking the door open, she burst into the gallery. All four men stared at her as though they'd seen a ghost, but only one of them appeared to be very happy about it.

"Alex! My God!" Arlie jumped up and rushed over to her. "Where have you been?! What happened to you?!"

Alex collapsed in his arms, flooded with relief. "For now, let's just say I had to fight my way out of a paper bag."

Chapter 47

AGAINST ARLIE'S WISHES, Alex refused to go down to the infirmary to be checked out because she might have to "lie next to a guy in a coma," as she had put it.

"I'm okay, really, Arlie. I just need to get more oxygen in my lungs; put some ointment on my wrists and ankles; clean up my bloody knee; pop a couple aspirins for my headache and sore muscles, and take a hot shower. Then I'll be fine."

Arlie held her by the shoulders and stood back to look her over. "You should probably be treated for shock after what you've been through."

Alex scoffed, "Save that for Danny, Frank, and Horatio. They're the ones who were shocked."

"I'm serious, Alex. You look terrible."

"Thanks. I don't smell great either, but I look better than Walter Sneed, and I'm more alive than Victor Garza. Besides, what you see is mostly smeared makeup, wrinkled wet clothes, and frizzed-out hair. All of that can be fixed."

"Well. . . if you say so. I'll take you upstairs and we'll see how you do. Marks and his guys are taking the three of them down to lockup. He'll transmit an initial report to the FBI on the fraud and their admissions to killing Garza and attempting to kill Sneed, and then you. They'll be turned over for prosecution in New York. When you're up to it, I'll take down your full statement."

"Oh, I'm up to it. I'm just now getting mad. Those creeps were going to dump me overboard to let me drown without even giving me a fighting chance!" Her voice broke.

Arlie put his arms around her. "I know, Babe. I know. Let's get you upstairs and you can give me all the details."

Alex pulled away and dabbed at her eyes. "Okay. I don't know why I'm getting all teary-eyed now and streaking my mascara even more. Not that I give a damn what I look like at this point, but I hate to scare the people who are on the elevator."

* * *

AN HOUR LATER Alex was comfortably settled on the sofa in her room, wrapped in one of the complimentary white terry robes. As she had predicted, she felt restored after taking a long, hot shower and tending to her injuries. Arlie had contributed to her recovery by fixing her a tall, iced Bloody Mary.

Sitting down next to her and putting down his own drink, he turned her face towards his and softly kissed her. "You look like your old self, but I can't believe you're anywhere near back to normal after being terrorized by those goons. Good thing you're so resourceful since you didn't have a very smart detective looking for you."

Alex patted his knee. "At least you were *there* and didn't think I had gone *shopping* like Marks tried to tell you. Anyway,

I wasn't so smart, either. If I hadn't told that old couple about the forgeries, right in front of Danny, I wouldn't have gotten into trouble."

Arlie stirred his drink. "That's what broke open the case. I might never have figured out that Danny Hawkins was running a massive art forgery scheme and killing, or trying to kill, anyone who discovered it."

Alex looked up. "Is that his name — Hawkins? I guess that's why he had a hawk tattooed on his forearm. Must be his nickname. Anyway, it wasn't hard to get Danny to talk after he figured he could send me out to sea to die like an elderly Eskimo."

Arlie chuckled. "I don't think they do that anymore. Danny just couldn't resist trying to impress you with what a great artist he was, although he was an even better con man. Imagine the money they were making with cheap prints, forged signatures, and his copies of originals. They had to have been splitting up like half a mil every cruise. Not evenly, of course, but the total the gallery took in must have been about twenty-five million dollars a year.

"Security will get the receipts for sales on this cruise and give people their money back in exchange for their artwork. The FBI can investigate further if they want to and civil suits will probably follow."

"That's good. The Wilsons will be happy about that, I know. And I'm glad they'll be repaid for Toby's help."

Arlie stroked his chin. "Y'know, it's always a small detail like that that trips up a murderer. They become so fixated on their hatred, or their greed, or their revenge, or whatever, that they overlook something that's an important clue to investigators. Like Danny denying that he had seen you in the crowded gallery. I knew that he would have noticed you."

Alex put down her drink. "There was only three of us there. But, speaking of murderers, as we are so often of late, what about the attempted murder of Victor Garza with the potted tree? Was that someone from the gallery, too? I seem to remember that Victor went down there when Jasmine was getting dressed for the wedding."

"Maybe he did and got them worked up and thinking about silencing him, but I know that they didn't push over the pot, because I know who did."

"You do? You wanna tell *me*?"

"Not right now. I need some genuine surprised reactions when I reveal who it is when I meet with the group tomorrow morning. Then you'll find out along with everyone else."

"What are you, some kind of Hercule Poirot who points at the murderer in front of all the guests of the hunting party at the end of the weekend?" She pulled at a make-believe waxed mustache for her imitation of the fictional detective.

"No, actually, I'm going more for Perry Mason — in the last act, when he's in the courtroom. I want to trick the villain to stand up and blurt out something in the heat of the moment, thinking I know it, anyway — but I don't."

"I thought you said you know who it is."

"I do. I just don't know who the target was."

Arlie reached over and folded Alex into his arms, drawing her close. Nuzzling the back of her neck he murmured, "Mmmm. Enough talk about murder."

"Fine with me," she whispered.

Turning her body to face him, he kissed her deeply. Then, standing and scooping her up, he carried her over to the bed.

Pulling down his head, she cooed in his ear, "Okay, but who pushed the tree over the railing?"

"Hah. Nice try — but you'll have to do better than that. You'll find out tomorrow."

Chapter 48

ARLIE AND ALEX had just finished dinner in their suite when the phone rang. Arlie picked up.

"Oh, hi. Uh . . . yeah. I think so, but just a minute." He put his hand over the receiver.

"It's Jasmine. She and Tony want to come down and see you. She says they won't stay long. Just wants to see how you're doing. Okay?"

Alex screwed up her face. "Oh, I'm not put together enough to see Jasmine. My hair is sticking out funny. I'm not dressed. My nails are *destroyed*."

Arlie nodded and spoke into the receiver. "She'd be happy to see both of you," he said, easily, ducking a sofa pillow thrown at his head. "She's doing fine. Yeah. Okay. See ya. Bye."

Five minutes later Arlie responded to the knock at the door. Alex cringed at the sight of a perfectly made-up Jasmine, every hair in place, in a lime green shift that showed off her tan. Tony followed, smartly dressed in nautical blue and white.

Alex sank into her sofa cushion and pulled the collar of her robe up around her ears. "Hi. Thanks for coming. You both look great."

"Hi, Alex! I'm so glad to see you sitting up!" Jasmine exclaimed, taking a seat next to her and giving her a hug. "I can't believe what you've been through, and you look— you look— fine."

Alex tucked her hands into the folds of her robe and forced a smile. "I'm not really at my best."

"Of course not. Lieutenant Marks told us how you uncovered the scam in the art gallery, and then were held prisoner, bound and gagged and wrapped up. I can't believe you escaped. You're like a Houdini!

"We just wanted to tell you how amazing you are, and how much we appreciate your getting to the bottom of what happened to Victor. The poor man was killed trying to do the right thing; what you succeeded in doing."

Alex gave a modest shrug. "I probably would have suffered the same fate if Arlie hadn't shown up."

Arlie gave a little snort. "Yeah. I showed up. And that's all I did."

Tony put a hand on his shoulder. "Somehow, I don't think you would have left without finding her."

"That's right," Alex put it. "But we don't have to debate who did what. What's important is that Victor's killers are behind bars, and that's probably some comfort to you."

Jasmine looked over at Tony. "That, and the fact that we're no longer suspects ourselves. It does give us some closure, too. You probably heard that we had his body cremated. We picked up the cremains this morning." She let out a sigh. "I've arranged with the ship's pastor to have a memorial service tomorrow at eleven — in the same chapel as our wedding, of course. It's all so unreal."

"Oh, we'll be sure to attend," Alex said, glancing at Arlie who nodded in response. "So — let's not be too gloomy. This was your only full day in Bermuda. What did you do?"

Jasmine brightened. "Oh, we rented scooters and rode up to St. George's to tour Verdmont House. And then we had lunch across the street at uh . . ."

"The Specialty House," Alex filled in. "Did you like it?"

"Oh, it was charming. And then we rode back to Hamilton and did some shopping on Front Street. We each bought a cashmere sweater, and I bought a Spode tea set. By then we needed a rest, so we took a carriage ride around town."

Alex sat up. "That's exactly how I *planned* for you and— oh. . . for you to spend a day in Bermuda."

"I know. For me and *Victor*. Don't worry. I know it's awkward for Tony and I to be together — even before Victor's funeral. And we plan on staying together. I've told people that I'm expecting, but no other details. I'm starting to show, as you can see..."

Alex peered at the barest rounding of Jasmine's stomach and sucked in her own. "What about the galleries? Will both of you be involved?"

Tony responded, "At this point I've inherited equal ownership with Sunny. Hopefully, she won't make it a legal challenge. She doesn't want anything to do with the day-to-day operations, anyway. She wants to tour Europe and find new talent — on an expense account, of course. That's fine. Whatever she wants to do. Also, it will give Jasmine and me some space to manage the business back here."

"Tony has some great ideas," Jasmine broke in. "For instance, he wants to invite everyone who's on our mailing list to a champagne cocktail party every three months for a one-night sale."

Tony added, "Not too original. We saw how effective it is on the ship, so we might as well try it, too.

"At the other end of the spectrum, I think we could serve the community by starting an art school for children since so many school programs have been defunded. We could even offer several scholarships to promising students who can't afford to pay.

"Sunny's totally opposed to that, of course. She says it's like teaching grafitti to vandals."

Alex rolled her eyes. "That sounds like Sunny."

Jasmine shook her head. "Yeah. At least she's consistent. She never wants to help anybody."

She glanced at Tony. "We'd better get going, huh?"

"Alex, it's great to see how well you've come through your ordeal. We'll see you tomorrow."

"Yeah, at the Memorial service, but Arlie's getting us all together before then to catch people up on the arrests and everything."

Arlie got up to show the guests to the door. "Right. Nine o'clock in that bar next to the casino, where we met before. Good to see you both. Thanks for coming."

He turned towards Alex after closing the door. "Don't we all sound so polite and proper? No one would guess that we're talking about meeting to learn who attempted to murder someone, and then to attend the funeral of the victim."

Chapter 49

THE NEXT MORNING the casino lounge was buzzing as soon as members of the group arrived to wait for Alex and Arlie to appear. All the talk was about Alex's daring escape from the gallery operators who had been arrested for the murder of Victor Garza, the attempted murder of Walter Sneed, and for selling art forgeries.

At the height of the din, Rudolph Perino made a grand entrance swirling a long bluish-green jacket over his skinny black pants. He was followed in by Damien Loren dressed all in midnight blue except for a psychedelic magenta silk tie. Spotting Alaana and Lola, the two men waved and walked over to join them.

"Did you hear the news?" Lola asked, excitedly. "Isn't it amazing that Alex captured the murderers? I think she had to shoot her way out of the gallery before security showed up."

"Oh my God, really?" Rudolph responded. "This would be a smash hit on Broadway if they made it into a musical. It would be like a combination of *Chicago* and *Catch Me if You Can*. Amy Adams could play the part of Alex. She can really sing and she looks a lot like her, anyway."

"That would be fun, wouldn't it?" Alaana clapped her hands. "It's just too bad that Vincent Price is gone. He could be made up to be a dead-ringer for Horatio Krumm. Of course, I don't know that he sang."

Damien looked down, shuffling his feet. "I'm so disappointed that Horatio was involved in this whole mess. He seemed so refined, and he's such a good dresser. Oh, speaking of which, how do you like Rudolph's new jacket?"

Rudolph cut in, "This is what I bought that's Bermuda Green. Remember, Alaana? I told you that I'd show you whatever I got in this color."

"It's lovely, dear. It brings out the frosted streaks in your hair. Of course, I like your outfit, too, Damien."

"Thanks. I'm wearing the dark blue for the funeral, but I put on the pink tie for just a spot of color, you know."

Lola's face brightened as her attention was drawn to the doorway. "Look! Here come Alex and Arlie, now!"

After everyone had become aware that they were in the room, conversation ceased as they all gaped at the couple.

Eloise Brown called out, "Well, let's not keep our hands in our pockets! The woman had to do the 'jimmy riddle' on herself to tear a hole in the paper she was wrapped in. Let's hear it for Alex! Hip! Hip!"

Enthusiastic applause followed and Alex nodded and smiled in response. "Thank you! 'Jimmy riddle' sounds a lot more respectable than the reality, which has probably gotten around to all of you. It was a pretty bad situation that I was in. I can tell you more, later, if you're interested, but for now let me say that I was lucky that some things went my way, particularly that Detective Tate sensed that I was in trouble and came to look for me.

"As you know, he has been investigating the tragic events that have occurred on this cruise and we're all together for him to bring us up to date on where everything stands. Arlie?"

He stepped forward. "Everyone have a seat, please." Taking a quick count he satisfied himself that no one was missing.

"First, I want to say that Alex is downplaying her courageous and ingenious actions yesterday. I was only there as a witness. As she said, she'll give you the details, later. I don't think she'd like me to. But I will tell you that she escaped a situation that could have resulted in her death. If any of you ever find yourself trapped, either by natural causes or by someone who wants to do you harm, don't ever accept your fate and just give up. Keep moving, yelling, or whatever you can do to call attention to your predicament or to alter the conditions of your situation.

"But that's not what I'm here to talk about this morning. As Alex said, I'm here to give you a report on my investigations over the last few days. I need to clear up some misinformation as well as to make more arrests." Several people gasped and furtively looked around

Arlie continued. "During what should have been a pleasurable honeymoon cruise, the groom was murdered and there have been two incidents of attempted murder, as you know.

"I was asked to start an investigation Monday morning, three days ago, when Security contacted me that someone had pushed a potted tree over the railing of the Sun Deck onto the Garza balcony, narrowly missing both Victor and Jasmine.

"As there were no cameras filming the spot where the pot went over, there was no way to know then who was responsible. From the difficulty in accomplishing the act, I had to assume that it wasn't an accident. Furthermore, it was only reasonable that it had to have been done by someone in this group who knew the intended victim.

"The first thing I did was to photograph the Garza balcony to show that the pot landed exactly in the middle of where the two people had been sitting.

"I next collected the broken pieces of pottery and took them to a crime lab in Hamilton to be dusted for prints. Presumably, if there were any fingerprints on a stationary floor pot, they would belong to the perpetrator of the crime.

"There were no eye witnesses who came forward, but there were two hearing witnesses. Dame Edith Herrington and Eloise Brown were sitting out on their balcony next-door to the Garzas at the time of the incident; although, there's a wall between the two. Both ladies reported hearing two high-pitched screams right at the time of the crash. The fact that there were *two* screams didn't strike me as being significant. Although Jasmine remembered screaming only once, she was in shock and could easily have been mistaken."

"But I was sure about the *two* screams," Eloise Brown inserted, "and so was Dame Edith, weren't you, Milady?" Dame Edith nodded and put her finger up to her lips.

"That's all right," Arlie responded. "Anyway, after I interviewed everyone, only a few people had solid alibis I could eliminate as suspects. I had to hope that there were good latents on the pot that the crime lab could lift when we docked in Bermuda. Frankly, I wasn't too hopeful.

"However, the next morning before I could take the pottery pieces off the ship, Security again contacted me. This time they told me that Victor Garza had been strangled to death the night before, and that his body had been found dumped in a basket in a laundry room on Deck Seven, where we are now.

"After examining the body, the ship's head physician estimated the time of death was after midnight. Therefore, I was able to eliminate most of you here in this room as you used your room key cards for the last time, *well before* midnight." Murmurings were heard as some felt it necessary to share comments with their neighbors.

Arlie raised his voice to talk over the voices. "Quiet, please. I'll try to get through this quickly, but I want you all to be aware of the painstaking process and the facts that were uncovered in this case.

"In the area of physical evidence, since the body of the victim was left on top of other people's laundry, the scene was contaminated, preventing me from collecting any hair or fibers that could be isolated as belonging to the perpetrator.

"What was left behind that was determined to be the murder weapon was a woman's scarf known to belong to Jasmine Garza. It was found under the victim." Several people looked sideways at Jasmine who continued to gaze steadily at the detective.

Arlie continued. "It seemed likely that the murderer was the same person who dumped the pot over the railing. He or she hadn't been successful in the morning, so wanted to make sure to get the job done that night. However, that theory would eliminate Jasmine, who was one of the few people who had a possible motive and the opportunity."

"We know now that she had sod all to do with it, right, Guvnor?" Eloise Brown asked.

"That's right," Arlie agreed. "I'm giving you all the chronology of the investigation. Up until yesterday afternoon Jasmine Garza couldn't be eliminated as a suspect, along with a few others. If it weren't for Alex eliciting a confession out of the art gallery operators after she uncovered their other criminal activities, several of you would still be suspects in Victor Garza's murder."

"But, let me pick up on the sequence of events starting with Tuesday morning, after finishing up with my inspection at the murder scene. I next paid a visit to the Hamilton's police department's Crime Lab with the pottery pieces and the scarf.

"Fortunately, the technicians were able to lift one whole print and one partial off the clay shards. Unfortunately, the prints didn't match any in the data base, meaning that the perpetrator didn't have a police record and hadn't been in government or security.

"Returning to the ship, I questioned everyone to gather information about Victor Garza's murder, concentrating on those who hadn't entered their rooms until after twelve o'clock the night before and had opportunity. They included the Garza family members, Dame Edith, Eloise Brown, and Edmund and Juliana Devers.

"Frankly, only the family members looked good for the murder, as they were the only ones who would profit from Victor's death, or had any strong motives.

"Developments yesterday changed everything. Coincidently, after Alex confirmed that the art gallery had been cheating the public, a young boy told her that he had overheard Victor Garza accusing Horatio Krumm of selling forgeries. Later that same night Victor had been murdered.

"When Alex went down to the gallery in the afternoon, the operators realized that she could bring down their illegal business. While holding her, they admitted to killing Victor and pushing Walter Sneed down the stairs. As you know, they had similar plans for her and were almost successful in carrying them out.

"Meanwhile, I had fingerprinted those of you who had come down for her morning meeting. On the ferry going over to Hamilton, I ran into others in the group who allowed me to fingerprint them. But there were two people who refused to be printed. Unfortunately, these were the same two people who were my prime suspects." Another murmuring of voices followed this statement as many looked around, trying to identify who the suspects were.

"Let me continue," Arlie said. "Once off the ferry, in the tradition of detectives and private eyes everywhere, I followed them and waited for them to touch and discard something that I could fingerprint: a Styrofoam coffee cup or a cigarette butt.

"They didn't but, fortunately, when I was on the ferry I had anticipated a problem and had hedged my bet. In casual conversation with these two people, I had brought up the subject of lunch, and had raved about the food and atmosphere at the Barracuda Grill, which happens to be the only restaurant I know in Hamilton." Someone gasped, but Arlie didn't hesitate and went on.

"My ruse paid off when, at a little after twelve, the pair went into the restaurant. Then it was a simple matter to take the waiter aside and have him pick up their water glasses with gloved hands and replace them, explaining that the first glasses were smudged which he found in violation of the high standards of the establishment.

"I lifted the prints on the glasses and rushed them over to the Crime Lab with the others that I had collected.

"It didn't take long to get the results. As I expected, the ones on the water glasses were perfect matches to the prints on the pottery. Not one of them. *Both* of them.

"You see, in visiting the site where the potted tree had been dropped, several things struck me: it was in the same area where we had all danced at the wedding, reinforcing my theory that it had been the work of one of the guests. Also, in locating a nearby potted tree of the same size, I found that it weighed a hundred pounds or more, which one person could not reasonably pick up, steady on a rail, and control to have it land on a particular spot. Therefore, I knew that I was looking for two people who were equally motivated, and who were confidants of each other, who wouldn't betray one another.

"That narrowed my suspect list down to the married artists, Rudolph Perino and Damien Loren, Roman and Monica Gregg, and Sunny and Carlo Giovanni.

"The artists had been vocal about their discontent with Victor, which wouldn't have been a smart move if they wanted to try to kill the guy. And the theatre designers didn't have a motive. So that left the Greggs and the Giovannis: a short list, but both couples had both motive and opportunity.

"Then I remembered the testimony of Dame Edith and Eloise Brown. While I hadn't found the two screams significant,

Alex was sure that they had come from two different women, since the first scream came before the pot landed, when Jasmine was still unaware of it.

"Why would a woman who was trying to sneak up and kill someone let out a scream that would attract attention? Again, it was Alex who argued that the murderer screamed when she saw that the pot was not going to land *on the right target*.

"Jasmine had told me that a split second before the pot crashed, Victor had turned back towards her to hear what she was saying

"Who would be so concerned that Victor would be killed instead of Jasmine?" He paused and looked at the one person who fit that description. Everyone's eyes followed his to stare at Sunny Giovanni.

Sunny leapt to her feet. "All right! All right! I've heard enough from you! I would *never* have killed my father! What kind of a monster do you think I am, Detective? I was his princess! He LOVED me. He gave me anything I asked for, until SHE came along and turned him against me." She glared and pointed at Jasmine. "I have nothing without my father! Nothing!"

"But you have me, sweetheart!" Carlo had spun off his chair and was reaching for his wife, who viciously shoved him back down.

"Fuck off, Carlo! You're the one who pissed him off so much that he was willing to listen to her! He saw you for what you are — a worthless drunk and a gambler. I don't know which is worse. And I thought I was marrying into *royalty*. Your family has nothing but a goddamned crest, if *that's* even worth anything. You and 'sweetness' over there have taken everything from me! I hate you both!"

Sunny suddenly started swinging wildly at Carlo who covered his head with his arms. "Ouch! Ouch! Sunny, darling, please!"

Arlie quickly grabbed her, holding her arms behind her back and clicking handcuffs onto her wrists.

"Oww! That hurts! What do you think you're doing?!"

"Just putting you under arrest. You and Carlo. But I want to thank you for filling in the blanks for me, Sunny. I figured you for a killer, but I wasn't sure if it was for love or money.

"If it had been only for the money, you wouldn't care if it was Jasmine or your father that you killed. But you were motivated more by the loss of your father's love than his money. And you perceived his love for you had been stolen by Jasmine when she became the 'other woman' in his life."

Sunny was breathing hard, her face contorted in rage. She kicked a spiked heel shoe at Arlie's shin but missed and yelled, "Go to Hell!"

Epilogue

ARLIE AND ALEX stood close together at the railing on the Sun Deck to watch as the *Bermuda Queen* sailed into New York Harbor.

Alex turned and gazed at Arlie as his sandy hair was being ruffled in the breeze. "Well, we're here and our cruise is over. Considering what we've both been through, I should be happy, but I'm not really."

Arlie put his arm around her shoulder. "I'm not either. I always like being with you, no matter what mayhem is always going on around us." He shook his head and rolled his eyes.

Alex chuckled. "Now, some good things came out of the trip. Jasmine and Tony are together, like they should have been in the first place; and it sounds like they'll treat their artists fairly as well as make a contribution to the community. But you gave them the biggest gift of all, by telling them that Victor was, in fact, Tony's father."

Arlie shrugged. "The Crime Lab came up with that one. I had them run the DNA on those swabs I took of everyone in the family, not knowing at the time that there would be a paternity issue. When there weren't any good DNA results on the scarf, I asked them to compare the samples of the family to see whether Victor could be excluded as being Tony's father. They told me that he couldn't be excluded. The chances are billions to one that no one else is."

Alex nodded. "That'll protect his share of the estate, and with Jasmine being entitled to a third under Illinois law, that gives the two of them controlling interest in everything in the estate — galleries, homes, stocks, bonds, cash, the works."

"What will happen to Carlo and Sunny now?" she asked.

"Well, I can't be sure. Security will be handing them over to the FBI agents at the dock. My report emphasized that the elements of attempted murder had been met; that there was malice aforethought, and an expectation that the action would result in death for the intended victim. Jasmine was just lucky that she wasn't sitting a foot to the left and that Carlo and Sunny didn't have better control of the pot.

"The FBI will have their hands full. They'll be taking Danny Hawkins, Horatio Krumm, and Frank Baggins into custody, as well. I hope they brought a couple of vans.

"I'll be kept in the loop as the cases go forward. You and I will probably be asked to get more involved, particularly you, as they'll need your testimony against the three gallery operators."

Alex nodded as she waved at the people on the dock who were meeting friends and relatives. "I need to follow up with Walter Sneed, too. Dr. Briggs thinks that he should have a full recovery. It was great news when he came out of his coma last night, although he doesn't remember anything about how he ended up falling down the stairs. It doesn't matter. Danny bragged to me about Frank 'silencing their critics,' as he put it, including both Victor Garza and Walter Sneed.

"Briggs is having Walter transferred from the ship by ambulance to a hospital here in the City. It's a good thing Walter lives here as does his brother. I called Harold last night with an update. He sounded relieved to hear that his brother was out of the coma. I'm sure he'll visit Walter and take care of his needs."

"Well that's good, anyway," Arlie agreed.

"Yeah. Oh, and Bruno Rasconi told me he dropped by the infirmary after I gave him the news. Bruno said he wanted to be sure that Walter knew he wasn't responsible for his fall. I think he feels Walter got much more than he deserved.

"Hopefully, it'll make Bruno control his temper more in the future. And maybe Walter will be more objective in his reviews."

Arlie brushed some strands of hair off Alex's face. "Speaking of the future, what are your plans? Do you have another trip in mind, yet?"

"No, not right now, but if I don't hear from clients in the near future, I'll come up with a tour proposal and contact them. Why, what would you suggest?"

"Oh, I don't know. How about something quiet and peaceful— like a bird-watching trip?"

Alex's face lit up. "Good idea! We could explore the jungles of Costa Rica or Belize."

Arlie groaned. "Alex. You beat everything, did you know that?"

Acknowledgements

Details relating to the reproductions of particular paintings referred to in this book are a result of my research, or have been dredged up from my memory of my studies in art history. However, the use of the information is in a fictionalized context, entirely made up out of my own imagination, and does not have a factual basis.

Similarly, I researched actual locations in Bermuda to put the reader into the setting, but these descriptions may have been altered, as needed, to facilitate my telling the story.

I have several people to thank in helping me with this book. My friends in the Authors Guild of Tennessee are constantly supportive and offer advice when asked.

I would like to thank my friend Paul Buie who previewed the book. I highly value his opinion of the story and the characters, and any suggestions he made.

I want to especially thank my good friend Marilyn Neilans, who is a skillful writer and publisher, and her husband John, as they both carefully proofread the manuscript. Any errors that remain are my own after some rewriting, or due to my overlooking any of their corrections.

Of course, I want to thank my husband Jim who is my constant support and guide. His comments are always helpful to make my story more interesting and to keep my characters consistent.

Made in the USA
Charleston, SC
26 September 2015